Raised on the high seas as an avaricio  her back on her roots, but she can't see... to stem the ancient magic that courses through her. Del is a soft-spoken soldier who seems to know more about Aela's inherited powers that she does. Brynne's the crofter's daughter who's reluctantly learning to become a princess, if she could just get a certain swashbuckling someone off her mind.

Originally hired on (okay, blackmailed) by the King of the island nation of Thandepar, Aela's light monster extermination gig takes a fast turn into kidnapping-for-profit. Del tries to ignore family issues by searching for a long lost friend, and ends up getting both for the price of one. Brynne's prepared to give up her heart for her country until her own personal heartbreaker shows up with the most terrible timing.

As the three of them become more entwined in their own political predicaments, and each other's lives, they may discover that the legacies their parents have left them aren't as solid as they seemed. In fact, they may just slip through their fingers, leaving all three fumbling to forge their own future, before the kingdom comes crashing down around them.

A NineStar Press Publication

Published by NineStar Press
P.O. Box 91792,
Albuquerque, New Mexico, 87199 USA.
www.ninestarpress.com

Run in the Blood

ISBN: 978-1-947904-76-7

Printed in the USA
First Edition
December, 2017

Also available in eBook

ISBN: 978-1-947904-70-5

Run in the Blood

A.E. Ross

For Geoff, who made the world bigger.

Acknowledgements

Thank you to Tessa and Mugs for taking time to read this book in its early stages and giving me vital feedback. Thank you to Murray, for being a constant source of support and the best friend I could ask for. Thank you to Raevyn, Jason, Sera, and the NineStar team, not just for agreeing to help me tell this story, but also for inviting me into an amazing community. Finally, thank you to Natasha Snow for giving this story a beautiful cover.

Chapter One

A SHARP BLAST of seawater hit Aela Crane square in the face, soaking her curls. As she gripped the rim of the crow's nest with dark knuckles, the surface of the ocean seemed to rise up to meet her as the brigantine listed at a dangerous horizontal angle. The captain was throwing out all the stops to catch up to the mercantile cog just ahead of them.

Just below, her shipmates flew through the rigging, raising and lowering the sails as the ship made a shuddering turn to the right. On the deck, she could see a familiar spark of flame as their archers held lit arrows nocked to their bows, ready to release them into the air.

The corsair ship, faster and sleeker, gained on the struggling cog. Aela knew that their captain, the infamous man named Dreadmoor, would not give up his quarry. He did not like to lose. She heard his voice call out gruffly from the fore as he ordered the archers to release the flaming shafts. The arrows arced up and over, some sinking into the cog's starboard side with a dull thunk, while the truer ones found their targets. Screams rent the frigid air as the brigantine finally veered within spitting distance. Several grappling hooks sank into the cog's side, stabilising the two vessels.

The dull sound of boots on soaking wood thundered below her as the corsairs swarmed across a boarding plank, their swords ruthlessly singing with the blood of the merchant sailors. Aela leaped down from the crow's nest; her hands burned on the coarse rope as she swung herself down to the deck where her own salt-weathered boots landed with a wet thud. The rigging above her head shook as the lookout boy scrambled down, eager to cross the planks and join in the fray. He landed beside her and slipped a dull blade from his belt. Shaking back his shaggy red hair, he grinned up at her. She clicked her tongue in reply and hefted her speargun with muscular arms, scarred by the marks of a dangerous life. Knife wounds and near misses were etched into her powerful limbs, evidence of her trade.

A corsair almost since birth, Aela Crane had grown to womanhood in the crow's nest, her only masters the sea and the sword. She and the freckled boy, Timlet, made for the gangplank and the merchant ship, but as Timlet took a step onto the cedar board, it lost its purchase on the other side and fell free, crashing into the ocean below. Aela grasped Timlet's arm and pulled him stumbling backwards before he could follow the plank down into the waves.

"Thanks." Timlet smiled graciously, blushing. Aela released him as he took several steps back, readying himself. He burst forward towards the side of the ship and then leaped off the edge and across the gap to land safely on the other side. Not a moment after landing, he flew into the fray, confronting a young merchant sailor who had naught but a trowel to defend himself.

Aela stepped back, considering the jump. The gap between the ships wasn't large, but she didn't have the same acrobatic knack as Timlet, and above else, valued style over substance. She aimed her speargun into the mast of the merchant ship and let it fly. The spear arced through the night sky, and the spear tip buried itself deep into the mast, pulling the line taut. Aela took a run and swung herself across the gap to land up on the aftcastle.

Knees bent, she scanned the action. Her fellow corsairs fought man-to-man on the deck below. She could see Timlet dodging the young sailor's trowel, bobbing and weaving as he prepared his attack as she had taught him. He ducked and danced away from his opponent's lunges, letting him tire until he could get in behind and slit the throat. As he pulled his knife across the boy's neck and released his blood, the body fell backwards, collapsing onto Timlet. Aela shook her head. The boy still had a lot to learn. As Timlet struggled to free himself, another man fought his way along the deck, past the body of the young sailor.

The man swung and jabbed at every corsair he could reach, seeming to search the boat until his gaze met Aela's as she stood on the aftcastle. Here was the captain of the vessel. It was clear in his purposeful stride, which hastened after he saw her and made his way towards the stairs. Trying to think quickly, she tugged on the line of her speargun and flipped the retraction lever as the steel tip came free of the mast. The line reeled back into the gun and the sharp metal shaft came shooting back towards her, clicking as it locked back into its place in the barrel.

The merchant captain was almost upon her as she pulled her long dagger from its sheath and turned to block his first swing. She scanned his form. He wore a vivid purple coat. Its crest featured the North Star, a sign of his patronage to the king of Thandepar, the frozen country in whose waters they currently sailed, and whose merchants they currently slaughtered. She smirked as he lunged again, and blocked him easily.

"Don't worry. We're here to relieve you of your extra cargo." She grinned, lowering her gaze as she flicked his curved sword away with her blade. She circled him, daring him to strike again.

"What goods? We've nothing but a hold full of bodies, thanks to you." His hair was grey, and his skin was sickly pale. Still, there was something familiar in the ridge of his nose and the set of his brow. The captain tried to gauge her skill as she stepped around him, dancing away as he tried another strike. She clicked her tongue at him.

"Oh come on. You've got to have something good down there, sailing in the dead of night like you are. No lights. No noise. Quiet as a thief." She lunged in with her blade, not to cut but to tap him on his waist, teasing. Furrowing his brow, he jumped back out of his range, a curious look in his pale blue eyes.

"So quiet we were, one almost wonders how you found us." He raised an eyebrow and stepped aside quickly as Aela pounced forward for a true strike. He was spry, which surprised her. He was much sharper than he seemed, in his delicate purple coat.

"Come closer," she said, still taunting. "I can make you a free man." Her tongue brushed her lower lip as she stepped in close, tucking her blade between his arm and abdomen. "One plunge of my dagger and you'll have no king but the patron of the dead." Aela jumped back rapidly as the captain struck at her shoulder. She was too quick, and his sword cut only air. He sneered.

"You corsairs are all the same. You think you are the only free people in this world." His voice was strained.

"Yes, as that is the case." She mocked him smugly as she sidestepped another blow.

"Ah, but is it? I have land, I have a lord, and I have—" He stepped in towards her, catching her off guard. "—a family." He thrust his blade against her outer thigh, pressing its sharp edge through her rough trousers, splitting threads and drawing blood, but barely wounding. "And your lifestyle will not allow you those things. Is that freedom?"

Aela jumped back, feeling his blade slide free of her flesh. She gave a quick glance down to the deck to see Timlet scrapping with another sailor.

"What is it you people say?" the captain continued. "I pledge allegiance to the sea. Landless, lawless, honour free?"

She spat at his feet. "My crewmates are my family, and this ocean is my land." She thrust forward, but the captain stepped free of her blow. She was becoming irritated, and she knew that it made her vulnerable to attack, but she pressed onwards, striking again and again but failing to land a blow. He had made her angry, and the heat rolled off her body, warming her blade, fueling her fire. She tried to blink it away, but it was too late—she could not recover her concentration. The captain lowered his sword as he gaped at her. She knew that her eyes had blazed from their usual deep brown to a candle's twin. Blazing orange, flickering like a flame, and the pupil ringed with blue. Before this moment, she could have been any woman to him, from any place. Her complexion was not unusual; deep brown eyes with skin the colour of a sequoia tree, its strength echoed in her muscular frame. Her head was crested by a bluster of curls, the sides haphazardly shaved for ease of maintenance at sea. Besides the profiteer's attitude, the sea-dog smell, and the uncanny bloodlust, she would have been passed without notice in any marketplace.

"*Monster.*" He choked out the word. His eyes were locked on hers. She allowed herself a moment to hate the familiar fear in his gaze before she lunged forward, striking at him, forcing him to defend himself.

"Do you want to keep staring? A second ago, you wanted to kill me." Aela sliced into his leg, letting the blade bite before ripping it back.

She burned on, forcing him backwards. She had him up against the railing of the aftcastle, her dagger at his throat, the sea at his back, ready to finish him off when she heard a noise behind her. She glanced back, expecting a sailor come to defend his captain, but she could see the battle had ended. It was only Timlet, scrambling up the stairs towards her. That one look back cost her the chance for a killing blow. The captain pushed her back, and before she could strike him, he leapt over the railing and into the sea, swimming clear of the rudder and away from the cog. Timlet joined Aela at the railing as they stared out at the sea and the merchant captain swimming away in the waves. Aela's eyes still burned.

"You little bastard, you let him jump!" She swore at Timlet, and a red blush spread under his freckles as he edged away to avoid her wrath.

"It was an accident! I was only coming to make sure you were all right!"

"I protect you. It doesn't work the other way around."

"Well, he'll never make it to land anyways! He'll just bleed out in the water or get speared by a narwhal or somethin'," Timlet stammered. Aela stepped towards him and he flinched as if expecting a blow. Instead, she let out a laugh. The fire faded from her as she put a hand on his shoulder and squeezed.

"Speared by a narwhal? You're ridiculous." She gave him a slight push backwards and turned back to the sea. She pulled her speargun from its holster on her back and set it on the railing to steady her aim. She found her mark through the sight and pulled the trigger, sending the metal spear flying through the night. It landed with a *thunk* in the captain's back, as his desperate swimming ceased with a shriek. His body bobbed on the frigid waves, spear sticking out like a dorsal fin.

She cut the rope that connected the spear to the gun. She would buy replacements on their imminent return to port, and had no desire to keep this one as a reminder that she had failed to keep her cool. Timlet squeaked behind her. She turned to see him rocking on his heels.

"He wouldn't have made it far before drowning," he remarked to his feet. Aela returned her gun to the holster and stepped towards him. She could hear the sound of the other crewmates' celebratory hoots as they carried goods from the merchant ship back to the brigantine.

"Ah, but drowning is a long and painful death." She shrugged and guided Timlet back down, across a new gangplank, and onto their ship. They would break the cog, sinking it with the sailors' bodies inside, and find a less conspicuous spot to spend the night.

THEY CHOSE A deep cove to drop anchor in until the morning. Its patchy evergreen forest was part of a small strip of land along the southern coast of Thandepar that its people referred to as the green belt. That coastline was one of the few fertile places on the northern continent where crops could be grown in abundance. The only others were a handful of deep river valleys tucked between the glaciers, the meltwater carving out hollows where the people of Thandepar had settled their major towns. It was a country made beautiful by its desolation. The valleys and the green belt produced the majority of the food for the small nation, but its trade wealth lay elsewhere.

Dreadmoor directed his corsair crew as they carried their bounty deep into the brigantine's hold. It contained a rich cargo: gold from Thandepar's deep mountain veins and vibrant dye squeezed from its tundra lichen. The refugees from Old Ansar had found it that way when their ships arrived on its shores. Empty. They came from southeastern lands of heat and spice, overcome with brimstone, to a world so penetrated by frost that it could scarcely feed their children. Gradually, they rebuilt their civilization, digging deep in the mountains for gold to trade and squeezing what little life they could out of the permafrost. Their capital, called Ghara, was built in the ruins of a stone stronghold they found etched into a high peak, its previous inhabitants long gone. But not entirely gone...

Aela floated on the surface of the ocean. Her evening swim was a chance for solitude. She could reflect on her thoughts without interruption. Heat radiated from her body, warming the water in her perimeter, another aspect she had inherited from unknown ancestors.

Tiny chunks of ice bobbed by, lazily melting as they entered her range. She tried to rein in her feelings, considering how the merchant captain had broken her practiced cool. He had known what she was, so she had killed him.

Aela dipped her head back into the warm water, letting it pool around her temples and in the hollows of her ears. It would have been a lot more therapeutic if she wasn't jolted to reality by the sound of Timlet hollering at her from the deck. She jerked upright, flipped onto her stomach, and swam towards the rough rope ladder that hung down from the deck.

She climbed up, hoisted herself over the edge, and grabbed her worn pants and light-weight tunic from where they lay, then pulled them on as Timlet waited patiently. He had his usual expression of half-cocked excitement, but there was an odd pall behind his cheerful expression. He had seemed alarmed when she killed the merchant captain, although he himself had dispatched a young sailor only minutes earlier. He was easily her favourite crewmate, maybe because he was so different from the others. There was no question of their archetype—like her, life under the sign of the Corsair had made them reckless, charming and avaricious. Timlet, on the other hand, seemed like he might be more at home under the sign of the Merchant, working at a bakery or a grocer. He was a fair-weather *fiend*, but a true friend—almost like a younger brother. Aela didn't think she'd enjoy her days half as much without the chance to ruffle his ginger hair or coax out his ragged smile. She meant what she had said to the merchant captain. Her crewmates were her family, for better or worse.

"Captain's called a moot in the galley," Timlet said, sweating slightly as he averted his gaze from the damp linen hugging her form. Aela considered him for a moment with a wry grin and then made her way to the meeting.

AS SOON AS Aela stepped into the ship's galley, she was hit with a hot blast of salt, sweat, and aging pork. The furnace was lit, the flames roaring behind Dreadmoor as he shouted orders at the crew.

"We'll make port tomorrow morning at the city docks. If any one of you shit-brained amateurs draws the attention of the guard, you're on your own." Brine-aged ale sprayed from his tankard as Dreadmoor slammed it down on the table. Aela smirked. As much as he played the rough sea dog, she knew that the captain was a family man at heart. After all, he was the closest thing she had ever known to a father.

She rested her forearms on the cool surface of the ice box, listening to her crewmates chatter about the prospect of fresh food. After weeks of nothing but stale bread and salt pork, Aela was salivating at the prospect of a nice ripe orange or a handful of figs. She couldn't wait to slip unnoticed through the dockside souk and grab some fresh piece of paradise, letting the juice of the fruit run past her teeth as she bit through its flesh. But those weren't the only fruits she was looking to pluck. While every port had its own special delicacy, the city of Marinaken held her favourite—a crofter's daughter by the name of Brynne. Aela traced her teeth with her tongue as she thought about the smell of hay and the warmth of sunbeams that highlighted scattered freckles, that thread of common themes came to Aela each night as she slept. She always woke with a fleeting internal warmth that could never seem to be replicated during her waking hours.

"Seabitch!"

Aela's reverie snapped in half as Dreadmoor roared his name for her and shook his tankard. She wiped flecks of salty ale from her cheeks and bared her teeth at the old captain.

"Aye, Captain?"

"Something tells me you haven't heard a word I said," he barked.

"Memorized them, Captain." Aela grinned, standing to attention. The captain gave her a dark, humourless glance.

"You better watch your shit-eating mouth. One more insolent word and I'll declare open season on your hide." His lips parted to show crooked, rotten teeth as Dreadmoor brokered a threatening smile. At his words, lude jeers and slurs erupted from the rest of the crewmen and women. Timlet shrunk back, appearing genuinely concerned. Aela peered around and raised her eyebrow at the hardened crew as she shifted into a defensive stance.

"Good idea, Captain. We've been riding a bit low with all the new cargo. Could stand to throw a few bodies overboard."

Her hand rested against the smooth leather of her dagger's hilt as she anticipated a brawl. Aela was used to the captain testing her ever since she arrived on the ship as a child. She had assumed he was trying to prepare her for the realities of corsair life, and if so, he'd succeeded. She moved into a crouch, ready to cut the first bitch or bastard to try to prove their mettle against her.

Before anyone could reach her, Dreadmoor's tankard hit the slick deck like a shrapnel round, spraying ale and glass shards into jockeying crewmen.

"Get out of my fuckin' sight, all of you!" he roared as his crew tried to flee from the blowback, piling out on to the deck. As they scrambled, Aela backed up and stepped discreetly down the narrow stairs that led below deck. She slipped into the belly of the ship, taking a shortcut through the cargo hold, and paused to run her hand over the looted crates. A surprisingly good haul for a mercantile cog of that size, especially one so close to the coast. Normally that kind of ship would be carrying food and supplies up to the river valleys, but the cargo in the hold was full of Thandepar's best trade goods. Each crate featured a violet seal bearing the North Star, some holding high-value dyes, others good-quality seal pelts.

Aela poked and peeked, checking out the haul. Definitely one of their better ones in quite some time. Along with the crates were a couple of bulging gunny sacks. The first one made a clinking noise as Aela kicked at it with the tip of her leather boot. She raised her eyebrows and bent down, her suspicions confirmed as she opened the top to see that it was absolutely stuffed full of gold coins. Her breath caught in her throat as she realized she was looking at enough currency to establish a small estate. She picked up a gold piece, sliding her thumb across the design. One side bore the familiar North Star. The other side featured a profile of the Ansari king, his small tight mouth and high cheekbones standing out in stark relief. Aela stood up, flipping the coin across her knuckles, and tucked it into the lining of her tunic.

She left the hold, her head spinning over their newfound nest egg. Surely Dreadmoor had plans for it, but she had a few suggestions in mind now that they were apparently filthy fucking rich. But those could wait for tomorrow, she thought as she climbed up into the crow's nest to watch the sun rise.

THE CLOUDS SPLIT open, bloody hues sinking down behind the buildings of Marinaken as the ship shuddered into its natural deepwater harbour. Reedy stretches of land reached out on either side of the boat as they slid up into the mouth of the estuary. Farmland spread out on either side, meeting in the middle at the crooked port. Like most towns in Thandepar, the buildings tipped the past into the present. Ancient stone foundations were topped by timber refits as the community built itself upon the bones of unfamiliar ancestors.

As the ship reached its mooring on one of the many rickety finger docks, Aela slipped down the rigging and landed on the deck with a thud.

She stalked across the ship, then vaulted over the side and down onto the salt-stained planks to help secure the brigantine along with the other crewman before taking a look around. After being so long at sea, the sounds of the harbour rang in her ears. The main marketplace for the country's breadbasket, the dock area was full of every kind of salesman— fish, produce, baked goods, and those identifiable few selling something slightly more intimate. Aela smirked to herself. She had learned her lesson years ago in the southern ports. Young and hungry, she had handed her gold to the first woman to give her a peek, and ended up with a delicate and painful rash that made the local medic blush.

In the centre of the square, a crier stood on a raised platform, barking the horoscopical advice of the day for each of the archetypes. Not unusually, the Corsair was not included. Aela toyed with the gold piece from the hold as she approached the end of the dock, trying to decide which pastry seller seemed the most desperate. One sweet bun to get her energy up, and then her only plans involved freckles and moans.

As she stepped off the dock, she lurched forward, thrown off balance as Dreadmoor's massive arm landed around her shoulder.

"Aela, dear. Spare a moment for an old sea dog?" He bared his ugly grin and offered a hand as she tried to regain her balance.

"Can it wait? I have somewhere I need to—"

"Oh I wouldn't worry about that little ginger muff. Word on the cobble is that she's up and moved." He pulled Aela in conspiratorially.

"How do you know about her?" She knew that the captain didn't give a shit what she did once she left the ship. She was instantly put off by the idea that he would bother to find out. Had he been watching her? Anticipation began to grow in her chest, prickly and strange. It was not a feeling that Aela Crane was used to. She tried to take a step away as he dug his fingers in tighter.

"Oh come now, pip. I know everything. What kind of captain would I be if I didn't have all the information? After all, information is worth a lot."

Aela's stomach flipped as she stared at Dreadmoor. His blank expression was a threat. Not aggressive, not victorious—all business. Behind her, she could hear the townspeople scatter to clear the square at the sound of marching boots drawing near. The sound of the barker abruptly ceased as he quit the square, his monetary advice for followers of the Merchant abandoned midsentence.

Aela shuddered as she gazed past Dreadmoor onto the dock, where the crewman were lined up behind their captain. Not a single eye met hers—except for poor Timlet. He was peering around, concerned and confused. The idiot, he had no idea what was about to happen.

Aela knew. She knew that the person she trusted most had just bent her over a fucking barrel. She knew who she would see when turned around. She had his face tucked inside her tunic, imprinted onto the gold coin that rested against her skin.

"You sold me out," she hissed at the captain, as she turned to face the king of Thandepar.

HE WAS REGAL and refined. His skin wasn't so different a shade from the coin itself. It was a deep bronze, his expression far from welcoming. The skillful etching on the metal's surface had the same tight mouth and rigid cheekbones that framed a crooked general's nose and two eyes like fine marble. His deep purple general's coat matched the uniforms of the score of soldiers standing in formation behind him, the North Star insignia embroidered over their hearts.

The king cleared his throat pointedly in the midst of the awkward silence that had fallen as Aela looked him up and down, calculating. His attention lifted past her to rest on Dreadmoor, who still kept his arm firmly around his furious charge.

"I trust you received the payment?" His tone held no mirth. It was merely official, like chalk on slate.

"Like fish in a barrel." Dreadmoor smirked. Aela shuddered at her own idiocy. Two full bags of Thandepardine gold on an inland trader? She bit her lip in fury, the taste of blood dancing on her tongue. Dreadmoor gave her a rough shove forward and she stumbled to her knees.

"Go south." The king spat his words at the corsair captain. Clearly dealing with his kind left a poor taste.

"Move out, boys!" Dreadmoor shouted, herding the crew back towards the ship as the king's soldiers surrounded their new captive. Aela tried to think quick, but her mind felt sluggish. She tried to rise, letting out a guttural cry as the nearest two soldiers slammed her to the ground, prone. The adrenaline fought its way through her veins, blocking out sight and sound. She hardly heard Timlet's shouts. She only barely registered his body flying off the dock, knife bare, in the direction of the soldiers. What she did feel was the warm spatter as his arterial spray hit the cobbles of the dockside market.

"Up!" barked the king as the soldiers lifted her roughly to her feet. Now upright, she could see that he held the young sailor by the collar of his tunic as blood flowed loosely out of the gash in his neck. Red bubbles slipped out between his lips like glass orbs. Aela's heart pounded viciously against her ribs as the taut string inside her snapped. She roared, furious and wild. Heat radiated across her face as her eyes ignited, burning as her veins caught fire. She lashed out with every limb, every ounce of strength remaining. The guard scattered and re-grouped, coming at her in fours and fives, overcoming her once again. They had order, control, and military training. She had only desperation and rage. She lunged her head and chest forward as two soldiers pulled her arms behind her, the metal irons ringing as they were clasped around her wrists.

"The longer you struggle, the less chance he has of surviving." The king spoke evenly, devoid of emotion. Aela's gaze snapped back to Timlet. He gasped raggedly. For a bare moment, his eyes met hers, projecting desperation. Breathing deeply, she tried to centre herself.

"What...do you...want from me?" She stumbled on her words as she tried to calm the bloodlust that controlled her. The soldiers' grip held tight even as she swayed on her feet.

"I need your help with a task. And if you care about this misshapen pup as much as you seem to, you'll agree to assist me." He gazed down at her, his expression unreadable. This king seemed to have a knack for mystery. It suddenly occurred to Aela that she didn't even know his name. Call it a perk of living the corsair life, but there was no need to pay attention to local politics. Aela turned from the inscrutable king to Timlet. Her instinct was to resist, to be self-serving and stubborn. But in the end, he was the only person from her so-called family that cared about her fate. The rest of the crew was already scrambling onto the ship, preparing to make sail.

"If I help you, you'll get him to a medicinary?" she asked, hesitant to trust the strange monarch.

The king nodded.

Aela bit back the urge to keep fighting, her temperature dropping as she continued to breathe. "Then I agree."

As two soldiers left the pack to carry her bleeding friend in the direction of the city's healers, she cursed his idiocy under her breath. She always knew that he didn't belong among the bruisers in their crew. There's no place for a hero on a corsair ship.

WITH WHITE-GLOVED HANDS digging into her arms on either side, Aela let herself be half marched, half dragged across the square to the nearby teahouse. A tiny bell hanging from the lintel chimed softly as they entered the fairly well-appointed establishment, startling a plump shop woman who dozed at the counter. The stone floors were covered with soft hand-woven rugs, giving an air of cozy sophistication. This was not the worst scrape that Aela had gotten into, as a career corsair. The prim atmosphere of the teashop was alarmingly calm, a juxtaposition given the events that led her there. It was not the kind of place that made Aela feel comfortable; she preferred the hay-and-piss stench of shithouse taverns.

The good shop woman mopped her gray bangs out of her eyes and then jumped up to bring her sovereign of a fresh pot of tea and two cups, at his signal. The high, strained whistle of a kettle sounded from the kitchen. She must have been in the process of making herself a morning cup, only to have it co-opted by the man to whom she already gave a quarter income in fealty. Thandepar was not a nation made rich by coincidence.

Jerked roughly into a chair at an intricately carved wooden table, Aela resolved to keep quiet until she figured out exactly what the king wanted from her. As he sat down opposite, he smoothed the rich fabric of his uniform and stared back at her, impassive. She studied his face, trying to pick out any thread of humanity that she could exploit. Like any good brigand, Aela knew that finding the human side of your enemy could mean finding their weak spot.

His fingers were slick, long creatures. He held the teapot in one hand, pouring it into two cups held with the other. She wondered about his family. She wondered who he asked for strength at night, when he scanned the stars. He had a military look, so perhaps it was the Guardian, but there was something about his demeanour that didn't seem to fit. Aela had learned to pick out the constellation of the Corsair from a young age, though she had never stepped foot in one of his few blood-soaked temples. Dreadmoor taught her well in that regard. Aela flinched as she tried to squeeze that late fond feeling out of existence. Across the table, the king failed to hide a smirk. He had found her humanity first. She had lost their unspoken contest. He slid a cup of tea in front of her and signaled to her left guard. She heard the iron scrape as he unshackled her wrists. Aela resisted the urge to rub them as she stared hard across the table and repeated her question from the market square.

"What do you want from me?"

The king flicked his gaze up from his tea to meet hers as he took a sip. The steam from Aela's own cup rose in front of her like a soft breath across her lips and nose. She took the cup in her hands, letting the warmth spring through her aching muscles. The king opened his mouth to speak, pausing slightly before his delivery.

"I knew your father," he said.

Aela surprised herself by laughing sharply. Maybe she had overestimated this character if he thought that was going to help his cause.

"Congratulations. I didn't." Strangely, she thought she caught sight of a well-repressed smirk on the king's lips as she took a sip of tea.

"Aela Crane, I have a proposition for you." He poured himself a second cup as he waited for her to respond.

She didn't.

"Perhaps you've heard of a little problem we've been having in the mountains surrounding the capital."

Aela shook her head. "I'm afraid I haven't been paying that much attention to the local gossip of your country." Aela shrugged.

The king plowed on with his pitch. "The short version is that we're having something of a pest problem. A certain type of beast that your family is particularly...proficient in hunting." She didn't like the way his gaze bored into her as he spoke.

Aela raised her eyebrows, skeptically. "Well, I don't know what you've heard about me, but it can't be much, because I'm not a hunter, and my parents didn't teach me a damn thing."

"Trust me, you may not know it, but you're a natural-born hunter. And you'll have four of my finest men to accompany you." He gestured to his uniformed guards, standing in formation outside the empty tea shop.

"You mean guard me?" Aela glanced at the guards on either side of her chair.

"Not at all." He paused to sip the tea. "You'd be leading the expedition."

Aela stared at him, scrutinizing his every movement as he spoke, searching for a tell. She was waiting for the other boot to drop. So far nothing about this interaction added up.

"I'm sorry. Let me get this straight. You paid off my captain and crew to deliver me to your feet so that you could ask me for a favour?" Aela sat back, crossing her arms.

"Let's just say you're a difficult woman to get ahold of, and I was happy to do whatever it took to make that happen." His cold expression wasn't giving away any secrets as he spoke, so Aela decided it was time to push her luck a little. She kicked her feet up on the table and swigged the remainder of her tea.

"And what's in it for me?" she asked, dropping some swagger. The king shook his head almost imperceptibly, his mouth tightening.

"A room in my household and a position as the Master of Hunt." His lips twitched upwards at the corner as if he might attempt a smile. "The position your father once occupied."

Aela pursed her lips, confused. This strange hard man was offering her something she had been purposely avoiding her entire life: security, patronage, and a link to her roots. Aela smiled, knowing her decision was an easy one.

"Sorry, man. That's not really my thing." She pushed her chair back and stood up. "But thanks for the tea and bloodshed." The king signaled the guards to let her leave.

"Well, you're more than welcome to go on your way. We'll always be able to find you if we need you." He broke into a truly terrifying facsimile of a grin.

Aela smiled. If that was the threat she was waiting on, it was one that she could live with. She shrugged and walked away from the table. Already, she formed plans in her head: a new crew, a new boat, and the waves beneath her once again.

As she hit the door handle of the tea shop, the king called out: "But I'd worry about that young friend of yours if I were you. Modern medicine can only do so much."

Aela froze, her stomach dropping. Timlet. The king had managed to zero in on the one thing that made her human. Her blood flowed hot as she thought about the only person in the world she cared for, and realized that she should have let him die rather than be held over her head as a bargaining chip. She turned back to the king. He didn't even have the decency to smirk victoriously. He was as blank as ever. It was the Bureaucrat, Aela realized. That was the patron that he looked to in the sky in times of need, if he even had any.

"When do we leave?" Aela said, through gritted teeth.

Chapter Two

DEL FELT LIKE whistling as they marched through the foothills of the green belt, but he was pretty sure that soldiers weren't supposed to whistle. It was hard to hold the feeling in, though, with the meltwater streams tumbling down past grassy banks as his boots marched up the muddy path. He stretched his arms out in front of him, letting the dappled light fall over his golden-brown skin.

It had been a few days since they left Marinaken, marching back towards the capital city of Ghara and spending nights camped out under the stars. He didn't mind that he didn't have much to talk about with the other soldiers, but couldn't help feeling discomforted by the silent fury of their so-called leader. She marched ahead and slept apart. She wouldn't share the campfire and didn't know how to build her own, but then Del guessed that she didn't really need one anyways. She was like a mean joke, and he was still trying to figure out the punch line.

He couldn't dwell on it when the sun was shining onto the green belt. He loved that part of the country, though he didn't often have the chance to see it. It was so full of colour and sound, with farming towns that dotted the landscape. When he thought about the direction they were marching, his stomach dropped. Each step closer to Ghara, with its cold stone halls carved into the mountainside, made his feet leaden. He shook off the thought and let the spring return into his soles and his heart. He caught sight of a speckled finch lifting off from a tree branch, its talons leaving marks in the soft brown bark and shaking the buds.

As they marched uphill, the trees thinned and the incline grew steeper. The morning had begun with them shaking off the thin layer of frost that encased their hide sleeping sacks. Except for Aela, of course. She slept without a hide, basking in the open air, untouched by the chill. But as the permafrost crept down towards them, each morning became more difficult for Del. Every step was heavier, stiff and cold.

BY THE TIME the sun was high in the sky, the path took a sharp turn upwards as they came to a semivertical rock face. Tentative handholds stuck out of the rock, appearing trustworthy. Average merchants travelling between the capital and the coast would surely choose to take the under roads for safety, but Del knew that his companions took the rougher overland route to avoid being seen.

The ancient roads tunnelled underneath the ground all over the island nation of Thandepar and created the basis for the modern system called the under roads. While convenient enough, with entrances by most major towns, Del avoided those subterranean networks as often as he could. Every well-travelled road beneath the earth led past several sterile, empty villages that honeycombed through the rock. That was how his father's people had found this land, stillborn and abandoned. Del didn't believe in omens or portents, but he couldn't deny the shiver that traversed his spine every moment that he spent buried under dirt and stone, surveying the result of some inexplicable exodus.

Del shook off the thought as he stared up at the rock incline in front of them. Jetty sidled up beside him, shielding his eyes from the sun's glare.

"Don't worry. We'll get you up to the top, no problem." As Jetty grinned, Del felt the warmth of embarrassment spread across his cheeks. He had expected the special treatment but in no way wanted it. He had passed his survival training just as they had, and with the addition of his engineering specialty, he had no doubts that he could tackle the rock wall. Jetty's grin faded. The unruly blond hair that fell across his brow swayed in the breeze. Del didn't mean to jilt the other soldier with his silence, but couldn't help resenting any treatment that he perceived as extraordinary. He forced a smile in return as Crantz and Tern loped up beside them.

"Don't worry about me. Come on. I'll race you." Del slapped Jetty on the back as he moved forward to the base of the wall where Aela stood, staring upwards with a discerning eye. She didn't acknowledge his presence beside her as she scanned the rocks critically. Del decided to try his luck, not expecting it to go any better than his previous attempts to start a conversation.

"We've got rope and climbing gear. Tern will go up first and anchor the rope." He glanced at her sidelong, checking for any sign of a reaction. She was relentlessly solemn, her face like stone. He watched as she silently took a step back before launching herself onto the rock and starting her ascent. Del stepped back to avoid the falling chunks of stone as she attempted to scrabble her way up the cliff face. She was athletic and determined. He could give her that much. Unfortunately, as Del knew too well, sheer desire was so often not enough. Aela crept up the wall without support, scraping her body against the sharp protruding rocks, but as she stretched out for a handhold, it dislodged from the wall. With a sharp shout of surprise, she fell away, slamming back down to the ground.

Jetty, Crantz, and Tern held back as Del approached her. She lay in a heap, blood drawn on her bare arms, as he extended a hand to help her up. She looked up at Del, and he could see the anger that boiled under the surface as she ignored his gesture and pushed herself onto her feet. Del ran the scorned hand through his teak-coloured hair as he watched her stalk away to sit on a nearby stone. Back to brooding, apparently her favourite pastime.

Tern stepped up to the wall, equipment ready. He took a deep breath before lifting his body up to the first handhold. Slowly and methodically he made his way up as Del stood below with Jetty and Crantz. He was constantly surprised by the temerity of the other soldiers. They were only carrying out their mandatory three-year term service in the military, but tackled every task without fear or hesitation. Even now, when faced with a hostile, unpredictable force like Aela, they didn't complain or question their orders. It was a lot more than Del could ask of himself. He was constantly questioning the wisdom of their mission, especially his insistence upon being included. He had begged and pleaded with the king, not expecting even for a second to have his request granted. Now, here he was, with boys who had left heart and home behind to follow the king's orders.

Tern yelled from the top of the wall as he threw down the anchored rope for the rest of them. Jetty ushered Del forward and helped him attach his climbing harness to the rope. As Del made his way up, his hands sliding over the sun-warmed stones, he took care to place his foot carefully, knowing that even slightly too much force could dislodge enough rock to seriously injure those climbing below. It took a little under an hour for him to reach the top, with Crantz, Aela, and Jetty following beneath. He hauled himself up over the lip of wall and rolled flat onto his back on the grass of the plateau. Staring up at the blue sky as he caught his breath, Del's gaze followed several columns of smoke as they drifted across the sun. Confused, he raised himself to get the lay of the land. The plateau onto which they had climbed was dominated by an alpine meadow. A flat tableau of land in the shadow of a glacier with small farms surrounded the only settlement for miles—a collection of large, round yurts that were currently ablaze.

Del looked over to Tern, who stood staring across the meadow at the embattled village. Townsfolk grouped around the buildings, trying to quell the raging flames with pails of water before their homes were reduced to piles of ash. Tern's gaze caught Del's as they shared an unwelcome thought. Together they turned to the cliffside to help pull the rest of their compatriots over the side and pack away the climbing equipment.

While Del removed his harness, he caught a glimpse of Aela, catching her breath. She stared across at the burning village, her eyes wide. There was something almost childlike in her expression as the flames danced, reflected in her deep-brown irises. As he watched her, Del felt the air expand his chest as nostalgia bloomed between his ribs. Pushing that feeling down, he shouldered his pack and followed Tern into the village.

DEL MOVED THROUGH the small crowd of villagers, trying to get a better view of the damage. Ash lay on the husks of smouldering crops surrounding the smoking yurts. An older woman with a broad chest and sharp nose stood and directed the others as they tossed barrels of water onto their homes. As she spotted Del and the small troupe of soldiers approaching, and she began waving her arms to flag them down. As he reached her, the woman grabbed his forearm, her long fingers gripping around his wrist.

"Please, help!" She pulled Del towards her, eyes wild with fear.

Recovering from the initial shock, he placed his palm over her weathered and cracked knuckles where she gripped him. "That's what we're here for. Let us know what you need." He tried to keep calm and act reassuring, but he could feel the heat from the blaze on his face. When he inhaled, the thick smoke lined his throat. The woman released her grip on his arm and swung around to point towards the village hall.

"My daughter—she was right in its path." She seemed stoic and strong. Del had a feeling that the fear he could see was just the surface of a bottomless well. She shook his arm and his entire body reverberated. "Do you have any medical supplies?"

Del nodded, adjusting the pack on his shoulder. He turned back to the others only to find that Tern, Crantz, and Jetty were already running to the local well to help combat the flames. Aela, on the other hand, was just standing in the middle of the village, staring up at the flames. As Del approached, he could see that her eyes were glassy. He waved a hand in front of her face.

"Aela? Come on. I need your help." Her expression didn't change. Del didn't understand what was going on in her head, but that was nothing new. Grabbing her hand to drag her behind him, he snuck a glance back. The edges of her irises were flickering like a candle flame. "Not here. Bad idea," he hissed, trying to shake her out of her reverie.

Gulping down a quick pang of panic, Del turned and headed towards the village hall, pulling Aela behind him. As they got up to the steps of the building, she seemed to come back to herself. She didn't speak, just glared as she ripped her hand out of his and followed him up.

The village hall was the most significant building in the small alpine burg. It consisted of an open row of columns on either side, and a roof of beams and thatch. Linen walls had been rigged up between the columns to break the wind, leaving the interior to be lit only by a central fireplace. One of the only inhabitants, a teenage boy, kneeled over a young girl who lay on a clean sheet away from the fire. She hissed sharply through her teeth as he poured cool water over her shoulder and arm.

He stared up as Del and Aela approached and then shuffled away, panicked. Del swung his bag down onto the floor, sending dust rippling across the stones. He squatted down beside the little girl and took in the extent of her injuries. The skin across her upper torso was cracked and peeling. It was eroded, her dark red flesh scalded and burned as it stretched over her chest, right shoulder, and down her arm. The smell was uncannily close to roasted pork, and Del gagged slightly as he reached into his bag for a small jar of light green salve. He held it out to the teen boy and then stuck his own fingers in and spread the paste across the girl's burns. Her nostrils flared as he massaged it into her shoulder. The soothing effect was instant, Del knew, but it would a difficult and painful recovery for this young girl.

Del's breath hitched in his throat. That morning he had felt free, happy to be out of the capital. Now he was faced with the harsh realities of a task that he had begged to be a part of. He glanced up to see the teenage boy staring at him, wary.

"She's going to be okay. If you need to go and help, we can stay with her."

The boy squeezed the young girl's uninjured hand and stood up to go. He hesitated.

"You're a soldier." The boy stared down at Del, his dark eyes appraising. "I'm going to be like you in a few years."

Del forced a smile, feeling dishonest. "Yeah, you will."

The boy looked grimly down at his young charge before stalking out of the hall to help with the fires.

As he left, the young girl reacted. She tried to rise and search for him, but the moment that her body moved, she cringed in pain and fell back to the stone floor. She reached out her unburnt hand, asking for reassurance. Del could only register shock as Aela moved behind him and knelt to take the girl's hand. He glanced over at her, but she refused to meet his gaze. Shaking his head, he put his grimy but cool hand over the girl's forehead to check her temperature before applying another layer of the burn salve.

DEL WASN'T SURE how long they sat in the dimly lit hall in silence, although it seemed like a very long time. He would have expected an awkward silence, but that wasn't the case. The light from the fireplace danced across the walls as he pressed a cool, damp piece of linen over the young girl's forehead. Across from him, Aela sat, holding the girl's hand. Occasionally, he lifted his gaze to meet hers. It made his stomach turn with anxiety until she turned away. He was afraid of her, of the anger that always seemed to be simmering just behind her eyes, except for those brief moments in the village square when her mind seemed a million miles away.

The clatter of boots on stone caused Del to turn as the other soldiers stepped into the village hall in the wake of the woman who had directed him there. She had a hard look that softened the instant she caught sight of her daughter lying on the floor. Like the other villagers, the woman and her daughter had sharp noses and golden-brown complexions with dark brown hair. Unlike Thandepar's few metropolitan cities, full of expats and visitors from sundry foreign lands, the high-altitude mountain plateaus were populated by the same nomadic folk that had lived on the plains of the old world. Their sharp features and hazel eyes were shared by Del, passed down directly from his father.

"Thank you." The woman put a hand on Del's shoulder as she knelt beside her daughter.

"It's no problem at all. We're here to help." He handed her the small jar of salve. "You'll need this. We'll give you as much of our supply as we can. It will be a long recovery."

She gestured solemnly. "My name is Dorje. I'm the matriarch of this community." Dorje took the salve from him and extended her other hand. Del clasped her hand in his, an expression of deference. "We ran out of our medical supply about a week ago. This is our sixth attack this month."

Del was shocked by the number. "Any idea what has the creature so active?"

"There's been a corps of soldiers trying to extend the under roads up to reach our village. That could be it. But the daughters—they don't need any reason to go on a rampage."

Del glanced over at Aela, but quickly turned away as soon as he met her stare. He silently cursed himself when Dorje noticed. She gestured towards Del and Aela, and then to the benches circling the hall where their travelling companions were already sitting, slumped over and smudged with soot.

"Will you stay and sit awhile? Please have a cup of tea."

"It would be our pleasure." Del leaned back over his young charge and smiled. He squeezed her arm before rising to join the others. Aela followed suit.

It wasn't long before he and the others each had a hot cup of tea in their hands. Despite the fire, a chill was already starting to set in since the sun was beginning to set. It was notoriously cold in the mountain plateaus above the tree line. Del could already feel his lower limbs becoming stiff and painful. He held his cup up to his lips and took a sip.

Unlike the imported brews in the teahouses of Marinaken and Ghara, the folk living up this high had a penchant for a kind of tea unique to the upper reaches of Thandepar. Made with butter fresh from the wooly steers that roamed the upper steppes, this tea had a creamy texture and a salty taste. Del sipped it patiently, letting it warm his mouth and throat. He and the other soldiers were used to the unfailing hospitality of the villages they stopped in, and no strangers to the hearty brew.

Between sips, Del glanced over to see Aela holding the drink up to smell it. Her nose wrinkled slightly and her brows knitted together in confusion. He stifled a laugh, but not well enough. He couldn't help it. It was too amusing to see her puzzled expression replace the trademark glare she usually wore. Instead of reverting back to her sulky expression, she sniffed again and lifted an eyebrow at him. He raised his cup again and took a sip, smiling theatrically. Aela seemed skeptical as she followed suit, taking a sip of the butter tea. Her mouth quivered into a grimace as it passed over her tongue. Sputtering, she coughed down the tea like it was a cup of poison.

Del tried not to snicker as she shot him a despondent glare. He knew that look. It was one he never thought he'd see again. He tried to push down the feeling in his chest, like his heart was expanding to fill its cavity. He couldn't help but grin, but as soon as the smile stretched across his lips, it slid away as he remembered their mission. He drained the rest of his tea as he stood.

Turning to Jetty, Crantz, and Tern, he picked up his pack and shouldered it. "It will be dark soon."

Tern abruptly rose, all business. "We'll find a place to camp and make our final push to the cave tomorrow." He collected their cups and flagged down Dorje as she bustled by, filling the village hall with supplies from the ruined yurts. "We must be on our way."

Jetty smiled a handsome crooked smile at their host. He was all smooth edges as opposed to Tern's sharp corners. "Thank you so much for your hospitality. We'll check in again on our way back down the mountain."

Dorje raised her left hand, making the sign of the soldier, a local gesture meant to bring goodwill. "Thank you all for your efforts to help our village. Your sacrifice means hope for our children." She placed a hand on Jetty's shoulder. "There is a mountain spring and some rock cover a half hour up the path. It should make a decent camp for the night."

"Thank you," Jetty replied as Crantz and Tern prepped their packs and hefted them onto their backs. With Tern in the lead, the small squad stepped out of the village hall and into the fading light. As he walked, Del scanned across the results of the fire. The yurts would need some repair and there were burns to be healed, but no lives had been lost. In small villages such as this one, that meant a lot.

As they left the outskirts, Del spotted the teen boy that had been in the hall earlier. He was helping to shift supplies out of a damaged structure. Catching the boy's eye, Del held up his hands in the sign of the soldier. Turning to follow the path high up into the mountains, Del wondered if he would make it for the return trip down.

AS DORJE PROMISED, a rocky overhang jutted out of the mountainside just up past the village, creating a tiny cave; an ideal place to make camp for the night. Del checked over the dirt floor for any pointy rocks or stones before shaking out his bedroll and laying it down. The others did the same as he sat down with the pile of wood and kindling he had collected on the walk, and began to configure it for the evening fire. Jetty, Crantz, and Tern grabbed the empty waterskins and headed out in the direction of the spring.

At the beginning of their expedition, Del had resented being left behind as the soldiers stalked out in search of game and fresh water, but the colder it got, the less he was bothered. Filled with exhaustion, with his limbs stiff from the evening breeze, he was happy to stay behind and try to build a fire on the damp dirt floor. After trying a few times to spark a flame with the damp pieces of wood, Del sighed with frustration. Up this high in the mountains, even the most experienced needed some time to properly start a blaze without some kind of cheat.

He looked to the mouth of the cave where Aela leaned against the rock wall, staring out at the drizzling grey sky. His sight followed the line of her profile, from the determined set of her chin to the loose crest of curls that rustled in the mountain breeze. Her expression was stony; her jaw, clenched tight. She turned her head slightly, as if to express with irritation that she was aware he was staring. Del swallowed his nerves and held up a piece of firewood, trying to seem nonchalant.

"Could I get a hand here?" he asked, expecting to be ignored. Instead, she rose and walked over to join him.

"I think I've proven that my survival skills are useless," she said, sitting down cross-legged before the inert fire pit. Del hesitated, not sure how to respond to self-deprecation. Scratching his nose, he gazed at the ground and tried not to say something stupid.

"Well, I'm sure if we were on the sea right now, you'd be the only one left standing." He looked up to see her smirking. Probably because she knew it was the truth. "Besides," he continued, "you can do something I can't. I told you, I need a hand." He held up his own to demonstrate, placing it palm down on the damp, cold dirt. Aela lifted an eyebrow at him shrewdly before following suit, her rough, scarred fingers inches from his smooth ones. The minute that her palm hit the ground, he felt it. The moisture leached out of the earth, his palm drying as the ground became warm to the touch. Her hand appeared as it had just a moment ago, with no sign that it was doing anything out of the ordinary, but Del could feel the heat emanating in the space between their fingers. Her eyes were closed tight.

"It's harder to control up here," he stated matter-of-factly as her eyes snapped open with irritation.

"How do you know that?" She glared, lifting her hand off the ground and flexing it into a fist. Del shrugged and tossed her a piece of firewood, watching as her long fingers spread across the rough surface and warmed away the moisture. She brandished the now-dry piece of kindling at him. "You honestly have no idea how you seem to know more about me than I do?" Del raised his eyebrows, surprised. Clearly he had not been as discreet as he had intended.

"I don't know what you're talking about." He scoffed, grabbed the wood out of her accusatory hands, and replaced it with a damp piece. With the flint rock and the steel blade of his sword, he set to work with the newly dry wood, attempting to ignore Aela's inquest.

"Look, there's no need to play coy. I just want to know what your deal is," she said. Del avoided her glances as he focused on his work, creating a small spark. Carefully, he directed all of his attention towards nurturing the flame, trying very hard not to focus on her difficult expression as she spoke. "In the village, you saw my eyes. You knew what was about to happen and—" She broke off, handing Del more dry firewood as he built up the now pregnant fire pit.

"Is that unusual? I've heard of people like you before; we all have." He nodded to the empty bedrolls, referring to the other soldiers, and then brought his gaze up to meet hers. He was surprised to find that her expression was more frustrated than angry.

"That's not what I— Most people just think I'm a monster or some kind of legend. But you...seem to understand it." She stared hard at him, like she was searching for some kind of tell. Del shrugged again.

"I don't—"

"Never mind. It doesn't matter." She clenched her angular jaw again. For a moment, Del thought her eyes flared up, but it could have been the reflection of the growing fire. He sighed deeply and scooted closer to the fire to chase the cold from his legs. Holding his hands over the flickering flames, he tried to picture his entire body made of steel, sharp and unforgiving.

"I knew someone like you." He glanced up to see her sitting there, silent. She scanned his golden cheeks, studying him.

"Who?" she asked hungrily. Del thought for a moment that he couldn't imagine what it would be like to be that lonely. And then he remembered.

"He was my...mentor, I guess you could say." Del focused on the fire, roaring healthily away. "He taught me to build a fire, to hunt, to find shelter in the wilderness. He taught me to survive."

"He's dead?" She was blunt. There was something about her manner that Del felt oddly comforting.

He gestured his assent, visualizing the metal rivets marching across his steel-banded heart.

Aela smirked in a way that made Del want to crumble. "I had one of those once. He's not dead, but he sure as fuck will be when I catch up with him." She bared her teeth in a full grin, hungry for blood. For a minute, she had almost seemed tame. Del wanted to believe that she had just been raised by wolves, but he knew that she had started out feral and grown into a full-blown disaster. He shook his head as the sound of military boots heralded the return of his compatriots. Aela raised an eyebrow, peering out into the darkness until Jetty, Tern, and Crantz got close enough for the firelight to wash across their faces. Dusting off her hands, she rose and stalked back to the cave entrance to take up her solo vigil.

Del stood too, and his muscles creaked painfully with each step. As he helped Jetty skin and prepare the rabbits they had caught, he kept finding himself glancing over towards her. The moonlight hit her squarely, catching the lip of each scar that stretched across her muscular arms. It had taken him most of his youth to find her, and when he crawled into his bedroll that night, the warmth from the fire at his feet, he tried to ignore the nagging thought that by the next sunset they might both be dead.

Chapter Three

THE SUN'S RAYS stretched from peak to peak as the expedition set out in the early hours and followed the rough path farther up into the mountains. Aela shifted her pack, keeping herself several strides behind the soldiers. Despite spending so much time in their presence, she still refused to let her guard down around them, though she noticed herself slipping with the soft one. He seemed different than the others, motivated by more than simple duty. Every time she glanced his way, their gazes met, as if he had been staring for some time. Lately he had been less inclined to look away bashfully.

So far out of her element, Aela knew that she couldn't afford any vulnerability. The world was different so high up. She didn't think she had ever been this far from the sea. She missed the sharp smell and the salt spray on her skin. Even though the cold didn't bother her, the dry crisp air in the mountains made her feel light in the head.

The path they followed was nothing more than a thin rutted track of mud. Jetty, the one with the easy grin, had pointed out that there were no villages this far up, and so the only folks who took this trail were foragers or miners, heading out to find a new vein of gold. Anyone who ventured to this altitude was aware of the danger inherent in knocking so close to the home of the nearby naga, the beast that Aela had agreed to dispose of.

It had been on a quiet evening during the second or third day of their journey that Del had described the creature to her. They had sat by a creek as the sky began to darken, Del telling her tales of the nagas' destructive ways. The other soldiers dipped and swam in the clear-flowing water, their armour and underclothes strewn along the bank as they rinsed off the day's dirt. She declined their offer to join in by way of a measured glare. Del reclined on the bank, and she noticed they hadn't pressed him to join. She lay back on the soft grass of the riverbank, focused on the darkening sky as Del spoke. She tried to maintain her indifference even as he described the vicious beast they would face at the end of their journey. It wasn't really a conversation. He spoke, and she listened without reply.

A great scaled beast, he said, that lived high in the mountains, eating livestock, spraying tongues of flame, and laying waste to local villages when some minor action left them inscrutably displeased. Called naga by the locals of Thandepar, these beasts had inhabited the land's peaks long before the refugees arrived on its shores. As Aela wondered if her own long-gone people had dealt with the beasts as well, Del mentioned that there were dusty leather tomes in Ghara's library that referred to them as "Daughters of Balearica." They were written in an ancient tongue. Aela was surprised that he could read her people's language. Like Aela and her corsairs, the majority of the population here were illiterate in their own language, the common tongue.

Even then, Aela thought to herself as she climbed the rock-scrabble slope, something had seemed off about this young soldier. He was capable, but something about him felt weak. He reminded her of Timlet when he laughed, making Aela suck in a sharp breath, pushing a rising tide of emotion back down her throat.

AFTER SCRAPING THEIR way up a slope covered in varying sizes of loose rock, hands dry and rough, Aela and the others hoisted themselves up onto a plateau of rock that stretched between two tall snow-capped peaks, its width no more than an eagle's wingspan. Almost as soon as she rose up to her full height, Aela dropped flat back down to the ground. Suddenly there was no comforting hill rising just in front of her feet. On either side of her was a dizzying drop.

If she looked down the way they had come, she could see their entire journey so far laid out in front of her. At the foot of the moraine, the zigzagging, rutted track ran down to the alpine plateau with the burned village. Farther down, the hills grew smaller and smaller until they were nothing more than lumps rolling across the green belt, stretching out to meet the distant sea. The port city of Marinaken was nothing more than a hazy blot that Aela could barely make out.

Aela inhaled sharply as she peered over the other side of the ridge. The land fell steeply away into a snow-covered valley, until it rose right back up again toward more distant icy peaks. Shaking, she tucked her legs beneath her, rising on the balls of her feet. As she stood, she could see the other soldiers scouting ahead along the ridge. Except for Del, who stood beside an old stone structure that seemed carved out of the very rock on which they stood.

She stepped forward gingerly and approached him from behind as he ran a hand across the delicately patterned rock lintel.

"What is this?" she asked. He turned to acknowledge her. She tried to will her body into a dignified stillness, but her nerves betrayed her. Her knees seemed to insist upon knocking together.

"I'm not sure. It doesn't look like a traditional shrine, but it seems to have been used that way." He pointed to the floor, where dried blood was collected in the crevices between the smooth flagstones. At the back, a worn copper idol sat on a shelf beside a shallow bloodied bowl. "I think the villagers have been making sacrifices to the naga, like you might make to the Corsair."

She furrowed her brow. Aela couldn't think of any other patron for which blood sacrifices were a regular custom. "Maybe they think that if they bring it fresh meat, it might not make a meal of their children." She ran her hand across the stone above the door. Figures were carved into the rock there. "Do you know what this says?"

Del peered at her in confusion. "You can't read that?"

"No, I can't read common. If you think that's a vital skill for a corsair, then you really don't understand what we get up to." Aela peered hard at the markings, willing them to make sense.

Del shook his head. "It's not common tongue. It's Sarkany."

"Oh." Aela felt warmth spread across her cheeks as she recognized the Thandepardine word for her people. Remembering herself, she shrugged and stepped inside the makeshift shrine, spitting onto the bloodstained floor. She had been right. This kid did seem to know more about her than she did, or about her people at least. But then, to know anything would be more than she did, really.

As Aela rubbed the toe of her boot around in the crusted blood, it happened again—that same feeling that she had in the village square, as she stared at the flames dancing across the taut fabric of the yurts. It felt as if an unbearable silence was pounding in her ears, blocking out all of her other senses. The only thing to which she could compare the phenomenon was when she had been caught too close to a barrel of gunpowder as it exploded. The wave of heat knocked her off her feet and onto the deck of the ship, a commandeered military vessel in the Southern Sea.

Aela hunched over, her back pressed against the stone structure that perched precariously on top of the ridge. She could see Del in front of her, his expression panicked as his lips moved soundlessly in slow motion. Her head ached, the pain splitting from one ear clear through to the other, as if an unfamiliar seed inside of her mind was trying to bloom. She could feel herself sliding down to sit on the bloodied stones as the alien discomfort in her mind seared through her skull, forming into language.

"I know why you're here."

The echo bounced off her nasal bone and rattled down her spine. Aela shuddered, bile rising in her throat, as if purging her stomach would clear her mind.

"What are you waiting for? Come on and try me."

As quickly as the wave had crashed through her mind, it receded, leaving Aela to attempt to regain her awareness, with only a dull throb in her temples to prove that anything had occurred. First, she registered the feeling of her body crouched against the wall, her ass firmly planted on the floor. The second thing she noticed was the sensation of Del's smooth bronze hands gripping her upper arms as he crouched in front of her, his green sea-glass eyes filled with the utmost concern. Thinking only of her vulnerable state, she instinctively lashed out, her elbow connecting with his nose. He fell back against the opposite wall, lifting his hands up to his face as a small trickle of blood rolled down towards his upper lip.

"What the fuck?" he shouted. He didn't seem angry so much as shocked. Aela launched upright, realizing where she was and what she had done.

"I'm sorry! I don't—" She broke off as the other soldiers appeared in the doorway, returning at the sound of Del's shout. "I didn't mean to do that, Del."

Aela's back scraped against the stone wall as Tern grabbed her by the arm and jerked her swiftly out onto the ridge. He held her firm as Jetty ducked into the shrine, helping Del onto his feet and into the sun. The blood was smeared across his face and fingers. Tern grabbed Aela's wrist and twisted, causing her to cry out as he pressed her down into submission.

"Okay. What the hell just happened here?" He was staring impatiently at Del, who was trying to stem the flow of blood with a dirty handkerchief. Del glanced down at Aela, concern still in his eyes.

"I don't know. Something strange just happened to Aela." He dusted himself off, holding out a bloodied hand to help Aela up, quickly intercepted as Crantz placed himself between them.

"Whoa. I'm sorry. Something weird? Like her monster mind activating and causing a crazed bloodlust?" Crantz puffed up his chest as if trying to protect Del from Aela. She stayed crouched, her wrist in Tern's grip as she tried to assess the situation.

"Del?" She tried to appeal to him. He clearly had some feeling for her, even if she didn't understand it. "I didn't mean to hurt you. I don't know why I did that."

Tern shook his head sharply and bent down and grabbed the knife hanging off of her belt. "I'll be holding onto this until you reach your destination." He released her, tucking the knife alongside his own. "Come on. Let's get this over with." Tern stepped out into the lead, expecting the others to follow. Crantz seemed hesitant to remove himself from between Aela and Del as she stood, gingerly rubbing her wrist. Finally he turned away, sneering at Aela as he steered Del forward to walk ahead of him. Jetty fell in behind Crantz, and Aela followed up in the rear, left to try to understand what had just transpired. She caught Del trying to look back at her several times as they walked along the steep and dangerous ridge.

Whatever had come over her, it had been happening with increasing frequency since they started climbing. Usually it was during the night, and no one had been aware that while they slept, she lay frozen against the ground, the sound of the soldiers' snores stretching out in slow motion. The only other time someone had noticed was in the village square when Del took her arm and pulled her into the village hall. He had thought that she was about to unleash, but to her, that feeling was one that was as familiar as sadness or joy. This new phenomenon was an entirely different one that she had no idea how to control. She turned back to see the shrine shrinking in the distance, and then forward towards the icy peak that rose up at the end of the ridge.

THEY WALKED FOR several hours as the sun reached its full height in the sky. With every step, the peak in front of them drew closer, and the shrine at their backs stretched away into the distance. Aela tried to peer around the others, shrewdly searching for some sign of what they were heading towards.

Finally, they reached the massive vertical wall of rock that reached up to the craggy snow-capped summit. Scanning the base, she saw it: a small dark slit that stretched out where ridge met rise. The cave's mouth was a thin horizontal wound, no more than two feet tall. Aela quirked an eyebrow. Any creature that called that place home couldn't be that large. Where was this terrifying beast she was tasked to dispose of?

Tern stopped a few feet away, letting the others catch up to him. Reluctantly he reached into his belt and pulled out Aela's knife, holding the handle out for her to take. As she grabbed it, their eyes met. His distaste for her was palpable.

"So what's the plan here?" Del piped up, fidgeting with his scabbard and looking from the mountain to his compatriots.

Jetty rolled his eyes. "She goes in." His expression hardened as he turned to Aela. She wished she could feel surprise, but what point was there? She knew the minute she'd agreed to go on this mission that there was a pretty good chance that she was going to be handling this alone. It was the price that she had agreed to pay for Timlet's life, and right about now, she was starting to curse whichever useless fucking tender feelings had managed to anchor themselves in her chest.

Del, on the other hand, seemed shell-shocked. "Wait, she goes in to scout, and then we follow?" His gaze drifted from Crantz, to Jetty, and finally to Tern's icy gaze as he put the pieces together. Aela scoffed. What was it about her that seemed to attract people that couldn't spot a sacrificial lamb if it kicked them in the sac?

Standing behind Del, she put a hand on his shoulder as the other soldiers visibly tensed up. "It's fine. Just stay here, I'll be right back."

Aela flipped her knife up into the air and caught it deftly and then turned her back on the soldiers. Her boots crunched against the rock as she approached the cave.

"Wait! I'm coming with you!"

She looked back to discover Del running after her, unaware that just behind him was Tern, leaping to tackle him down to the ground. Del groaned as his breastbone slammed against the rock. Aela backtracked, approaching his prone form, Tern sitting on his back to make sure he didn't move. Aela shook her head as she squatted down beside the soldier.

"Sorry, kid. I don't think you're allowed into this party, but I will take this." She slid his sword out of the scabbard attached to his belt, then stood and placed a foot squarely on Del's. Aela was more confident with a knife than a sword, but as she walked away from the soldiers and towards the naga's cave, she thought that really, more steel couldn't hurt.

AELA CROUCHED AS low as she could and peered inside the cave. The scree sloped down swiftly in a scatter of rocks towards a smooth, worn floor. She hunched down and pushed herself through the opening, her tunic catching on the sharp protrusions from the rocky ceiling, which scraped across her back.

Failing to keep her balance on the loose rocks, she scrambled down towards the cave floor. Stones bounced across one another, carrying her downhill in a mini-avalanche, the sound of which echoed off the walls. She jumped to land on the floor of the cave. *There goes the element of surprise.* The only light source she could see was the entrance she'd just come through. Glancing back up at it, she could only make out a thin ribbon of blue sky.

Aela gripped the leather sword hilt in both hands and held it up in front of her, trying to reflect the dim beams of light into dark corners to feel out her surroundings. Three giant pillars of rock rose up from the floor to meet the ceiling, and the cave seemed to stretch out endlessly behind them. Standing with her back to a pillar, Aela angled Del's sword to try to get a reflective peek at what lay ahead, only to be nearly struck blind with the sparkling shine that blasted off the surface weapon.

"Hello, shiny," she whispered, peeking out from behind the pillar to peer into the half dark. Small shafts of light drifted down from odd angles in the wall, like veins of illumination forming a wide semicircle on the wall of the cave. What Aela found more interesting, however, was what they revealed.

In the middle of the cave floor was a massive pile of gold. Coins were piled and stacked, bulging out of burlap sacks and iron-banded chests. Even after a life of piracy, Aela had never seen a stash this big. She crept forward, swept a hand through the clinking mass to pluck out a thick gold coin, and held it up into the shifting beams of light.

Aela held the coin steady as the light moved across it. Sharply, she jerked her head up as she became aware that the light hadn't been moving a moment before. She scanned the cave and found the veins of light in the cave wall growing and morphing as a horrible realization hit her squarely. The light wasn't moving at all.

It was flowing in full force from an opening in the side of the mountain the size of a ship, previously blocked by the shifting creature now rising up in front of Aela's eyes. Its scales glinted and gleamed, reflecting the blinding sunlight that poured in from a hole full of blue sky. She was pretty sure the breach led to a straight vertical drop.

Aela looked around the now-bright cavern to see that it was massive, essentially the mountaintop itself, hollowed out.

"I guess I came in the back door," she said under her breath. Stepping away quickly, she pocketed the thick gold coin as she began to fall under the sway of that unfamiliar numbness. Aela crumpled, her knees hitting the rock, her body slumped against the nearby stone pillar. Her mind prickled with pain as words echoed through it, bouncing off the facets of her skull.

"Are you here to kill me or just to steal?"

Aela turned, scooting her butt back against the pillar. She grasped the sword hilt in one hand, her fingers begging it to bring her back to reality. She tried to blink the pain away, only to see the full form of the naga above her, punctuated by sunlight from the cave mouth.

Rising like a manor house, every inch of its body was covered in dull copper scales. Four lean, powerful limbs gave way to feet with violent talons the length of Aela's thigh, which could gut a yak in one quick swipe. The magnificent scales rippled across its breasts and neck, and led up to a terrifying head. A reptilian snout stuck out above long, curved fangs, but the worst part was its eyes. They flickered and flared like the fire that licked along the village yurts. Ringed in gold and crimson, with an ice-blue halo undulating wildly around the pupil, the familiarity choked Aela's throat closed in fear.

"Well? What's it going to be?"

The voice stampeded across her mind as the creature lowered its head to Aela's level in one smooth movement, its feathered mane flowing along an uncanny spine. Aela fought the urge to throw up as she rose to her feet, her back moving against the stone pillar. She winced as the rough rock scraped over her raw skin. The pain broke through her clouded mind like the sunlight thrusting across the cave. Gritting her teeth, she hefted the sword and moved forward towards the naga's face.

"How about both?" she said, spitting onto the stone floor and sinking down into a fighting stance. The king had told her she would have some kind of familial knack for fighting this beast, but so far, she didn't feel like she had any more advantage than usual, even if they had the same eyes.

She leapt to the side instinctively as the naga rushed forward, snapping its jaws at her. The teeth were long and sharp enough to puncture straight through her chest. Aela struck out at its lip with her blade and then danced back across the shifting pile of gold. It might as well have been quicksand for all the purchase it allowed her. The beast reared back, and Aela's mind was mired once more as it spoke inside her head.

"Too bad. The gold is mine. I earned it," it hissed. *"What is it that you truly desire? Wealth? Honour?"* It leapt forward, shaking the cavern and sending piles of gold tumbling down on top of her. Aela brushed the coins off of herself and crawled free of the pile as she tried to think straight. The naga pressed its mental offensive. *"Or are you here to please your little king?"*

Aela choked out a laugh. "I have no king. I'm here for me." She ducked swiftly as the naga struck out with its claws.

"Why do you lie? Is it because you know that he found your weak spot? That he played your heartstrings like a harp?"

Aela shuddered, rising as its vicious voice ripped through her.

"Or have you not even realized that yet?"

Aela bared her teeth and growled. She could feel herself losing control as the monster continued, raising her ire with each pointed question.

"Oh look, it's getting angry. You are so fun to play with. Too bad you're almost extinct."

Aela was sure she saw a smirk spread out behind the naga's fangs. She wasn't sure if it was talking about her or her kind. She put a hand to her head as the pain increased.

The creature let out a shriek of joy. *"Don't give up on me now. I haven't even brought out the real firepower yet."* The naga reared up and sprayed a thin spiral of smoke and sparks out of its ridged nostrils.

Aela gritted her teeth as the pressure built inside her head, her temples throbbing. One hand on her sword, she used the other to draw the knife from her belt. Trying to keep steady, she shifted her weight. In one smooth motion, she drew the knife across her thigh, letting the blade bite into her flesh. Aela winced, choking out a gasp as the pain shot through, clearing the naga's influence from her mind and igniting the fire in her chest.

The naga reared up, striking towards her with its sharp claws and a jet of flame as Aela spun away from the fire into a crouching position. She grinned, overtaken by the frenzy of bloodlust, her eyes glowing to match those of the beast. As she ducked and wove between the naga's powerful claws, she realized that this wasn't like any other fight. She didn't have to be afraid that anyone would see her for what she truly was. She inhaled the fresh air and gave into the fight as she slashed out with knife and sword, cracking the beast's worn copper scales.

Aela tucked and rolled away from another violent jet of flame, working on pure instinct. Not only that, she seemed to be anticipating the naga's moves. They were connected in some way that she didn't understand. With every lunge of its claws, its forearms planting down like tree trunks, she jumped and rolled and dove away, knowing where each attack would come from, her single-minded battle fury blocking its attempts to communicate.

The naga screamed in fury as Aela pressed it back towards the gaping front door of its home. She stabbed out with either weapon in turn and jammed them between its toes and under its shining scales, drawing thick red ropes of blood. With every advance, she felt euphoric, like she was perched on top of the crow's nest, arms outstretched as her ship raced at full speed across the wide blue sea.

Suddenly the beast was the one scrambling across its vast piles of gold, trying to stop itself from being forced off the edge of the crevasse, straight down into the valley below. Its cries rent the air, claws dug into the rock walls on either side of the cave's mouth, its mouth and nostrils blasting an inferno. Aela dashed back into the fray after narrowly avoiding a jet of flame, laughing maniacally as she launched herself off of a treasure-crammed chest to land squarely on the naga's snout. Its eyes opened wide as she landed, inches from the wavering flames that glowed just behind their glassine surfaces. Smiling wide, she tucked the knife back into her belt in order to hold the sword with both hands. Her thighs straddled either side of the monster's snout, just above its smoking nostrils. The heat rose up into her body.

"You're so fun to play with," Aela said as she raised an eyebrow briefly before narrowing both in a violent mask of fury. "Too bad you're almost extinct." Using all of her upper-body strength, she plunged the sword into the beast's left orbit, puncturing its flickering eye. A spray of hot blood hit her body as the naga raised its head, letting out a powerful scream. Aela raised herself, ready for round two, ignoring the way her feet were sliding across the beast's scaled and bloody snout, and deaf to the sound of its claws grinding through the rock wall as it lost purchase.

Suddenly, Aela lost her balance and slipped back across the naga's snout towards the curved fangs that rose up from its jaw like a herald's horn. Gripping on to the yellowed protrusion with one hand and her sword with the other, she looked up at its claws, about to lose contact with the rock. Without a second thought, she leapt down to the floor of the cave just as the naga disappeared from view with a shriek, dropping down into the valley below.

Breathing hard, Aela knelt on the cave floor where she had landed. She remained in that position as the bloodlust drained from her body and her eyes returned to their usual shade of brown. Deep grooves marred the walls where the naga's claws had dug in as an attempt to save its life. She was shaking as she stood, surrounded by the piles of gold, spattered with blood and broken copper scales. She couldn't quite grasp what had just happened. She usually tried at all costs to repress her true nature when she fought. This time, she had fallen into it fully, and she wasn't sure how to feel. Unsteady was as much as she could decide at this moment.

She pocketed a handful of gold coins and headed for the cave's back door where the soldiers and Del would be waiting. If she didn't tell them about the treasure haul, she could always come back for it later. Trying to find her way, she stumbled as she kicked a bright, bleached vertebrae, sending it skittering across the rock. Now that the place was sharply lit, she could see the countless bones piled against the wall and littered across the floor. She climbed the slope of loose rocks that led up to the slim slot of sky that she had come through, trying to be careful where she placed each hand and foot.

Just as she grabbed a large knobbled stone, a pained shriek rent the air. Aela stiffened as she stared up at the opening, trying to see what had made that noise. A familiar shadow swooped low in front of the cave's thin mouth, blocking out the light that filtered across her field of vision. Aela peered up to see that the naga had returned for another round. As it flew closer, it was clear that one of its large eyes was damaged and dripping. The beast crashed down onto the ridge outside, the force of its landing shaking the entire mountain. The percussion sent Aela tumbling back to the base of the debris, sharp stones fell and tumbled over one another, pelting her, as if they were running away from the source of the sound. Landing hard on the stone floor, Aela reached out across its pitted surface, trying to drag herself out from under the blanket of loose gravel and rock that covered her body.

Failing miserably, Aela dropped her arms, exhausted. She lay still, her cheek pressed against the cold stone, and listened intently for any sounds of battle on the ridge as she tried to summon the strength to move again. She heard only the low shudder of the naga's claws scraping across the ground as it moved. She was sure the beast had returned to finish her off. Another earsplitting scream cut through the air, punctuated by what she recognized as the hiss and crackle of fire pouring from its snout. The blowback hit her seconds later. A hot dry breeze poured through the mouth of the cave, carrying on it a few flickering embers and the smell of roasted meat. Aela's eyes shot wide open. She summoned every last shred of effort and rolled onto her side, shifting as much debris off of her back as she could, and then kicked her feet out of the gravelled quicksand and rose, her body aching in protest as she tried to climb up to the cave's mouth once more.

She stepped gingerly from stone to stone up the incline until finally Aela could touch the rim of the rocky opening with her hands. Peering out, she could see the naga perched, facing away on the ridge several feet from her. Its long feathered mane shifted in the breeze among curls of smoke. Aela couldn't see past the beast, but from the pungent smell of the roasted flesh, she had a pretty good idea about how the soldiers were doing. A pang of hunger sprang unbidden, and she tried to push the morbid feeling back down into the pit of her stomach.

She unsheathed her sword and threw it out onto the surface of the ridge before placing both hands on the edge of the cave mouth. Using her muscular arms, Aela lifted herself up and over the lip, then crawled out onto the ridge. Flat on her back for a brief moment, her eyes watered as the full power of the smoke hit. Quickly she rolled herself onto her stomach, jumped into a crouch, and grabbed her sword where it lay. In front of her, the naga stood its ground, long and leathery wings drooped on either side of its thick spinal column. There was barely room for it to plant its feet on the thin mountain ridge.

The beast threw its head up into the air and screamed again before launching itself off the ridge and spiraling out across the blue. It swept the sky, wings outstretched and cutting through the air. Aela glanced up at the place where it had sat moments before. Just beyond the gutted claw marks sat a pile of smoking debris. She staggered forward, towards the still-smouldering bodies. Kneeling in front of the slumped husks of the soldiers, she recognized Tern atop the others, his skin cracked and charred. Jetty and Crantz were curled on either side, and underneath them...

Aela peered at the naga's victims, well aware that she had little time with it still airborne nearby. Poking Crantz's ashen arm aside, she jumped up, stifling a shout. Underneath, lay a soft unburnt hand. Aela crouched back down, hurriedly. She reached between the bodies, grasped Del's wrist, and was rewarded with the sight of his hand gently flexing. Aela peered up at the sky. The naga had disappeared from view, but she was certain it would come back for its meal, and for her. Shifting the corpses of the soldiers away, she uncovered Del's upper body. His eyes were heavy-lidded, and he was not without his share of burns, but he appeared as if he might make it.

Aela grasped his hand and pulled Del out from under the others. He opened his eyes wide and blinked at the sun, registering her presence. He opened his mouth as if to speak before choking violently on the smoke caught in his lungs and the smell of his dead friends. He swung his other hand up as he coughed, and Aela grabbed it, yanking both of his arms toward herself until his legs slid out from under the others' bodies.

Aela brought her face down to his. "Can you make it?"

Del assented, still coughing.

"Good, then get the fuck up and don't look back," she snapped as she grabbed his hand in hers and stood, leveraging her own weight to pull him to his feet. She clapped him on the back as they stepped across the bodies of the soldiers.

Together, they stumbled along the ridge, trying to find the trailhead that led back down the mountain. Aela couldn't see the naga but doubted they were home free. It was very intelligent and clearly pissed. That thing was far more than a wild animal, and besides being a vicious vindictive piece of work, it seemed to have it out for her in particular. She thought about her sword ripping into its flame-ringed eye and mused that she might kind of deserve it. Beside her, Del seemed to regain his composure as he jogged, his footing getting surer with each step. He peeked over at Aela, inhaling sharply as he noticed the blood that was painted across her body.

"I didn't know that was going to happen. That they would make you go in alone." His eyes were big and wide and pathetic.

Aela shrugged. None of that mattered now. "Save the heart-to-heart. Just keep going." She pulled ahead, the sight of the old shrine in front of them bolstering her confidence that they might actually make it out of this alive. With a well-timed retort, the naga's telltale scream filled her ears. She paused and turned back as Del raised his chin to see the naga soaring over his head. It wheeled through the sky and hurtled down towards the ridge to block their escape route.

"Get the fuck down!" Aela grabbed Del by the shoulders and pushed him facedown onto the ridge as the naga landed, its body slamming into the ground, shuddering through the very rock of the ridge.

It perched just beyond the shrine, blocking their chance to slip past and head down the way that they had come. Aela jumped to her feet and turned to help Del, but he was already dragging himself up. He stared at the beast, transfixed, before jerking his head towards Aela. She looked back at him. His skin was raw and red across his cheek and arms. He must be in an incredible amount of pain.

"I don't think I can kill it," she said. Her body ached. Her limbs were fighting every movement, and the muscles in her chest and legs screamed with pain.

Del gestured up to the naga's damaged eye, blood still seeping from the punctured orb. "Did you do that?"

He stared at Aela as she violently shook her head once more at the naga's intrusive presence. She focused on blocking out its distractions, trying to use the intuition that had flooded her senses back in the cave. Full awareness floated just out of her mental reach. The naga perched itself a ways down the ridge, daring them to try to get past.

As Aela tried hard to think of another way out, she felt Del grabbing at her arm and pulling her forward towards the naga. "Are you crazy? Do you want to end up like your friends back there?" She pulled back and found that she hardly had the strength.

"No, and we definitely will if we don't find a way off of here," Del hissed, dragging Aela down the path until they were mere feet from the beast, its body towering above them like a trebuchet. It raised its head, one good eye burning intensely. Aela could feel its violent hatred piercing her mind as they drew level with the shrine. Her mind leapt into action one more time as the beast reared up in front of them, smoke preemptively jettisoning out of its nostrils in lazy curls. With a pained whine, it jerked towards them, spraying fire out across the ridge just as Aela pushed Del into the shrine and dove in behind him.

The flames flicker past her, the heat rolling across their skin where they slumped on the floor just inside the doorway, barely protected by the stone wall of the shrine. Aela stared at Del, whose gaze was locked inscrutably on the floor. She could hear the naga's claws moving across the ridge rock as it repositioned itself for another attack. This was really not where, or with whom, she had expected to die. She had always thought she'd go out like a maniac, blood spraying as she was struck again and again and again by enemy corsairs or retributive merchants or do-good soldiers. She definitely had not expected to die side by side with a do-good soldier.

The structure rocked as the naga slammed its body into it, obviously trying to bowl it over to get the sweet reward inside. Tiny stones rattled against Aela's feet as its assault continued. Cracks spiderwebbed across the flagstone floor. Beside her, Del moved, crawling forward. Surely he knew any move he made now was pointless. This little shack would barely last one minute more, and one side was as good as the other.

Sure enough, with concussive force, the naga headbutted the tiny building just as the floor caved in beneath them and the walls gave way. Aela clung to the makeshift altar, trying not to slide down into the yawning darkness. Beside her, Del laughed triumphantly, grinning like a fool.

She looked over in confusion, barely a second to register what was happening before he grabbed her hand and pulled her down into the widening hole at their feet. They fell through the dark. Aela choked back a cry as her back slammed into a sharp stone edge when her body hit the ground. Arching painfully, she stared up at the circular opening they had just fallen through, now high above. Rocks came rattling down towards her as the naga rummaged through the wreckage of the shrine. A blast of flame lit up the space all around Aela. She could see Del beside her. She reached behind her to feel the protrusion that she had landed on, only to find that it was the smooth angle of a step. To her left, a stone column rose up out of the depths where a set of stairs descended around it. They had fallen into the conch-like well of a spiral staircase that fell away into the unknown dark. Up above on the ridge, the naga rampaged, unable to find its prey. The ridge shook with its fury, the sky glowed hot with fire, and Aela smiled, having escaped certain death once again.

Chapter Four

FOOTSTEPS ECHOED FROM the adjacent chambers as Brynne Halloran ran her fingers across the dark purple satin of the dress lying on her bed. Here in the capital city of Ghara, sound moved in different ways. It slammed upwards from below and drifted sideways between tiny cracks in the crumbling masonry. The clatter resonated through her chambers; though small by the standards in Ghara, they were much larger than her old attic room in Marinaken. After stepping out of her day-dress, Brynne curled her toes against the cold stone floor. A mountain breeze flowed in through the open window, nipping at her skin and turning the tips of her breasts hard as marble. She'd had her pick of living arrangements when she arrived. The lower the room, the warmer the air, but Brynne had jumped at the chance to have a view. From her window, she could see out across the glacial fields that surrounded the city.

Even though she had heard bits and pieces about the city from travelling merchants in her mother's marketplace fruit stand, she never could have imagined the immensity of the place. Rather than a collection of separate buildings, like Marinaken or any normal city, the capital was one massive complex honeycombed into the side of the tallest mountain in Thandepar. Wide stone halls led to separate households spread across dozens of levels, and at the top was the king's household—the most opulent and well decorated of them all. The walls were covered with ornate carvings created by the people that had abandoned them decades ago. Brynne stared at the mysterious tableaus at night as she tried to fall asleep, their stories churning in her mind. Great winged beasts were a regular fixture, flying through fire and smoke. They seemed to tell of a world where nothing was certain and myths stood as tall as men.

She pulled on the smooth satin dress, fastening the buttons up the side with clumsy fingers. She sighed heavily as she gazed at herself in the floor-length mirror. She would rather be wearing this beautiful gown for some kind of ball or royal function, anything but her father's funeral. She bit her lip as her mind dredged up the memory of his last departure. He was leaving for a routine trade run up to the northern river valley. It was a journey that he had made many times a year. He was his usual stern self as she hugged him goodbye, but she couldn't help feel a gnawing in the pit of her stomach. Corsairs were a constant source of danger along the Thandepar coast, and rough waters could rip the planks from any hull. Giant masses of ice moved through the water like whales coming to the surface, their true hulking nature submerged and unseen.

She slipped her feet into a pristine pair of shoes from the royal cobbler and tried to take a few steps, wobbling warily. She was used to tromping through hay and mud in her bare feet on the way to the souk with a crate of peaches hefted in her plump arms. Everything was different up here. These delicate slippers with the heightened, pointed heels were popular couture in Ghara, and her tutor Charmaine had had her practice in them for special events, but Brynne still felt unsteady as she made her way to the door of her chamber. When she stumbled into the doorframe, Brynne gave up and plucked them from her feet and carried the shoes by hand. She needed to get down to the open court for the ceremony, and she wasn't going to fuss about.

One negative of life at the top of the city was that it took longer to get anywhere. Brynne crossed the hallway and peered around at the adjacent doors as she approached the lift. All were imposingly shut. The only other residents this high up were members of the court, and despite being here for at least a month, she had yet to see any of them in person. Brynne rang the large brass bell outside the lift shaft the correct number of times and waited for the telltale grinding of wood on stone. Little by little, the box jerked into view, hovering above the long drop down to the city's bowels.

She stepped inside, took hold of the interior bell, and tugged out the sequence that corresponded to the open court, listening as the ringing of the bell carried through the floor to some unseen mechanism below. Brynne didn't understand exactly how the lift worked, despite Charmaine trying to explain it several times, but she just knew she preferred it to an absolutely unthinkable number of stairs. She swung the safety bars shut and watched as the stone floor in front of her rose upwards, until there was only solid rock in front of her eyes.

Brynne always took great interest in the other floors as they passed by them. She peered out of the lift, trying to figure out what each level might hold. Some were smoky parlours where she could catch a glimpse of nobles smoking long perfumed pipes. Others were kitchen levels where the scents of cinnamon, honey, and pistachio drifted out to meet her.

About ten floors later, and ten stories lower, Brynne stepped out into the brisk air of the open court. One of the city's many courtyards, it was by far the largest and the most grand. This was where all of the royal events were held, from balls to diplomatic meetings to high-level judiciary hearings. The elegant stone parquet stretched out in front of her, punctuated by meticulously kept gardens and topiaries. Tall columns rose in lines at either edge to hold up a great stone roof. Outside the perimeter of the court, the mountain's exterior sloped away steeply but gracefully, occasionally dotted by an ornate balcony or window frame.

Brynne liked to come to the open court to study or practice for her lessons when it was empty, but today, the court was packed to the brim with city residents and members of the royal court alike. Many wore white silk armbands in mourning, symbolically admitting surrender to the inevitability of death. At the far end, she could see the dais set up, with the four royal thrones perched upon it. Brynne searched the crowd for her mother or Charmaine, worried that the ceremony would start before she could spot them. As she craned her neck for any sign of them, she felt a gentle tap on her shoulder and spun around to see one of the king's guardsmen standing in front of her.

"This way, Your Highness." He gestured to a doorway a few feet down from the lift. Brynne thought his name was Sam or maybe Gerard. She was still struggling to keep so many names straight.

"I don't think you can call me that yet. We're only just engaged." A hot flush crossed her cheeks as her capillaries dilated. She had just learned about capillaries. She insisted upon reading about subjects of the prince's interest just so that they would have something to talk about upon his return. "Not to mention, we've never actually met," she mumbled. Brynne didn't know much about the prince, except that he was interested in medicine and biology and that he was handsome and well-read. That he was away on an important military mission she knew absolutely nothing about. She didn't know if he would like her. She didn't know if she would like him. She hoped that she would be able to love him, but she wasn't sure that she knew what it felt like to be in love.

She followed the guard and soon found herself in a small antechamber, face to face with Charmaine and her mother, Aisling.

"Mother!" Brynne cried, sweeping her mom into a hug as Charmaine stood to the side, tapping her foot impatiently. Aisling stepped back, holding her daughter at arms' length. She gasped.

"You look absolutely beautiful, darling. It seems this mountain air has done you some good after all." Aisling brushed the long red hair that fell across her daughter's shoulders, the same as her own. Brynne noticed that her mother's face seemed more aged than it had at her reluctant departure. Wrinkles spread out across her forehead, soft and sweet like the dates she spread out in the sun to dry. Brynne worried that her mother had too much work now that she was no longer around to help with their orchard. She brushed her thumbs against her mother's cheeks, pulling her into another hug.

"I'm so happy to see you." Brynne sighed, breathing in the familiar scent of hay and blossoms that made her immediately homesick.

Charmaine clucked her tongue, moving forward to snatch the shoes out of Brynne's hand.

"Were you planning to wear these or just tote them around like a basket of figs?" Charmaine's well-plucked eyebrow was raised in sharp relief. She was a city girl, through and through, and fully unimpressed that she had been saddled with an unworthy charge like Brynne. Clumsy and self-conscious, Brynne was the complete opposite of her confident tutor. Her hair was frizzy while Charmaine's was sleek and well-kept. Her body was curved and plump like a peach, while Charmaine could fit into the latest fashions with no issue. In fact, Brynne had been a constant source of frustration for the royal tailor since her arrival.

Brynne pulled the delicate shoes onto her less-than-delicate feet and tried to steady herself as a knock came at the door. The guard stepped forward to open it. Outside was another guard. That one was definitely Gerard. Brynne attempted to commit Sam's dimpled cheeks to memory so she could call him by name. Sam turned back to the three women as he ushered them out of the antechamber and into the open court, which had fallen silent as the horns began to play.

Brynne followed behind the guard named Sam, who led them up the side of the court towards the dais. The king and queen were just stepping onto the platform to solemnly take their seats before the crowd. Outside the columns of the court, the sun was just beginning to set. The sky was shot through with lilac and red, painted softly onto the lining of the clouds. Sam took Brynne's hand as if to help her up the steps and on to the dais. Quickly she turned back to kiss her mother on the cheek and squeeze her hand before being ushered towards the two empty thrones.

All eyes were on her as she passed the prince's empty chair, then the king, then the queen before coming to her own seat. Brynne sucked in her stomach and focused on her steps, trying desperately not to trip over her own feet. Finally she reached her destination and sunk down into the hard wooden seat. As she stared out at the throng of people shoved into the courtyard, they peered back up at her in expectation. In front of her stood a black coffin, closed tight and covered in flowers imported that very morning from the green belt. The sweet smell drifted up through the fading sunlight, hitting her senses as squarely as a punch to the jaw. She shuddered, overtaken by emotion. Her life was so different today than it had been a month ago. She felt as if she had woken up this morning to an entirely new room, new city, new self, with no idea of how she had gotten there.

Teeth clenched, she tried to subdue her reeling thoughts as the king elegantly rose to speak. His strong cheekbones jutted out above dry lips as he began his eulogy.

"Captain Bronagh Halloran was a brave man and a great loss to this kingdom..." the king began, the masses hanging on his every word. As he spoke, Brynne's attention drifted to the great stone roof that arched above them, every inch covered in ancient carvings. A massive inferno reached out from the centre, surrounded by beasts. At its heart was a jagged cluster of rock surrounded by billowing flames. The king's words passed over her like a slight breeze as she stared upwards. She allowed her mind to drift—frightened that if she let any of his words anchor in her, she might lose control entirely and spray great heaving tears all over the dark satin. She didn't care about the condition of the dress, really. She was pretty sure that it would be soaked in tears and snot as soon as she got back to her chambers, but she was determined not to show weakness in front of the king and queen. Someone had once told her that weaknesses were like fresh fruit, ripe for exploitation.

Brynne fought back the unwelcome smile tugging at the edges of her mouth as she thought about the person who had shared that particular bit of wisdom. Last time they met, she had slipped into Brynne's room as the moon hung high in the sky, her breath warm and sweet, and her skin as soft as a fawn's hide, despite her scars. Brynne tried to wipe the thought from her mind and attempted to concentrate on the carvings. She had to convince herself that those memories were from a past life and no longer had any use, but deep down, she was guilty of employing them thoroughly on lonely nights. She would have to make new memories, here, with the prince. She glanced over at his empty throne only to realize that the king and queen were both staring at her.

The king arched an eyebrow as he repeated himself. "Brynne? Do you have any words to share about your father?"

Brynne gulped as hot nervous fear rose in her throat and trickled down into her stomach. She had not realized that she would be asked to speak. She hadn't prepared anything. Her mind raced as she stood shakily to her feet, suddenly realizing just how many people stood in the court before her.

"My father..." she started, trying to gather her thoughts enough to avoid making an absolute fool of herself. "My father was, as you said, very brave. He was also very kind. He believed in honour and truth and family. One of his deepest desires was for me to lead a comfortable and happy life, and I believe that he can rest easy knowing that I have found one." *Short but sweet.* She looked over at the king who nodded, his steel-sharp gaze solemn. Brynne curtsied awkwardly as she sat back down, hoping that she would not have to speak again, the anxiety still solidified as a hard mass in her gut.

THE REST OF the funeral ceremony slipped by without incident. Brynne spoke to countless people as they passed through the receiving line and professed their sincerest sympathies for the death of a man they had never met. She listened to their words, holding their soft Bureaucrat hands in her own. Her skin was rough from a youth helping her mother in the orchards, but every day since she had arrived in the capital, they had grown smoother and less callused. She focused on the feel of their skin, on the warmth of the breath, so that their words would wash over her without really sinking in. It was the only way to make it through.

Finally the seemingly endless flow of people dried up as the last few individuals spoke to the queen, the king, and finally to Brynne before disappearing back into the honeycomb city. The open court was almost empty once again, just the way that Brynne preferred it. Glancing at the place where her father's casket had sat, she remembered the way the soldiers had come to carry it down to the crypts in their crisp, pressed uniforms. Was that what the prince would be wearing when he finally came home to meet her? Would she remember this difficult moment when she first saw her future husband? The sour lump in Brynne's throat grew painful as she turned and walked away from the open court.

Brynne and her mother didn't speak on the long descent towards the carriage house. The heeled shoes dangled from one hand as she wrapped the other around her mother's shoulders, burying her nose in Aisling's fading russet hair. She wanted to beg and plead for her to stay, but she knew what the answer would be. Her mother would rather return to Marinaken and work herself to the bone than stay in this strange city. Brynne exhaled, pressed up against the woman that had raised her, sure that these empty halls would never feel like home.

The lift sank lazily into the warm bowels of the mountain, sliding towards the city's transit hub. The "carriage house" was a hot, loud complex where the city's many horses resided. A large natural cleft in the side of the mountain opened onto a high alpine meadow where they grazed. As Brynne stepped out of the lift, she could feel a curious exchange of air bluster across her face. The fresh breeze blew in from the meadow, mixing with the still hot air of the mountain, which carried the smell of hay and dung. That scent was the closest thing to comfort that Brynne could find. She came several times a week for riding lessons, accompanied as always by Charmaine, who would complain bitterly the entire time.

Across the muddy stone floor and opposite the horse stalls, carriages lined up at the entrance to the under roads. Travellers stood in clumps, awaiting the vehicle that would take them through the mountains and on to their specific destination. Brynne remembered, like it was a previous life, passing through the green belt on her way to distant markets, seeing the entrances to the tunnel system rising out of the earth in a hump as if formed by burrowing creatures. Each one an ancient mystery; each one led here.

Brynne walked her mother to the carriage bound for Marinaken. The mud squished between her bare toes as she pulled Aisling in for a solid hug.

"Have a safe trip home," Brynne said. She searched for more words, something more meaningful, but her tongue came up empty. Her mother pulled back, and Brynne gulped down emotion as Aisling's weathered thumbs moved across her dry cheeks.

"You'll be all right here," Aisling said, more confidently than Brynne felt. "This is what your father wanted for you. I know that you'll do your best to live up to his expectations."

Brynne sucked the heavy air in between her teeth. She helped her mother up into the carriage as the rough-hewn driver called out for passengers. He tipped his wool hat towards her as the rest of the crowd tried to squeeze into the remaining seats.

"Your Highness," the driver wheezed between yellowing teeth. Brynne bit her lip and gave her mother's hand one last squeeze.

"If you say so," she said before stepping back to watch as the carriage driver spurred his horses forward into the arching mouth of the subterranean roads, taking her mother away.

BRYNNE LEANED HER back against the stone walls as she waited what seemed like an eternity for the lift to come. This wasn't the only one in the capital; she knew that there were a variety of them, all servicing specific areas of the city. This one was specifically for royal use, and judging by the time it was taking, it was currently in use by some high-ranking member of the royal house, if not the king or queen themselves.

Brynne didn't think she had ever spoken to either the king or the queen in a nonformal situation. They were just names, shadowed figures, just as they had been when she was nothing but a poor merchant's daughter. Even sitting beside them on the dais during the funeral, the person she felt closest to was cold and covered by a thick slab of marble. Charmaine had taught her to be civil and formal when speaking to the monarchs. Always be positive, she'd said. If you can't be sincere, then fake it. Brynne suspected that Charmaine faked a lot of things. She had the air of a woman who held herself extremely tightly, but then, she probably had her reasons. Charmaine's mother held a seat on the king's council, representing the wealth and cunning of the Merchant. Each archetype had a representative to guide the king in his decisions—five in all, for the Merchant, the Artisan, the Pilgrim, the Guardian, and the Bureaucrat. The latter was occupied by the king himself. The Guardian's seat had been empty since its representative, Sarus Crane, Master of Hunt, had died in an unfortunate accident nearly a decade past. The Corsair was not included. Anyone born to that archetype wasn't to be trusted, or at least, that was the common wisdom—advice that Brynne had failed to take more than once.

Finally the lift slid into view, and Brynne entered. She rang the bell, using the combination for her floor at the top of the city. She was exhausted, ready to crawl into her bed and let the floodgates open. She did a double take as the lift shuddered into life and began to move. The floor in front of her was sliding upwards, which meant that she was descending farther into the mountain. She grabbed the bell rope and pulled it in distress, railing on it again and again. The descent continued. Brynne exhaled sharply and slammed her hand against the lift wall, the heels she held tapping staccato against the wood. Hadn't this day been long enough already?

Brynne tumbled to the ground as the lift jerked abruptly to a stop as if it had hit bottom. Pushing herself up off the dusty ground, she rose to find a dark doorway opening onto an unknown floor. She rang the bell again, double-checking the sequence in her mind, but no matter how many times she tried it, the lift refused to budge.

"Okay..." she said, her voice echoing back to her. She reached up to grab the handle of the lift's lit lantern, hefted it off of its hook, and stretched it out in front of her to illuminate the darkness, in search of a stairwell. After pushing back the safety gate, she stepped out of the small enclosure, letting the flickering light of the lantern wash over the masterfully carved corridor. The lamplight dipped and swung over scenes that covered the walls from floor to ceiling. Brynne held in a breath as the figures in the reliefs seemed to move in the low shifting light. Sarkany lore held that no form could be trusted, and nothing was immutable. She held her breath, fingers tracing over the wall carvings. Horned creatures, more beast than man, and women with fire streaming from their eyes all felt like silk beneath her fingertips. She stepped forward, her bare feet pressing against the cool marble.

That was odd. Usually the lower you travelled in the capital, the warmer the air became, but she couldn't help but notice a palpable chill.

As she walked on, the corridor continued to appear ahead of her as the light from the lantern penetrated the unknown. On her right, several massive wooden boards came into her sphere of illumination. They reached up to the height of the ceiling, covering over part of the design where they were fastened against the wall. Brynne paused for a moment, placing the lantern on the floor. She tried to stick her fingers between the boards to see if she could pry one from its place, but they were heavily secured. She searched for a sign of what they might be covering up, but the surrounding images gave no clue. The walls on either side held only deep reliefs of the tall peaks surrounding the city.

As she lifted the lantern off the floor, she noticed a shimmer on the edge of her vision. She hefted her light source and moved in its direction, watching the strange reflection change as she neared. It led her through a nearby doorway into what seemed like a large empty cavern, roughly the size of her mother's barn. It was as if she had walked from one of the city's most well-appointed hallways into a regular mountain cave.

The reflection of the light danced and swayed in the centre of the room, and as Brynne approached, she realized what it was catching on. In the centre of the room was a small natural pool. The rest of the chamber was empty but for a rusted iron ring affixed to the floor beside it. Brynne crouched down and dipped her fingers into the water. She gasped and snapped them back quickly. The water was absolutely freezing—probably fed by glacial runoff. She rested her lantern on the floor and sat down at the edge of the pool to admire how the light moved across the water as she manipulated it with her fingers.

It reminded her of the way the sun hit the ocean, sparking on the caps of waves as they rolled against the hulls in the harbour. She used to stand on the planks of the slip as her father prepared for his latest journey, peering into the inky blackness of the sea. The longer she stared, the more she saw. First one single jellyfish would rise into view, bobbing along on the current. As soon as she saw the first, she would see another and another and another until it seemed like they extended down into the deep forever.

The pool was cold against her skin, but her tears were warm as they began to roll down her cheeks. She had to wonder—was this like the ice-flow-laden water where her father had lost his life? Did he feel this sharp painful cold in his last moments? More likely, all he felt was the agony of the corsair spear in his back. They said he washed ashore with it standing up straight like a mast, the rope tangled around his body. Maybe the water had merely felt like a gentle warmth ebbing across his skin as his blood diffused into the salt sea.

Brynne's face grew hot as the overwhelming emotions that had been pent inside her all day burst forth. Hot tears carved tributaries down her cheeks as she sucked in sharp ragged breaths of cool air. She dipped her whole hand in the frozen waters of the pool and held it under until it hurt before wiping the cold water across her face. Drops spattered her satin dress, chilling her skin through the thin fabric.

She sat by the pool until the flame in the lantern began to sputter. Pulling herself together, Brynne stood, carrying the lamp in one hand and her heeled shoes in the other. Inhaling a ragged breath that scraped across her lungs, she turned away from the pool and headed into the darkness.

She didn't search long before finding a set of spiral stairs that led up into the city proper. She climbed until her thighs ached and her calves burned. She climbed until her lantern stuttered and died. She climbed until the only feeling left inside was a dull throb in her empty chest. She rose through the darkness, dragging herself up through the heart of the city, to return to a room that didn't feel like home.

Chapter Five

HOW LONG IT took to descend the spiral staircase, Aela didn't know. It felt like days in the darkness. She kept her right hand against the grimy wall so that she didn't lose her balance. Del walked behind her, at times nearly slumped against the wall out of weariness. They didn't sleep; they barely ate. By the time they reached the bottom, they both collapsed onto the uneven rock floor of a dark and unseen chamber.

Every muscle hurt. They twisted under her chafed and broken skin as Aela lay prone, her head butting up against Del's akimbo arm. Finally, she could no longer hold onto her faculties and let a deep sleep wash over her fitful mind.

ORANGE LIGHT DANCED across the surface of Aela's closed eyelids as she begrudgingly awoke. The smoky smell of a campfire meandered into her nostrils.

As the stimuli crept up, her eyes snapped open, revealing a sight that reminded her exactly where she was and who she was with. The large dark cavern was only partly illuminated by a tiny fire. The light flickered across rough walls, dipping into the delicate arcs of carved tableaus that seemed to move in the firelight. Shaking her head as if to shed her sleepy fugue, Aela managed to pull herself upright only to feel pain spread across her back, the epicentre a hard knot at the base of her neck.

"You must be hungry." Del's words drifted towards her from where he sat by the fire. Aela approached tentatively to see that he had one of his cooking pots out over the fire. It was dented from the events up on the ridge, but like his pack, it seemed to still be functional.

"What is that?" she asked, kneeling down in front of the flames. The smell emanating from the pot was curious—savoury and crisp but in an unfamiliar way. Hadn't they run out of food on the descent? She thought she remembered having that conversation more than once. Her stomach clenched at the smell, and she began to salivate as her body rediscovered its need for sustenance.

A beautifully crooked smile spread across Del's face. "Have some water." He pressed his dirty canteen into her hands. That seemed to have survived the fight as well. She lifted the canteen to her mouth and choked with surprise as clean, crisp water flowed down her throat.

"Is this fresh?" She spat the words out as she coughed violently, trying to clear the liquid from her airways. Del pointed a few feet away where ancient channel had been carved deep into the floor, moving water through the chamber and into a hole in the rock wall. Aela glanced around her, adjusting to the low light. The walls were carved with decorations, the surfaces were well-worn. This place had been inhabited once. Someone had lived here.

Del took the canteen back as she finished and took a long draught before pausing at the confused look on her face.

"There are meltwater springs running all through these mountains. The people who lived here before were very good at making the most of their surroundings."

Aela realized very suddenly that she was at a disadvantage, her least favourite place to be. They had descended into a subterranean world that she knew nothing about but that her travelling companion seemed to be familiar with. Luckily, Aela still had one very useful card to play.

"So, were you going to tell me that you're the king's son, or were you planning on just keeping that to yourself?" Aela said casually, her eyebrow raised. Now it was Del's turn to choke, and that he did. Aela edged back as he sputtered cold spring water onto the fire.

"Excuse me?" he said, wiping a grimy sleeve across his face. He was as bad a liar as he was a fighter. Aela let out a low chuckle, her deep voice resonating throughout the chamber.

"Don't play coy, little prince." She smiled dangerously. She rose up into a crouch, one hand scratching at the water droplets in the dirt. It was a predatory pose. "Did you really think you were in disguise?"

In truth, she had only suspected there was more to this fool than met the eye until she saw the corpses of his fellow soldiers piled atop him on the ridge. There are few people that conscripted soldiers would give their own lives to save. Aela didn't mention that, though; better if he thought she was just plain omniscient.

Del opened the pot lid and stirred the contents with an errant stick. "So you know who I am then?" His long lashes pointed towards the ground. His voice was oddly light and strangely hopeful. Perhaps he was tired of pretending to be less useful than he truly was. Aela smirked and dragged her tongue across her teeth. In truth, he might not have realized just how useful he was to her, but he was about to.

"I know that your father will pay an awful lot to have you home safe. So here's the deal: you seem to know how to survive down here, and I'll bet you know the way back to the capital. You're going to take me there...as my prisoner. Once we get back, I'll give my ultimatum, he'll give me a big bag of gold, and I'll find the nearest boat heading for the Southern Isles. How's that sound?"

"If you think my father is going to pay any amount to get me back, then you clearly don't know him very well." Del glared up at her, brow furrowed. He didn't seem particularly regal. He didn't look particularly scared either.

"It's worth a try," replied Aela.

"And you think I'm just going to go along with this?" he asked skeptically.

Aela shrugged at him, teeth bared in a smile. She put her hand to her hip and pulled the long knife from her belt, letting the steel slide across the leather.

"Here's what I think. If you try to run, I'll stop you. If you try to fight, I'll kill you. I'm faster, stronger, and meaner." Aela slid the knife back in quickly, giving him her best stone-cold stare. To her surprise, Del shrugged casually.

"I really don't think this is going to turn out the way you want, so don't say I didn't warn you." He reached out to lift the pot off of the fire and placed it on the cavern floor between them. His eyes were heavy-lidded, the corners of his lips turned down. "Are you hungry?"

Aela leaned forward as he removed the pot lid. It was full of little brown pellets, crispy, glossy, and utterly unidentifiable. It smelled amazing in the way that anything will if you've barely eaten in days.

"What is that?" she asked.

"Termites," Del said, as he grabbed a handful and began popping them into his mouth. Aela tried to quell her gag reflex as bile rose up and tried to jump out of her throat. She stared at the roasted carapaces, thinking hard about what a waste it would be to starve to death after coming this far. Ignoring her rising gag reflex, she plucked a few from the pot and crammed them into her mouth. As she split through the husks, her tongue tentatively getting a taste, she mused that they were actually pretty good.

AELA SNORTED, HER laughter ringing against the ceiling of the cave as they walked through the low light.

"Delphinium?" She choked, giving Del a light shove. He staggered, the light from his torch shuddering across the walls.

"Reza Delphinium Ansari IV." He sighed.

"Let's just stick with Del." She grinned.

"Fine by me." He chuckled in agreement and relief. He was leading the way, choosing their path through an endless series of labyrinthine tunnels. Aela knew that her grasp on the situation was tenuous at best. There was absolutely zero chance she would escape without his help, but despite a brief moment of malaise at being threatened with a sharp knife, Del had bounced back quickly. He had cleaned up camp at Aela's word and was surely the most talkative prisoner she had ever taken.

He pointed out the rutted tracks worn into the stone floor, a lasting sign of subterranean trade routes, created long before the modern under roads. He talked about the carvings on the walls and the stories that they told.

"See how everything is halfway between one form and another? The Sarkany believed in a concept called 'metamorphosis.' Basically, that all beings change over time, until they reach their apex form."

"What does that mean?" Aela asked, raising an eyebrow at the detailed carvings. Women with bare breasts and clawed feet strutted across the tableau, wreathed in flame.

"I'm not sure. Truth be told, it's hard to know if I'm interpreting the texts correctly. I don't think it's necessarily literal, more of a metaphor. You know, 'everything changes.'"

Aela snorted.

"Well, you used to be a child, and you've changed a great deal since then, haven't you?" Del glanced over at Aela for a reaction. What she was supposed to be reacting to, she didn't know. The words had washed over her, undigested, as she used her tongue to poke at a stray bit of termite shell jammed between her worn molars.

She shrugged, hoping that was answer enough. Instead, Del shook his head in frustration. Dropping the lecture, he quickened his pace as they walked in growing silence.

At every crossroads, he would pause. He'd tilt his brow up and inhale, testing for something Aela couldn't fathom. After a good few minutes of glaring into the half-lit tunnels, he'd pick a direction and start walking with Aela stalking behind on the edge of the torchlight.

EVENTUALLY, THE SOUND of their footsteps on stone was joined by another noise—the urgent rush of moving water. It started out barely audible, growing to an intense roar as they walked towards the source.

Del turned a corner and led her through a doorway that opened onto a larger chamber. How large, she couldn't tell. The darkness seemed to stretch away forever. What she could tell was that this room was the source of the water they had been hearing. Following Del's torchlight, she walked across the corridor to a small balcony that seemed to jut out over a wide subterranean river. Cold spray flecked the left side of Aela's face as she turned to peer into the gloom. She could just barely make out the torrent of falling water that originated high up on the cave wall and spilled down across the jutting rocks into a wide carved channel that could barely contain it.

Del held the torch out over the balcony, trying to illuminate the dark. The chamber's ground floor and the swollen river were several levels down. The light scattered as it glanced off the currents far below. If the other levels were the same as the one they stood on now, they consisted of patiently carved galleries looking out over the falls, with small shallow rooms set back into the walls. The balcony on which they stood seemed to stretch all the way around the circular chamber, broken only by the waterfall. The carved stone balustrade that they leaned against was worn but sturdy, created from the bedrock itself.

Aela felt Del's eyes on her as she took in the chamber. Above them, more identical levels seemed to stretch upwards into the unseeable beyond.

"What do you think this place was?" he asked, his condescending tone implying that he knew the answer. She wanted to smack his haughty eyebrows right off his face, but the endless cave march had left her bone-tired and sore. Exhaling away her malicious thoughts, Aela glanced around and tried to answer in earnest.

"I don't know. Some kind of marketplace?" Her words echoed across the open space, bouncing off the opposite wall.

Del smiled. "Yeah, it's a trading post. Different communities would come here to trade supplies and food. The coastal Sarkany would bring produce and trade for minerals, fresh water, and other things that the mountain folk had better access to."

Aela thought on his words as she looked around. She could imagine people setting up their shops in the alcoves that punctuated the outer wall. People like her.

She made her way around, one hand on the balustrade, as Del followed behind with the torch. A winding set of stairs descended to the next level, and she took them one at a time as the light slid across each smooth step.

Another set of stairs later and they were on the bottom floor of the marketplace, directly opposite the waterfall. Flecks of water sprayed up and over the railings as the river thundered towards them and beneath their feet, carried through a wide opening in the floor and on to some unknown destination.

Aela looked over at Del. The torchlight glinted off his face. High-set cheekbones stood out above cheeks that were still in the process of losing their boyish chubbiness. A pitiful smattering of auburn peach fuzz scraped across the line of his jaw. Aela didn't understand how someone could seem so wise and so young at the same time. Maybe she had underestimated Del by considering him just some naive royal brat. If there was one person who knew that no one should be considered 'just' anything, it was her.

Del cleared his throat, pointing towards the overgrown waterfall, and raised his voice to be heard over its violent roar.

"Spring melt," he said. "This river is fed by a glacier, so it's going to be swollen until the autumn. It will run underground until it feeds into one of the river valleys." He gestured up towards where the falls fed into the chamber. "Your people had a way of controlling the volume of these rivers so that they didn't overflow and become dangerous. The locks have probably decayed by now."

Aela opened her mouth to ask a question she felt pretty sure she'd regret. "How do you know all this?" As the words left her lips, she grimaced, certain that she had already figured out the answer. What she wasn't expecting was Del's response, as he turned to her, eyebrows raised incredulously.

"How do you not?" He half-shouted, echo muffled by the roaring river.

"What do you mean?" She was taken aback as he turned towards her, eyes sharp to match his confrontational tone.

"These were your people. This is where you came from, but you don't seem to know a single thing about it." He gestured out to the marketplace at large as she stifled a haughty laugh.

"This is *not* where I came from. I came from a ship. I came from the sea. Those are my people. They're rotten fucking bastards, but they're my people." She stepped back from the railing, taut scarred arms crossed over her muscular chest. Del took a step towards her tentatively, brow wrinkled in confusion.

"What do you mean you came from a ship?"

"I mean that's my home. That's where I'm from."

"And before that?" He laid his words out cautiously, as if afraid to spook her. Aela could feel the ire rising in her chest. She didn't like questions. She didn't like it when other people asked them of her, and she liked it even less when she asked them of herself. She had stopped that practice when she realized she was unlikely to figure out the answers. She took a deep breath, looked Del in the eyes, and gave him the response that she had been pretending was good enough.

"I don't remember anything before that." Then she turned and walked away into the dark alcove behind them. The torch bobbed in tow as Del strode to keep up. The tiny open chamber was strewn with debris. Burnt wooden crates slumped against the stone, filled with ashen detritus. Del put a hand on her shoulder, and she moved her own instinctively to her knife as she spun around.

"Whoa," he said.

Shaking her head, she relaxed the mounting tension in her shoulders. It wasn't his fault, after all. "Sorry. Reflex." She tried to wring the embarrassment out of her voice. Aela removed her hand from the knife's handle and ran it along the wall of the cave, then rubbed the residue of cinder between her fingers as she decided to rip the bandage off. "You didn't answer my question."

Del glanced up warily. "No." A blush spread across his cheeks.

"How do you know so much about my people?" She paused, already a step ahead. "About me?" Del held the torch away from his face, throwing light across damaged shelving. Behind them, the rustling noise of the river seemed to grow deafening as it echoed through the small chamber.

"Like I said, I had this mentor." He shrugged, feigning interest in the ruins of the shop. He reached out and lit one of the wall sconces with his torch. New light flared into life as it shared the flame.

"Someone fit to mentor a prince..." she said. "Someone *like me*." Her voice had a lilt to it, leading him with her words. She wanted to hear him say it. She stepped in close to Del, purposely pressing the hilt of her belted knife into his hipbone as her sternum nearly brushed against his. She had learned early that if there's something you want to know, it never hurts to try a little physical intimidation. She learned that on her own; she hadn't been taught.

"Your father," he said, a tremor rising in his throat just as a massive object hit the ground behind him in a cloud of dust, blocking them inside the alcove.

AELA GRABBED DEL by shoulders as the storm of motes rose around them. He gave a surprised yelp as she shoved him roughly to the side before stepping towards the blocked opening, shielding him with her body.

Knees bending on instinct, she slipped into a low stance and pulled the long knife from her belt. Behind her, Del rose up out of the dirt and ash with a groan.

"You have got to stop doing that." His voice drifted behind her as he pulled himself to his feet. He picked up the dormant torch, extinguished in his fall.

"I'm trying to protect you," she said as she stepped forward to inspect the large dark shape in front of her.

"Well, I'm not cargo, and I bruise easily." There was a wince in his voice.

She couldn't help the smirk that spread across her lips as she reached up to run a hand across the foreign surface. Her fingers brushed across a swath of something soft and smooth, like leather, before her palm hit the fur. It was warm and musky. Del spoke from behind as her hand gently rose and fell according to a pulmonary rhythm that was not her own.

"Aela, get back. That's no rock." His words were a step behind her as she hopped away—just as the creature rose jerkily from where it had landed. Blind but blood-red eyes flashed in the torchlight as it hissed full force, baring teeth like a butcher's toolset. Stretching one great leathery wing towards them, the bat jostled at the cave entrance, desperate to reach the sweet reward inside. Its wingspan was the size of a summer cottage, with the body of a large bear.

Aela jumped out of its reach, knife at the ready as Del took a stiff stance beside her, his sword drawn.

"Leave this to me," Aela said, dancing forward with her blade. In one smooth movement, she slashed through the worn leather that stretched below its grasping claw. The bat reared back, emitting an ear-splitting scream that hit the back wall of the small alcove and shattered the quiet. Grabbing her temple with one hand, Aela lunged forward, disoriented. Her blade sliced through nothing but dust as the bat recoiled and recovered, then swung forward again to grapple for its prize. Aela let out a shout as its claws raked across her abdomen. She scrambled backwards and looked down at her worn leather tunic as blood began to bead on the skin where the beast had sliced clean through and grazed her.

Scenting blood, the bat retracted its arm and swung both wings up to anchor itself on the wall outside the alcove. Aela rose cautiously, one hand on her stomach as she staggered towards it once again. Red orbs gleamed in the dark as the bat shoved its snub-nosed face into the cave and towards them, jaw open in anticipation.

Barely aware of Del crouched low beside her, Aela lurched forward as he sprang in front of her, sliding low to run the full length of his sword into the bat's open mouth and through its palate, into its brain. The bat shuddered to a stop, its eyes dimming as it collapsed forwards onto him, Del's bloodied hilt hovering a bare few inches from his chest. Aela stared down at where the prince lay, head between her feet. She tried to shake her daze and comprehend what had just happened as he blinked up at her.

"That was...not the outcome that I had intended," he said, heaving slightly on the rank smell wafting from the bat's open jaw. Raising himself up on his elbows, he scooted back in an undignified manner, carefully pulling himself out from beneath the beast. Aela stepped in, holding open its maw for Del as he stood up and brushed himself off. He shifted forward and placed one foot on the bat's lower jaw for leverage as he worked his sword out of its lifeless form.

"Tired of termites?" he said, gesturing to the corpse.

Aela shook her head with a grimace as he shrugged and grabbed the lit torch from the wall sconce.

She headed towards the entrance, gestured for help, and together they shifted the lifeless mass of fur and leather to the side, or at least enough to squeeze their bodies past its bulk and back towards the river.

"How do we get out of here?" Aela asked, as they returned to the balustrade. Del gaped up at the waterfall, opening his mouth to speak before choking on the cold air. He clapped a hand over his mouth, and Aela followed his line of sight up into the gallery. Above their heads, as far up as their torch could penetrate the darkness, masses of dark shapes hung from the bedrock. Suspended upside-down from the bottom of the balconies, claws dug into familiar grooves in the rock, an entire colony of oversized bats hung swathed in their leather wings. Farther up, beyond even the shapes that they could make out, hundreds of pairs of bright red eyes glowed in the darkness.

Aela grabbed Del's hand and quickly dragged him away from the balcony and towards the stairs as an army of shrill voices pierced the marketplace with their cries. One foot in front of the other, she made her way, pulling the prince behind her as the entire chamber began to vibrate with the sound of leather beating on the air. Beyond the railing, just above the river, countless animals unfurled from their haunts and launched themselves across the marketplace. Their wings flapped loudly enough to drown out even the aggressive roar of the river.

Aela had one foot on the bottom step of the stairway as one of the beasts swung through the gap between levels, landing above her with a thud. Arms stretched out towards her, it shuffled forward, descending the stairs. Aela turned to face Del, whose jaw hung slack as the monster advanced on them.

"Run!" she shouted into his face, her nose inches from his, before sprinting away from the stairs and back to where the dead bat lay sprawled across the stone floor. Reassured by the sound of Del's footsteps behind her, she skidded to a stop. He knocked into her from behind, breathing hard as she turned to hold him upright.

"Which way?" She gasped, the cold air ripping through her already-strained lungs. One hand on either shoulder, she stared into Del's eyes. He peered into the darkness, losing his grip on the guttering torch.

"I think... Maybe—" he stuttered, searching for another way up or down. She felt the ground shake again as his eyes flew wide, fear washing away any of the wisdom that had lived there earlier. His hand flew up to her arm, his grip like a vise as he spun her around to face another one of the beasts approaching. Aela swallowed hard as the bat arched its neck, sending a shrill blast of rank warmth towards them as it communicated to its clan.

She stared at the beast for a moment before turning back to see the one that had landed on the stairs approaching them from the other side. Del's fingers still dug into her bicep as she looked him square in the face.

"Can you swim?" she asked, her question answered as all colour drained from his face.

"No... No!" He glanced from her to the balustrade to the water that flowed towards them. "I'm not... I can't—" He spat the words out, whole body shaking. Over his shoulder, Aela could see the bat getting closer as it laboured towards them, its wings rustling against the stone. Close enough to hear it whine as it drew each breath, its yellowed fangs flickering in the torchlight. She grabbed Del by the hand and dragged him bodily towards the railing that extended out over the river. Keeping her voice low and calm, she tried to reason with his base instincts.

"Do you want to live?" she asked, her hair blustering in the wake of the airborne maelstrom above them. Del looked up from the river.

"No," he said, the corners of his mouth lifting up slightly. "Just leave me here." His voice was too measured. His body went limp as he slumped down to the floor, his back to the water.

Aela didn't want to admit that she had considered that option, but in truth, as the icy spray from the river sparked up to lash her cheeks it crossed her mind. Her heart beat madly against her chest as she stared towards the approaching bat, knowing there was an identically ugly bastard looming in the darkness just behind her. It was close enough for her to feel its rancid breath wafting towards the back of her neck. She crouched down and jammed her arm behind Del's neck, wrapping it around his shoulders as she shoved the other under his knees. Rising up, she lifted him and used every bit of strength she could muster as she threw him over the balustrade, where his body hit the water and disappeared into the deluge. All sound was swallowed by the roar of the falls and the low whine of the monstrously sized bats approaching from either side.

Suddenly, the bat from the staircase lunged forward with its leathery wing, claws grasping towards her. Moving on pure instinct, Aela grabbed the balustrade with both hands and vaulted over. She hit the water with a slap and was shot like a cannonball on the current. She slipped through the opening under the cave floor into pure darkness, the glacial water warming as it slid over her skin.

Chapter Six

UNABLE TO HOLD his breath any longer, Del gasped, his sinuses burning as ice-cold water flooded in through his nose and mouth. Above him, the torchlight flickered beyond the water's still surface, just out of reach. Arms outstretched, he attempted to urge his body upwards even as his lungs began to tighten. Every movement was punctuated by the iron manacles around his wrists cutting sharply into his skin. One leg kicked feebly as the other hung below him, the only part of his body that wasn't cold as ice. From his calf to the sole of his foot, his left leg felt warm and oddly heavy. The last few bubbles slipped forth from between his lips as the weightless feeling between his ears expanded, blocking out vision and the distant sound of a heated argument.

DEL'S EYES SHOT open as the pressure in his lungs forced ice-cold river water upwards through his tightened airways. Sucking in a breath, he pushed himself up onto one arm and coughed up a small lake onto the riverbank. He thought he could feel his heartbeat reverberating through his entire body, but he would later realize that it was only Aela's firm hand patting his back as he choked up every drop of water remaining.

He flopped face-first onto the muddy grass, closing his eyes. One by one, his other senses returned to him. He could hear birdsong and the low rush of the river. The sun felt warm, but his body shivered uncontrollably. His lungs were strained and sore. His trachea felt irreparably torn, but nothing in the world hurt as much as his leg. Just below the left knee, the pain prickled and throbbed. Del bit his lip as it ripped through every nerve.

Only barely aware of Aela's presence beside him, he shuddered as she rolled him onto his back and pressed a hand to his chest. Ribbons of warmth spread across his skin, reverberating through his body to chase the chill of the river away. He blinked up at her. Her brow unfurrowed a second too late—he caught the concern that she tried to slide behind a cocky ease. Aela moved her hands up and down his arms and then down towards his thighs before he grabbed them.

"I'm fine," he said, gritting his teeth against the pain in his leg. She raised an eyebrow.

"You were basically dead. You're lucky you've been captured by such an experienced sailor. I've got a pretty good track record with drownings."

Del closed his eyes. He was sure she did, in more ways than one. And yet, she had saved his life. She had thrown him into that river instead of leaving him to the bats, and from the way the river water came rushing out of him, he was certain she had resuscitated him there on the bank. She wanted him alive, whether it was for a payday, or something else. Ignoring the hard questions, he tried to focus on his survival training. Past Aela, the sky was bloodshot, a purple bruise stretching away behind a low sun. Evening was setting on the floodplain. They would need to find shelter.

Aela stood by as Del tried to hoist himself up to his feet, putting all of his weight on the right. He tried to take a step with his left foot, but his fears were confirmed as he crumpled back down into the mud, breaking the fall with his hands. His hands tightened into fists full of grass as a sharp cry escaped his lips. Aela squatted down and rolled Del onto his back.

"Are you okay? You seemed fine when I pulled you out. I mean, besides the part where you weren't breathing." She put a hand on his shoulder, her dark eyes searching his. There was no way around it. He sucked back the fear that clamped around his airways. He wasn't going to be walking anywhere without her help.

He gestured down towards his legs. "The left."

She rolled up his soaked pant leg, revealing a tall leather boot. He stared up at the darkening sky as she deftly undid the laces and slid it off. She didn't gasp, didn't say anything. He leaned up to see her running her hand across his prosthesis and then glanced away. He hated to think about what he should or shouldn't be feeling as her fingertips brushed across the metal, whether it be in his phantom limb or anywhere else. She stared back at him, the corner of her mouth quirking up slightly.

"Better than a peg leg, eh?"

Del almost choked on the warmth that radiated from the smile spreading across her lips. She was right, though. It was a sleek design, his own. This was the fourth incarnation and the most durable by far. Hand-cast by the royal blacksmith using the lightest metal alloy available, his prosthetic leg attached just below the knee. It was easily disguised and allowed him to do almost anything that didn't involve being submerged in water.

"Come on, let's find some shelter. It's going to be dark soon, and I don't like being out in the open like this," he said, trying to change the subject. His chest was sore and phantom pains curled his absent toes, but Del knew he would need somewhere warm to try to fix his waterlogged prosthesis.

Aela watched as Del replaced his boot. She reached down to help him up, centering his weight over his right leg. "Can you walk?" she asked, eyebrow raised.

"Not on my own."

Aela nodded solemnly before putting an arm around Del's shoulder for support. "Well, let's get moving then. I'd hate for us to escape giant bats just to get eaten by wolves."

He scanned the horizon for some recognizable detail. In front of them was the outflow cave where the glacial river that had carried them emerged from under the ground. In the distance, behind its low rise, the long tooth of Ghara rose up to pierce the beaten sky. Del gestured west, towards the mountain, taking a step forward as he leaned on Aela. The rhythm took some time to figure out as they gradually made their way along the riverbank and up over the hill, towards the setting sun.

Del sucked in a breath and released it gently. He was sure that Aela already thought him weak and useless in a fight. He had been sure that if she discovered this part of him that she would have considered it the final nail in his worthless coffin. He knew the other soldiers had treated him differently, but it was impossible to know how much of that was the prosthesis and how much was his royal title.

Del's heart jumped into his throat as he thought about the soldiers that they had lost up on the ridge. Warmhearted Crantz, adventurous Jetty, and Tern, a born leader—at least far more than Del had ever been. He had known them only briefly, but they had died protecting him. Ever since he and Aela had descended the stair into the mountain, the grief and guilt had plagued him. Their shadowed forms marched across his mind, calling out his name in a rush of heat and smoke. Each time he remembered, he pushed the feelings down again, his heart hardening. It was the only way to keep going.

As he and Aela lurched across an unfamiliar river valley in search of a shelter, he made a promise to himself that he would not let their sacrifice fall silently behind him.

THE LANDSCAPE CHANGED as they walked. The sound of the river ebbed away behind them and the tree line grew thicker as they approached the foothills. Deep howls echoed in the distance. The river valley was a hunting ground at night, and not just for wolves. Thoughts like those kept Del moving forwards, leaning on Aela more with each lurching step. More than once, he found himself glancing up, picking constellations out of the darkness. Sarus Crane, Aela's father, had tried to teach Del to find his way using only the stars above. As long as he could find the right touchstones, he would always be able to make his way home, Sarus had said. It was never Del's strong suit. The glowing pinpricks swam in front of him as he tried to force them into recognizable shapes.

Aela paused to take a sip from her waterskin, thankfully still attached to her belt and not swept away as their packs had been. Making sure he was steady before she jostled the skin from her belt, she raised an eyebrow at Del as he scanned the sky.

"Who are you hoping to talk to up there?" she asked, prodding. "My money was on the Guardian, but now that I know you're not just a soldier..."

"All of them," Del said vaguely, staring hard and coming up empty. Aela pointed a slender finger up towards a small cluster of stars to the southwest.

"That there is the Corsair," she said, letting her finger drift across the sky. "See the curved blade? And beside her, the Bureaucrat. You can tell by the scales—and his smug face."

Del squinted, more confused than ever as she handed him the waterskin. "Face? How do you see a face?" He shook his head in exasperation before taking a long sip of water.

"I'm just joking, Del. They are whatever you see them as. Just use your imagination." She swept a hand across the sky, pointing out clusters of stars that spread scattershot against the dark. "The Artisan, the Pilgrim, the Guardian, the Scholar, the Merchant."

Del looked at Aela, wide-eyed.

"Surprised?"

"I guess I just didn't expect you to know this kind of stuff." Del wiped a hand across his mouth. "I'm supposed to be the trained scout." Aela let out a laugh like a bark and Del coughed up a bit of water as she clapped him on the back heartily.

"How do you think we get around on our little boats? You'd be lost as hell using only a map when you're drifting in the middle of the blue." She took the waterskin back and bared her teeth in a smile. "Here's the only thing you really need to know: pick the brightest one and follow it till you fall off." Her words echoed in his head in a different voice—older, rougher, deeper. Del stared at Aela, certain that her father's words had just come out of her mouth. Sarus had made the same joke during their lessons, making fun of the beliefs of the old scholars: that the world was flat like parchment and if you went far enough, you would fall right off the edge.

When Del was a young boy, he and the huntmaster would leave the capital, camping out under the stars where Sarus would teach him the survival skills that had saved his neck more than once. Rather than training with the rest of the military brats, the king's son had his own private tutor. Del inhaled sharply as the memory sparked a realization for him, ushered by the scent of candle wax and cedar.

"What's up? Are you okay?" Aela tensed, looking skeptically at Del as if he might collapse at any second.

Del grinned and brushed back his hair with one hand as he used his other to trace a path across the sky. Visualizing the connections between the stars, he followed the curve along the Guardian's bow towards the southwest. He turned to Aela as a new warmth spread across his chest, heartening him.

"I'll be fine," he said, "and I think I know a shortcut." He limped ahead, the pain in his leg ebbing slightly. Del motioned to Aela, beckoning her towards the dark forest that spread across the mountainous foothills before them.

THE MOONLIGHT MOVED in strange ways inside the forest. It slid across the underbrush, shifting up and down cedar trunks as wide as the stone columns back in the open court. Del shook off thoughts of home and the knots in his chest that accompanied them.

Aela followed just behind him. While the pain in his leg hadn't fully abated, the rush of adrenaline at being close to shelter allowed him to push through it. What happened when they reached their destination, he didn't know. At the cabin, they would need to rest. When they made it to Ghara? There was no way of knowing what Aela would do. At knife-point, she had claimed him a hostage, but he would never know that by the way she treated him. She laughed with him. She laughed at him. She had even been kind.

Del tried to slip through the underbrush without leaving a trace, the way he had been trained. It was difficult with his waterlogged leg weighing him down. The interior was separated into hollow compartments, creating the lightweight feel that he was used to. Thanks to the river, each compartment was filled with liquid, throwing off his equilibrium. He felt clumsy, like a child learning to walk.

Not that it mattered, because behind him Aela crashed through the forest with abandon. In her wake was a trail of crushed leaves, snapped twigs, and smeared footprints in the mud. Even the worst tracker would be able to find them with no trouble at all.

Almost as if bidden by his thoughts, Aela let out a yelp behind him. Del turned to see her caught, her tunic ensnared by a wayward branch. She wrestled herself free, ripping the dirty fabric, the bark scraping her skin beneath.

"All right back there?" Del asked, trying to hide his mirth.

"This is, hands down, the worst place I have ever been. And I've been to the Great Library in Barthenes." She grabbed the offending branch, snapping it in two, threw it onto the ground, and spat.

"Okay," said Del. "Not a fan of trees in any form, then."

"I like ships. Ship are good," she drawled, running her hand across a trunk. "This one would make a lovely mast." She recoiled, her fingers covered in dark sap. "Never mind."

"We're almost there." Del pointed ahead to a small clearing.

"Thank the Corsair," Aela growled, kicking at the undergrowth.

Del shook his head and started for the clearing, the telltale carnage of splintered branches from behind him beginning once again as Aela followed in his wake. When he stepped out from between the trees, Del was proud that he had managed to find his way to their destination. Before him was a small, roughly built wooden lean-to beside a stone well. He turned to see Aela standing, hands on hips, one eyebrow raised in an artfully practiced way.

"Sorry. I must be confused. I thought you said you knew a shortcut? This seems to be some sort of stomping ground for tramps." The sarcasm dripped from her tongue. Del rolled his eyes and turned back to the clearing, heading for the lean-to.

There was certainly some damage since the last time he had been there, ten or more years ago. It did seem as if someone or something had been using the structure as a temporary campsite. There were definitely signs of use in the rough straw that covered the floor. Regardless, he moved to the right side, next to the well, and shifted the roughage away to reveal a cellar-style door set into the ground. He turned back to Aela, who was examining the stones on the well.

"A little help?" Del asked, pointing to the rusted iron ring used to lift the door. Aela seemed to hear his words a moment late. She pursed her lips as she ripped her gaze away from the stones that formed the base of the well.

"Huh? Sure." She stepped to the cellar door, braced herself as she grabbed the iron ring, and pulled upward. It swung free grudgingly with the scrape of metal on wood. Del peered down into the dark hole that extended down beneath the open doors.

"Got a light?" he asked Aela.

"Hold on a sec." She ran back to the tree line. Del watched in amusement as she jumped up to wrap both hands around a branch and swung free for a moment before forcing it to break off as gravity pulled her down towards the forest floor. Grinning viciously at the tree, she stalked back towards Del.

"You might have an unhealthy grudge against the forest," he said, pulling out his flint and steel as she grasped the makeshift torch in two hands.

"I like to think we have a mutual distaste." She grinned as Del struck the steel and stone together, and sparks ignited the end of the branch. As the shy flames struck up an accord with the raw edge of the wood, the familiar smell of cedar rose up to hit Del's olfactory centres and warmth spread through his body.

After taking the torch from Aela he descended into the dark hole, his memory knowing that his feet would hit the stone steps that lay just below.

Beyond the short staircase, he emerged into the cabin proper, the light from the torch illuminating the stone chamber. The walls were identical to those in the underground marketplace, but the cabin itself was furnished with handmade cedar furniture. Del walked towards the centre of the room where the stone rose up to form a lip around the fire pit. Charred logs still sat amidst the ash while an untouched pile was stacked up against the wall nearby.

The glow stretched out to all corners of the room as Del lit the fire pit. Golden light danced across the sanctuary that his mentor had built. A rich feeling rose in his heart, reaching up into his throat. Behind him, the sound of Aela's feet on the stairs came to a stop. He turned to see her taking in the room, warily.

"Did he build this place?" she asked, her expression guarded.

"Sort of. The chamber existed already, an extension of the underground passages reaching out from Ghara. He just made it more...inviting." Del gestured to the finely crafted furniture—a four-poster bed, large table, and a set of low chairs that surrounded the fire pit.

Aela ran her hand across a tall bookshelf near the entrance. Beside some yellowing tomes sat a small collection of wax figurines, shaped into different forms. Nearly all of them seemed to be twisting halfway between person and beast. Del was curious as she plucked an odd one off of the shelf, staring at it.

"He made those, you know." Del hoped his voice didn't falter. It was strange how Aela had acted when they discussed her father previously. Full of anger but delicate, like a house on fire. With insides that were roaring and raging, crackling red hot, just waiting for the flames to gut a load-bearing beam and collapse the entire structure. Aela held the figure between her thumb and index finger.

When he walked over to Aela, he got a closer look. The one she held was the form of a small girl, her hair short and curly. The pose was dynamic, as if she were springing into action. He had known that little girl.

"How?" Aela asked, turning the figure over in her hands. Del grabbed a plain candle from the shelf beside the collection of figures. He held it out, pretending to manipulate it with his fingertips.

"Using the heat from his fingertips. It was an ancient art of your people. He would mould the candlewax using only his fingers until it matched the vision in his mind's eye. Delicate, painstaking work inspired by the Sarkany concept that all forms are mutable. It would take him hours just to make one." Del held the candle up beside the figure that Aela held. The fine details on the little wax girl were astounding. Del had always been amazed by Sarus's artistry.

Beside him, he felt Aela give off a wave of heat. Her eyes sparked to life, her irises dancing like flame, close enough to burn him. Between her fingers, the wax figure began to melt, warping and sinking into itself, until it was crushed between her fingers, a mess.

Del's heart sank, and the exhaustion of their journey shuddered through his body.

"We should get some rest." He turned back towards the fire. He sat on the edge of a chair and let the warmth of the flames wash over him as he rolled up his left pant leg. Gritting his teeth, he removed his boot and grappled with the straps that attached his prosthetic leg. After removing it, he set the metal limb against the fire pit in hopes that the water would drain overnight. While it would make the rest of the trip back to Ghara easier on him, it was only a temporary fix. The metal would begin to rust in no time. He would need to commission a new one upon his return.

Phantom pangs still chased up and down his leg, but exhaustion threatened to overwhelm. A drowsy calm drift over him. He rested his head back against the chair and listened to the rhythm of Aela's boots against the floor as she approached.

"You take the bed," he said, the edges of his vision blurring.

"Don't be stupid," Aela replied, standing before him. The fire in her eyes was ebbing as she bent to pick him up. Moments later, Del groaned slightly as his head hit the pillow. Aela grabbed a stray pillow after she deposited him, headed to a long sofa-style seat beside the fire, and hunkered down.

Del blinked groggily, the fog of sleep extending across his mind as his body sunk into the soft bed. The familiar smells of cedar and candlewax echoed as he opened his mouth to speak.

"Aela," he said. The name rolled off his tongue. Not with the light lilting joy that it held when he was young. It was older now. Scarred and confident. "I missed you." The fire flickered across the walls, impressed against his eyelids as sleep took hold.

Chapter Seven

AELA BLINKED IN the low light. The fire had burned down to embers while they lay sleeping in the underground cabin. She inhaled the overwhelming smell of wood and smoke. It held no love or nostalgia for her, not the way she could see that it did for the prince. Grasping the edge of the sofa where she slept, she could feel the hard wax on her fingers, still dried there from the previous night. She summoned a little heat and rolled the now-malleable residue into a small sphere. She held it between her fingertips, remembering the form it had taken before.

Her feelings towards her father had changed so much over the years. When she was young, she would become sad and sullen at the thought of what she had lost. She must have had memories of him back then, but as time passed, her melancholy turned to anger and erased any positive association. For whatever the reason, he had sent her away as a child and never bothered to try to reach her after that. He didn't need her, and as she grew into womanhood, she found that she didn't need him. And in that little teashop in Marinaken, when the king had told her that he was dead, she didn't feel anything at all.

But now, in this little cabin that was his, with a boy that knew her father much better than she ever had, it was hard to grasp what machinations her heart was working at. The little wax figure proved that he hadn't forgotten her, but what was that really worth at this point?

Her muscles tensed out of habit as she heard Del stir across the room. Her attention moved to his prosthetic leg, still resting against the lip of the fire pit. She had underestimated him. There was clearly a lot more to the doe-eyed prince than she had guessed, especially now that she had come to understand his strange familiarity with her. He had fallen asleep murmuring lost memories of their days playing together in the capital as children. But there was no little boy lurking in her memory, no matter how much she racked her brain. He was as absent as the man that had shipped her off to sea.

Regardless, Del's obvious attachment to her was going to make the next stages of her plan a lot more difficult. The endearing little fucker could be a goldmine, depending on how she played her hand.

Aela stood up and leaned forward, stretching her limbs until the muscles burned, then rose with the grace of a sailor and strode over to the bed. The sooner they left for the capital, the sooner she could return to the sea with a clear mind and a fat purse.

ONCE DEL WAS up and ready to go, they raided the cabin for nourishment. Surprisingly, it had a fairly well-stocked larder, full of food made to last ages and others that had not fared so well. Aela reached out to grab a container of mixed dried fruit and nuts and then threw a handful into her mouth as she deposited the rest into her pack.

"Dates, pistachios, some very stale flatbread," she listed.

"I'll be glad to have a break from termites." Across the room, Del filled their waterskins from a tap that seemed to feed directly from the well a few feet away. Aela shot him an optimistic smile.

"I don't know. I was kind of getting used to the crunch." Swinging the bag onto her back, she made for the steps up to the clearing, but Del stopped her as she passed with a gentle hand on her arm.

"Not that way," he said, turning towards the back of the cabin. "That way." He casually pointed at a large set of shelves. Aela frowned, as he strode to the back of the cabin where he examined the trinkets on the bookshelf with deft hands. Finally, he focused on a metal statuette, sculpted to resemble a crane. He jerked it towards himself and the bird tipped forwards like a lever. There was a dull grinding from behind the shelf as it swung backwards, revealing a dark stone passage.

"This would be the shortcut you mentioned," Aela said with a sigh. If there were two things she was getting sick of, it was forests and underground passages. She needed the sky above her and the gentle rocking of waves beneath. She made her way to the dark entrance and then stopped to grab their torch from the previous night and press it into the dying embers till it caught alight.

"This chamber is connected to the old tunnels that pass underneath Ghara. It will take us right where we want to go." He held a hand out as if ushering Aela into the passage. "Ladies first."

Aela let out a snort at Del's words, putting her free hand on his shoulder and gently pushing him into the dim tunnel.

THEY WALKED FOR a long time in silence, the path gently sloping upwards. Above them, the foothills must've been giving way to the sharp inclines of the capital proper. Del walked ahead for a time until the walls grew wide enough apart that they could travel side by side. Aela focused on the light bouncing off carved walls and tried to ignore the surreptitious glances he kept throwing her way until she could no longer stand it.

"What?" she demanded, the light from her torch dancing across his face with each step. It bounced off his plump cheeks and long golden eyelashes. Del inhaled sharply and opened his mouth as if hanging for a moment, unsure of where to begin.

"I was simply wondering if I might take a moment to try to convince you to reconsider your plan." His tone was diplomatic, trained. This was the voice of a king's son, practiced in lessons about policy, geography, and all that bullshit. It didn't seem to fit the boyish bounce in his step.

"You can try," Aela said with a smile, giving in to curiosity.

"It's just that it seems to be inherently flawed." Del spoke with a wide-eyed innocence that was certainly not sincere.

"How so?" she asked.

"Well," he continued, "your entire plan is predicated on the idea that my father will actually pay money to have me returned to him." Though he was trying to keep his manner light, Aela couldn't help but notice the bitter trimmings that adorned his words.

"And? He's a king. You're a prince and, from what I understand, his only heir. He needs you to carry on his legacy when he dies. Any other monarch would pay a great deal to have their heir returned to them." She tried to fancy up her words and mimic his eloquent form. It was just a little bit fun.

"Ah, but you see, that is where the issue lies. My father does not intend for me to inherit," he said, so lightly that she didn't quite grasp his meaning.

"What? What the fuck does that mean?" Aela asked roughly, forgetting their pseudo-intellectual game.

Del let out a strangled laugh as she broke character. "I'm not sure, to be honest. It was something I overheard him discussing with my mother. I was sneaking around the castle, as one does, and managed to eavesdrop on a rather peculiar conversation." He sighed, running a hand across the stone wall. "It seems that not only does he not want me as his heir, but that he doesn't seem to need me, either."

"Wait, what?" Aela said again, trying to wrap her head around Del's words. "You're saying he plans to just keep on being king?" She glanced sidelong at Del, who just shrugged.

"Or he's got someone else in mind." He tried to keep it light, but she could see a grimace tugging at the corners of his mouth. "The who and why are yet to be revealed, to me anyway."

"Well, surely he'd rather have you safe at home than dead?" She ran her hand across the knife at her waist. Maybe a little reality would peel the truth out. "He must be willing to pay for your life." Del's gaze locked on her hand, her thumb running up the hilt of her blade. He stopped walking, his eyes hard as he brought them up to meet hers.

"That's what I'm trying to tell you, Aela. He'd probably be elated if you killed me."

Aela scanned his face, trying to find a tell. If he was bluffing, he certainly hid it well, and her time spent with Del so far certainly made her doubt that was the case. Her focus ran from his open face down his dirty, torn uniform to his muddy leather boots. She thought she had him pegged from the get-go: a noble soldier, a little too learned, a little too kind, and about as experienced as a newborn kitten. Swallowing hard, she looked up to meet his glance. Now, seeing his tight wariness, she knew that she had been wrong. He was wounded in more ways than one, but still fighting. In the worst way, Aela realized that they weren't so dissimilar.

"So, what are you going to do?" He seemed to take her silence as a sign that she was considering his words. Aela inhaled deeply, her mind counting and recounting her options, considering the results of each open possibility.

"I'll let you know when I figure it out," she said through gritted teeth, before she turned and walked ahead into the dark passageway.

IT WAS DIFFICULT to tell how long they walked, but it seemed like the better part of a day. With no view of the sun, it was impossible to keep track as they travelled far beneath the mountain city. Aela stayed mostly silent, occasionally giving a grunt of assent or derision as Del ran his mouth about the various sections of the city. The boyish twinkle in his eye had returned. His body seemed loose and without its earlier brooding tension as he swung his arms and gesticulated with each description.

As they walked through the monotonously carved passage, he spoke about the opulent royal quarter, the open-air balconies that studded the sides of the mountain, and not least in his opinion, the city's massive library. As Aela listened, she tried not to think of the ache in her calves and lower back, hoping for her fourth or fifth wind to kick in.

"There are still a few tomes from the old population—"

"You mean the Sarkany?"

"Yeah, they're falling apart and hard to find, but there's one with a pretty good detail on all the back passages in the city. That's how we found this one."

"We?"

He gestured to the passage they were walking through, pausing suddenly to peer ahead into the gloom.

"Hold up. I think we're here."

"Where's here?"

"The way in." He pointed towards the wall ahead on the right. There was a large hole in it, loose bricks and debris piled up on either side.

Approaching the hole, Aela could see that there was a heavy piece of fabric hanging down on the inside. Del reached in, pulled it back, and gestured for her to step through into unknown territory.

She stepped over the low stoop of displaced bricks, walked a few paces into the dark, and stopped as Del bobbed in behind her, his torch illuminating the new chamber.

It was a small room, smaller even than the cabin they had just come from. Clearly it was somebody's living quarters, albeit unused for quite some time. The torchlight spilled amber across dusty blankets covering a small bed and several packed-to-bursting bookshelves. Behind them, there was no sign of the hole they had just come through. Instead, an old and worn tapestry hung against the wall. It showed a young girl, no more than six, her hair a mess of curls, her eyes aflame. Aela shook her head, her own curl-ridden mohawk wilting gently. Usually she would shave her head on either side of the tangled seaspray mane, but she hadn't bothered since their battle on the ridge. Her hair was growing back in, soft and new, resembling the girl in the delicate hand-weaving that she couldn't seem to tear her gaze from.

"These were my father's quarters?" she said, taken aback. "They're so small."

Del walked across to the bed then sat down and rolled up his pant leg.

"He said he preferred it down here. That it was more comforting." Del removed his boot.

Gazing around, Aela realized that she knew what he meant. Not the dusty trappings of the little room; there was nothing comforting there. It was a feeling that had been growing inside of her, the closer to the city they got. A warmth had been spreading inside her chest in a way she couldn't explain. She felt as if the space behind her ribs was filled with molten gold. She ran a hand across the books on the nearest shelf. The titles were a jumble of symbols and letters, but it didn't appear to be common tongue. For the first time since she made port in Marinaken, the mantle of loneliness that hung around her shoulders seemed to lift a little.

Aela shook her head, trying to clear the unbidden thoughts that were collecting. She didn't know this man. She didn't know his people. She didn't know the little girl on the tapestry that hung from the ceiling, ember eyes glowing in the torchlight.

"Okay," said Del. "Go collect your ransom." His voice had an edge of effort to it.

Aela glanced over to where he sat on the bed and raised an eyebrow. With a piece of rope looped around his wrists, he was tying himself to the bedpost. Gripping the end between his teeth, he pulled it taught.

"What are you doing?" she asked.

"Well, you'll want to make sure I can't get away. It would likely ruin your plan if I turned up just as you were making your demands. You'd look like a complete fool." He nodded towards his prosthetic leg beside him on the bed. "You'll want to take that, by the way. Pretty good proof that you're not full of horseshit."

Aela walked to the bed and ran her hand across the lightweight metal. It felt soft under her fingers.

"How did you lose it?" she asked, sitting down beside him.

Del frowned, his brow furrowed in anger.

"Look, don't screw me around here, Aela," he said, with a new sharp edge to his voice. "You have two choices. You can go find my father and try to get your money's worth, or we can go up there together."

"I just wanted—"

"I know. You want to know more about me. More about your father. More about your people. And if you stay here, I will help you find out anything and everything you want to know. But if you leave me here now, that door will close." His eyes bored into hers as he spoke. Aela shook her head, his serious tone bouncing off the stone walls. She stood abruptly and turned away from Del.

"I don't want to know about them. You should know by now that I don't care about any of that shit." The words seemed to have less truth by the time they left her lips.

"And me?" he said.

Aela was silent for a moment, her heart beating angrily in her ears as she turned back to face him.

"Right now, I'm the only link you have to your childhood and your family. Call me crazy but I'm pretty sure that if you were as ruthless and cold as you seem to think you are, I'd be dead already. How many times have you saved my life since we met?"

Ire rushed through Aela's veins like poison. Worse than being told how she felt, worse than the audacity of this irritating pretentious boy was the uncomfortable realization that he was right. If she was really the person that she thought she was, he would be dead. Her hands shook as the flames kindled to life, licking and flickering in her irises, and then she reached down and drew her knife.

Cold steel grew warm in her hands, the leather hilt so hot it blistered and warped as she raised it a few inches from Del's nose. Beneath the tip, his lips moved as he spoke.

"Go ahead. Prove me wrong." He refused to drop his eyes from hers. She pulled the blade back with a grunt of frustration, lifted it up over his head, and brought it down on the rope that he had used to tie himself to the post, severing the fibres in one slice. After tossing the knife onto the floor in frustration, she reached out with her other hand and grabbed Del by the front of his worn shirt.

"Let's go," she said, still alight with anger. Released back onto the bed, he rubbed at his wrists.

"It was a slip knot," he said.

"I know," she replied, mentally retracing her steps until she could pinpoint the moment in which she had lost the upper hand.

ONCE DEL REATTACHED his prosthetic and Aela managed to calm down, they discovered that the doorway from the chamber to the hall was blocked. Some kind of wooden barrier had been erected to block off the entrance to Sarus's quarters.

"This is new," Del said, running his hand across the boards.

"What's it for?" Aela asked, then groaned as she put her strength against it to see if it would budge.

Del shrugged. "Probably just a little gift from my father, to pretend that yours had never existed."

Aela raised an eyebrow.

"They didn't get along?" she asked.

Del let out a strangled laugh. "Putting it lightly."

"The king failed to mention that when we met," she said, thinking back to their conversation in the tea shop. He had been so impassive and restricted. That is to say, it seemed like he had a big old stick up his ass—it would explain his posture anyways.

"Which reminds me. We're going to have to tell him that we failed to bag his naga."

"We?" said Del.

Aela squared her shoulders and bent her knees in a boxer's stance and then brought up her fists and slammed one into the wooden board that covered the doorway. She could feel it reverberate from the impact. This would be easy. She ripped some cloth from the bedsheet and wound it around her knuckles before planting herself in front of the door.

"What are you—" Del began, his mouth agape.

"Believe me, you'd rather this happen to the wood than you, and it's about fifty-fifty right now on which one I'd rather hit." She smiled grimly, still frustrated.

Again and again, she sent high-impact punches into the same spot on the board until finally she heard the telltale crack as it split down the centre. Aela stepped back and swung her leg around in a powerful kick that sent the boards splintering outwards, leaving a ragged hole that she and Del could just squeak through.

As she stepped out into the hall, the air felt cleaner and clearer. The musty smell of her father's quarters didn't linger. Del stepped out in front of her and led the way up a hall that stood empty before them. Aela glanced down at her hands in the torchlight to discover soft spots of blood beginning to bloom on the fabric that stretched across her knuckles. She flexed into a fist and sucked in a breath, letting the sharp sting wash over her. She was hesitant, sure that she was about to step into a world where she knew neither the players nor the pieces. With every step, she contemplated turning tail and running, to keep her legs moving and her blood pumping until she reached some distant shore. She thought about how good that sea breeze would feel but knew deep down that it was a choice she could never make. Whoever she thought she was, whoever she really was, neither one was a coward.

AT THE END of the long corridor was an empty doorway with a large bell.

"What's that for?" she asked as Del reached out and tugged on it.

"You're not going to like this," he said, the corners of his mouth lifting a little bit as a grinding noise started from somewhere above them, descending haltingly.

He was right. She hated every moment of the slow rise up through the mountain. They stood on a small square platform, tugged up a stone shaft by unseen forces. Through the open doorway of the lift, she could see brief slices of life on the levels that they passed—a bustling marketplace, steaming kitchens, and numerous cool quiet halls stretching away before her until they slid down out of view. Ghara was much larger than Aela had expected. It was a full city, branching out endlessly beneath the opulent royal quarters that sat curled at the top of the mountain like a self-satisfied cat.

When the lift finally shuddered to a stop, Aela stepped out to find herself on the edge of the world. Before them, the stone had been cut away to reveal a wide balcony. Aela walked to the edge to discover the rock face falling away at her feet. Far below, the foothills smoothed away to velvet green fields before sinking down to meet the ocean. Even at this distance, the surface of the sea sparkled and winked, beckoning Aela back to her home.

Del put a hand on her shoulder.

"Come on," he said, motioning towards a pair of guards that had appeared at the entrance to the nearest corridor. They each had a hand on their sword, which hung heavy at their waists, their faces reflecting concern about the scruffy, unkempt intruders in their midst.

"That's far enough. What business do you have in these quarters?" The left one spoke sharply, his dimples showing even though his mouth was turned down in an authoritative frown. The right guard said nothing, his golden pompadour bobbing softly as if to add emphasis to the other's words.

Del stepped forward. His coat was so muddy and torn that it could barely be registered as military wear. Dirt and the odd bit of blood smeared his cheeks and brow, but he shone with the inner dignity that could only come from knowing your place is at the top of the pecking order.

"Sam." He looked to Dimples. "Gerard," he appealed to the pompadour with a warm smile. Aela could tell at a glance that they recognized his voice from the way their heads pitched up.

"Prince Reza?" Sam exclaimed, his eyes narrowing as if he was trying to peer through the grime that covered Del's face. As Del assented, both Sam and Gerard lowered to one knee, their heads bowed in a sign of fealty.

"Ehhh," Del muttered uncomfortably, "Stop that." He shifted from foot to foot, beckoning them up with his hand. As Sam and Gerard rose, he walked up to the latter and put a hand on his bicep, roughly level with Del's head. "Tell me, where is my father?"

Gerard gestured back down the corridor that he and Sam had come through.

"He's in the high court this evening; there are petitioners from the valleys."

"Then he's sure to be in good spirits already," Del said, the sarcasm jumping from his tongue. He threw a glance at Aela. "Let's go." He began to walk down the hall but stopped short after a second, realizing that the guards were eyeing Aela warily and standing together to block her passage.

Crossing her arms, she stared them down. Gerard raised an eyebrow and glanced at Del over his shoulder.

"Who did you say your companion was, Prince Reza?" His gaze drifted across Aela's muscular body and bloodied knuckles, clearly identifying a threat. Sam's hand moved back down to the hilt of his blade, his body shifting into a defensive stance. Mimicking, Aela bent her knees and shifted her weight into a more flexible position.

Del pushed back between them with some difficulty and rolled his eyes. "Sam, Gerard, this is my travelling companion, Aela." He reached down to Aela's belt and grabbed the sword that hung there, his own military issue. After pulling it free of the scabbard, he flipped it around and handed it hilt-first to Sam. "She won't need this, if that makes you feel any better."

Relaxing slightly, Sam and Gerard exchanged a thick-necked assent and stepped aside to let her pass.

"That's better," Del said, heading down the corridor. "Now come on, Aela. Let's get this over with."

Aela stood up straight, slightly incensed at having her weapon taken away. As she walked between the two hulking guards, she stretched her arms out to brush her fingers across their barrel chests.

"Sorry, Dimples, Pompadour. Next time, I promise it won't be me giving you the sword."

"Gross." She heard Del mutter up ahead as she hurried to catch up.

Ahead, the corridor gave way to a broad staircase. Against one wall stood a line of individuals waiting their turn to bring their concerns and requests to the attention of their king. Most were shabbily dressed, peasants or farmers, but some wore slightly more wealthy attire: faded military dress or nicely pressed and dyed clothes.

As Del and Aela stalked past the petitioners, those waiting in the line began to mutter under their breath, taking issue with the fact that they were jumping ahead of the queue. Aela noticed that while Del tried to move forward confidently, his head held high, he couldn't help but glance back into the faces of those that they passed. They were worn and lined, sun-baked from lives of hard work.

At the top of the staircase were massive double doors, hewn from the mountain stone. As Del and Aela approached the top steps, the doors swung open and a young farmer stepped out, stumbling towards them. From within the high court, a voice called for the next petitioner, but Del moved swiftly past the front of the line and through the doors, with Aela in tow.

On the other side of the doors, Aela was surprised to find a relatively modest chamber. "High court" must refer to its elevation, rather than rank. Windows set high in the wall on one side let in shafts of light to pierce the highly polished floor. Stepped seating ran in a semicircle around the left side of the room, creating a forum. On the right stood a dais with a tall throne atop it. In it, the king sat, awaiting his next audience. His posture was impeccable; his face was impassive but not placid, buttressed by the high ridges of his cheekbones. The long slender hands that Aela remembered so vividly were steepled together just below his grey eyes.

Beside the dais, the royal announcer peered at Del and Aela, mouth agape. Dropping back down to a long piece of parchment, he scanned the paper.

"Welcome to the high court of King Reza Ansari III, please— Hey! You're not on the list," he remarked, incensed. He gestured, and a pair of guards moved forwards from the shadows behind the throne. Ignoring their hulking presence, Del walked to the centre of the room and bowed low. Aela hurried to join him but declined to bow. As the guards reached either side of the throne, the king threw up one hand, halting them like statues.

"You've returned," he said, his voice low and gravelled. He raised his eyebrows in something akin to surprise. "Both of you." He paused, letting the silence settle into every corner of the room before continuing. "I have to say, I expected you back from your mission quite some time ago. I got word last month that the naga had been taken care of."

"We took a detour," Del said, using a tattered sleeve in an attempt to wipe the mud from his cheeks. Aela raised an eyebrow, stepping forward.

"What do you mean the naga was 'taken care of'?"

Del placed his fingers on her shoulder as if he thought his touch could restrain her tongue.

The king gestured to Aela, pointing one long finger in an accusatory joust. "You killed it, did you not? The beast was found on its back, wings spread across the plateau, having bled to death from an orbital wound." He swept a hand across the room as if to indicate the breadth of the beast. Aela and Del shared a quick glance, but she quickly suppressed her surprise, replacing the words on her tongue with more confident cousins.

"Of course I killed it. Nothing says oblivion like a sharp sword through the old eye hole, right?" Crossing her arms, she shifted her weight, her hip cocked.

Del shuffled forward to stand beside her. The king raised an eyebrow, rising to his feet. A deep violet military tunic stretched across his chest, reflected in the bronze crown that nested in his close-cropped hair.

"You had no idea it was dead," he said. It was not a question. His feet were strangely light on the steps as he descended towards them. Aela felt Del take several instinctive steps backwards at his approach, but she held her ground, teeth gritted. The king came within a foot of her and stopped, standing straight with his hands clasped behind his back. "Ultimately, I should not be surprised. It was your first. I should have expected you would be caught off guard."

Aela bristled at his words, familiar ire rising up inside of her. King Reza's marble gaze linked with hers as a telltale prickling began in her chest.

He simply shrugged. "But you felt it, didn't you? Your gift. You must learn to hone it as you would a sword. I can help you with that." His small, tight lips parted in a smile. "If you are willing."

Aela broke his eye contact to glance behind her at Del, who seemed to shrink away as if to preserve some sense of distance between himself and his father. He looked up at Aela, wary and small. She turned back to the king, shook her head clear, and held her ground.

"Are you suggesting that your offer still stands?" she asked.

"You did the task as requested, whether you were aware or not. My offer stands: a place in my household and your father's position. Royal Huntmaster." He held out one gloved hand.

Aela met his eyes. "I'm not swearing any oath of fealty."

"I did not request it."

"I serve no one but myself."

"You may leave at any time, Aela. No one is forcing your hand," he said, his own hand still hanging in the air between them. Knowing as he surely did that she stood to gain more than lose, she held her own hand out to take his, and they shook. "You won't regret this, my dear. There is so much for you to learn about the power inside of you. So much that you can do." His gaze scraped across her body like a notched blade. She tightened her grip on his long, slim fingers as they continued to shake firmly. He was intensely untrustworthy, as if she could almost see the motives dividing behind his stony irises.

"And you," he said as they broke their handshake, lifting his attention to Del. Aela turned to Del, who stood with his head bowed.

"Yes, Father." The relationship between the two of them made Aela greatly uncomfortable. If anything Del had said was true, it was hard to see it reflected between the two of them now. In fact, they seemed like any father and son but for the royal trappings and the fear that clearly nestled deep inside her companion. Del stepped forward and met his father's gaze.

"You're a very lucky man," the king said, nose like a crooked chimney stacked above thin, charmless lips. "You're about to be married."

Del's eyes widened in alarm for a split second before regaining his princely composure, in a manner that seemed like instinct.

"As you say, Father. I cannot wait to meet my bride." He smiled, wide but empty.

The king gave a wry smile before turning on his heel and striding back to his throne on the dais. "I'm glad that you have both returned in one piece. Your mother will be very happy to see you, Reza. Now, it's time you wash up and look presentable. We all have jobs to do." He gestured to the announcer, who had been watching the proceedings as if they were the latest theatrical play.

Surely this would be something to gossip about later, but for now, he snapped out of his reverie, pulling the parchment list up to his face before shouting "NEXT!" towards the opening stone doors.

ONE HAND FIRMLY on Del's shoulder, Aela steered him out of the chamber and back to the balcony in front of the lift. A light breeze blew across the mountainside, rustling through Aela's hair. The cold air made clear the damp sheen of sweat on Del's brow as he gazed out across the vista with a wan smile.

"I'm glad you agreed to stay," he said, gaze firmly on the rolling hills below their feet.

"For a while, anyway," Aela replied. She wasn't exactly sure what had compelled her to accept the king's offer, but one thought had nagged at the back of her head in his presence. He was so determined to have her take up her father's old position, and he seemed the sort of man who would reach his goal—no matter how it was achieved. She couldn't help but dwell on the memory of how he had gotten the best of her at their first meeting. He had read her so easily, playing on her emotional attachment to Timlet to get her to do his bidding. And even though she still harboured revenge in her heart for the corsair captain, Aela would never forget Dreadmoor's most valuable advice: know your enemy. Was King Ansari her enemy? Aela couldn't say for certain, but she was beginning to realize that there was a lot she didn't know. Whether she would regret it or not, she was determined to find out.

Chapter Eight

BRYNNE WINCED, HER shoulders rising sharply in reaction to Charmaine's long tapered nails digging into her side.

"Hold still," Charmaine demanded, her fingers moving swiftly to fasten the buttons up the side of Brynne's dress. It was long and flowing, panels embroidered with gold crisscrossing the bodice lifted her freckled breasts in a celebration of womanhood. It was far too much.

"This seems silly. We haven't even met. He's only just returned." In her mind, Brynne ran through every reason that she was not excited about the night's event.

"Well, luckily, what you think doesn't matter," Charmaine snapped. "The queen has been planning this ball for months. It's been the only thing keeping her sane while Prince Reza has been away." She finished with the last button, just beneath Brynne's armpit, and moved her attention up to Brynne's head, where she tucked flyaway hairs and checked the pins were tight. They were, in fact, painfully tight. "Her Highness is trying to celebrate the new addition to her family. Do not make her regret it."

Charmaine stared Brynne straight in the eyes with her own icy blues. Her usual expressions ranged from pissed to downright deadly. This one was off the charts.

"Okay," said Brynne, rubbing her exposed arms nervously. Charmaine picked a silken wrap from off the rack and thrust it under Brynne's nose.

"If you're cold..." she said, as Brynne took the square of fabric gratefully. She wasn't cold, just anxious. Moments away from meeting the man that she would be spending her life with, Brynne could only count the reasons that she was inadequate. Despite the months she had spent studying any topic that might have been deemed relevant— politics, medicine, the economy—she still felt like the rough-edged crofter's daughter that she had always been.

"Time to go," Charmaine crowed, one foot tapping impatiently against the stone. After taking a final scan of herself in the looking glass, Brynne tore her attention from the smooth, sleek, unfamiliar girl in the mirror and turned to follow her advisor, her uncomfortable heeled shoes clacking against the floor. At least she had learned to walk in those ridiculous slippers without falling on her face. Brynne took a deep breath and allowed herself a nervous smile at that small victory.

FAR BELOW THE safety of her small quarters, Brynne stepped out into the cool night air of the open court. Glancing around, she could not believe the transformation that had taken place. Just yesterday, she had been studying idly on a simple stone bench during the early hours, and it had looked the same as every other morning. Tonight, it seemed like another world. Massive glowing lanterns hung in the air, suspended from the stone vaulted roof. Colourful flower arrangements taller than the guards stood between the pillars like bright and fragrant statues, giving a more natural sense to the space. On the dais, an orchestra warmed up, playing soothing arrangements as the first few tentative couples took to the dance floor.

Tearing her gaze away from the decor, Brynne remembered Charmaine's instructions and walked towards the antechamber where she had met her mother only a month earlier. Her heart beat rapidly against her sternum as she entered the small room. She tried to ignore the memories that rose to the surface of the last time she had been here, and the lingering pull of grief. She strode to the staircase at the back of the room and lifted up the hem of her skirt with one hand, the other sliding up the stone banister as she guided herself upwards to a small balcony.

Two thrones stood side by side, nestled between sculpted columns. A guard stood at the parapet, gazing out over the open court. The hue of his military coat matched Brynne's soft silken dress; violet was the colour of the royal household, a symbol of their monopoly on the expensive dyes harvested from tundra lichens. Brynne's shoulders dropped, relaxing for a moment. She leaned over the guardrail, her attention lifting up to the glass lanterns, which hung like luminous baubles above the dance floor. The court was beginning to fill up with the well-dressed citizens of Ghara.

"Pretty impressive, isn't it?" he said. "How much gold can be spent on one frivolous party."

Brynne raised her eyebrows, surprised at the sarcasm in his tone. Every guard she had met thus far had been blandly polite, never offering an opinion on so much as the weather.

"Frivolous? The queen is celebrating the return of her only son. Is that cause not worthy enough for you?" Brynne broke her gaze from the lanterns to realize that she did not recognize this guard's face. His skin was the warm brown of an apricot pit and seemed as soft as its fruit.

"Sorry, you must be used to this sort of thing where you're from." His striking green eyes met hers kindly, peering out from beneath curly brown bangs. Brynne paused as she processed his words.

"In Marinaken? You've clearly never been," she said with a laugh. The idea of finding a celebration this opulent in the loud, messy port city was ridiculous. "The best party I ever went to back home involved five kegs, a bonfire, and a dead whale." She smiled. "Don't ask," she added when he opened his mouth, one eyebrow raised.

A small smile spread across his lips. "Marinaken? You mean you're not from some distant land, shipped here to strengthen the bond between our nations?" The man looked genuinely perplexed.

"Are you new? I thought the hot gossip about the prince's low-rent suitor had already made the rounds in the guard barracks." Brynne returned her attention to the dance floor as he laughed softly beside her.

"I'm sure it did," he said. "It just seems to have bypassed the prince himself."

Brynne's eyes widened in horror as the realization dawned on her. Tearing her gaze from the open court below, she stared back at the man standing beside her.

"Oh shit," she said, sure that somewhere Charmaine was twitching uncontrollably without quite knowing why. "Oh shit, shit, shit." Her hands flew up to her mouth in hopes of manually stemming the torrent of profanity that was brewing. "I am so, so sorry," she gasped, as the anxiety building in her chest cavity began to constrict her lungs.

He put a hand on her shoulder.

"Don't worry about it. You're making a pretty good first impression, to be honest," he said. Behind the thrones, the scuff of shoes on the staircase announced the presence of an actual guard. Brynne glanced up to see Gerard standing stiffly at the top of the stairs, his pompadour impeccable.

"Your Highness, the queen, requests that you and Lady Halloran make your way down to the party for her address," he said.

Looking at Gerard, Brynne began to notice the slight differences between his uniform and the prince's—the ones that probably denoted their rank, not to mention the prince's soft white gloves and the golden epaulettes that perched on his shoulders. Cursing her inability to know all things at all times, Brynne felt the heat radiating from her crimson cheeks.

"We'll be down in just a moment." The prince motioned to Gerard, who then retreated back down the stairs. The prince smiled at her reassuringly.

"Lady Halloran— May I call you Brynne?" he asked, testing out her given name.

Brynne nodded emphatically, afraid to open her mouth and make a further fool of herself.

"You can call me Del, if you like," he said. "Are you ready?"

"As I'll ever be." She replied. Del dropped his hand from her shoulder and curled it around her fingers instead as he led her towards the stairs. She took a deep breath and willed her feet to move.

"Is it too late to start over and try this again?" she asked, her voice shaken and nervous.

Del shook his head. "Yes. It's too late." He paused, gazing back at her with a smile. "I already like you."

DEL LED BRYNNE to the edge of the dance floor just as the queen appeared on the dais at the far side of the open court. The musicians held their strings as she rose up in front of the orchestra, stiff and regal, letting a silence sweep across the room.

"Greetings, noble gentlemen and ladies. A special welcome to our visiting ambassadors. Thank you for coming. We are here to celebrate the return of my son, Prince Reza Ansari." She gestured over the heads of those assembled to where her son stood on the fringes of the crowd, with Brynne shifting awkwardly beside him.

All at once, the sea of people parted to create a corridor for them to pass through. Brynne followed the prince carefully, heeled slippers tapping against the cold floor, aware that all gazes were directed at her. After stepping up on to the dais, she turned to face those gathered and inhaled a sharp breath. A slight breeze blew in from between the columns where the court was open to the night sky. Brynne pulled her wrap around her shoulders more firmly as she scanned the faces before her as the queen put a hand on her son's shoulder and continued her speech.

"I can't tell you how relieved I am to see this handsome face again. And speaking of handsome, I mustn't forget the other reason for this wonderful party. As you know, in his absence, Reza has become engaged to this lovely girl."

Brynne executed a curtsy that would make Charmaine proud as she looked out over so many unfamiliar faces. She had spent the past few months with her nose in so many books that she had yet to meet a great deal of the important aristocrats that orbited the royal family. As the queen droned on about their upcoming nuptials, Brynne thought she might recognize a few faces from the receiving line at her father's funeral. She saw the king's buff, bearded Royal Blacksmith with his slim bespectacled husband, the Keeper of Lore. Besides being figures of great import to the city, they were also two members of the royal Arch Council, representing the Artisan and the Pilgrim, respectively.

Alongside the councillors, several old women stood crowded together, whispering amongst themselves. Their wrinkles extended from their rubber necks down beneath their over-stuffed gowns. Brynne felt their judgemental stares scrape across her as the queen continued speaking.

"Again, thank you for joining us to celebrate the future of our family. Now please, eat, drink, and dance!" She flicked her wrist back towards the orchestra conductor who raised his hands, leading his musicians in a fast-paced polka. The dance floor cleared rapidly, leaving only those with the youth to keep up, including the blacksmith and his librarian beau. Del turned to Brynne as the queen stepped down off the dais to socialize with her subjects.

"Thank the stars that's over," he said, wiping his brow in overwrought relief.

Brynne smiled, but the feeling did not extend past her lips.

"Now, the sooner we start some dull conversations with vapid aristocrats, the sooner we can struggle to end them." Del held out a hand to help her down the steps to the dance floor. Accepting it, she peered out at the crowd of people, sipping from delicate crystalline glasses and faking polite laughter.

"I think I might need a little air first," Brynne replied. "I'm still not quite used to this." It was an understatement.

As she turned and walked away from her betrothed, Brynne put a hand to her chest. Claustrophobia was stirring up inside of her like a winter squall. After making her way past the edges of the vaulted roof, she placed her hands on the edge of the stone baluster, the only barrier between her and a near-vertical drop down an icy mountainside. With one finger, she traced patterns in the frost that had formed on the stone. Behind her, footsteps approached.

"Tell me," the firm voice rang out behind her as a shiver rushed across her shoulders. "How does a crofter's daughter come to find herself engaged to the prince of Thandepar?"

At those dulcet tones, Brynne's stomach flipped. In her chest, a familiar grip held every muscle hostage. She exhaled shakily and turned around. Before her stood Aela Crane, like a spectre made flesh. Brynne's gaze flicked up and down her body, from her freshly coiffed mohawk of curls to the finely tailored leather hugging her curves as Aela stepped closer. Brynne pushed past the breath that caught in her throat as she fought to reply.

"Why don't you tell me how a landless, bloodthirsty corsair comes to find herself wearing the royal seal." Brynne reached out to brush her fingers across the embroidered symbol over Aela's heart. She gasped as Aela reached up to cover Brynne's hand with her own and pulled it down to rest at her waist. Stepping close, Aela placed her hands on the guardrail, forearms on either side resting against Brynne's satin-swathed hips.

"Come on now, Bee. You know blood isn't the only thing I'm thirsty for." As Aela's lips moved against her ear, Brynne held her breath, the pressure in her chest increasing to an almost unbearable degree. Face to face with her former lover, Brynne couldn't help but run a hand up the length of her arm, fingers tracing the lines of scars old and new.

"What are you doing here?" Brynne said, her blue eyes fixed on Aela's brown ones, rich like a cup of coffee.

"I asked first," Aela whispered, their faces mere inches apart. Brynne could almost smell the sweet scent of the hayloft, feel the warm rays of sunlight sliding across their tangled limbs.

"I'm here to—" she started, remembering the rest of the answer before the words came out. She was here to marry Prince Reza. Or Del, as he had called himself. Shaking her head aggressively, she lightly pushed Aela away with one hand.

The corsair fell back without resistance, the forward momentum between them interrupted.

"We can't do this," Brynne said, wrapping her arms around herself.

"You started it," Aela said, placing her hands on her hips. She was aggressively arrogant, as always.

"You...took me by surprise," Brynne replied, struggling to argue. She bit her lip and opted for honesty. "I didn't think that I would ever see you again."

Guardedly, Aela nodded, her face softening. "Yeah. Me neither." Her words drifted out into the night to join the swirling eddies of snow that had begun to fall. The season was just slipping into summer, but you wouldn't know it up here, gazing down on glacial fields. A silence stretched between them, broken by Del as he walked towards them, a crystal flute of champagne in one hand.

"I know it's a bit shy of five kegs and a dead whale, but this might help your nerves." He grinned and held out the glass to Brynne. She took it as he looked over to see Aela standing beside her. "I see you two have met!" The grin that stretched across his mouth was too earnest to bear. Brynne flickered her gaze across to Aela and back to Del, his smile retreating at the pregnant pause between the three of them.

"Do you know each other already?" he asked, one eyebrow lifting lightly. Deciding quickly, Brynne shook her head, rustling free the loose hairs that Charmaine had carefully pinned.

"No. Not at all," she said, regretting the words as soon as they fell from her lips. The look on Aela's face was enough to turn her heart to ice. It was cold and impassive, unaffected, but in her eyes, a dim glow had kindled.

"I was just taking the opportunity to introduce myself to your lovely fiancée," Aela said, clearly in far better control of her emotions than the brash, impulsive girl that Brynne remembered. It used to be that Aela's eyes would spark up at the smallest transgression, her skin growing almost too hot to touch—not that it ever stopped them.

"Yes," Brynne said, now that they were both complicit. "She was just telling me the way by which she came to find herself here in Ghara."

"A very good story," Del said. "She may be the only reason I made it back here for this ridiculous party."

"May?" Aela retorted, crossing her arms. "Try almost certainly the reason you made it back."

"Well, you may have saved my life once or twice, but without me, you'd still be lost in a cave."

"If I couldn't find a way, I would have made one."

"Agree to disagree," he said, chuckling softly. As he glanced at Aela, it was impossible to miss his admiration. The ease with which they bickered seemed almost fraternal. Brynne took a long sip from the champagne flute in her hand and the bubbles flew down her throat to meet the tangled mass resting in her gut.

Aela allowed a small smile, directed towards Del. Brynne watched her closely, surprised to see that the prince's fondness seemed to be mutual. The smile dropped as Aela shifted her gaze to Brynne.

"Well, I'm gonna split. I'm a bit partied out—if you can even call this a party."

"Just as well. If we don't start talking to some of these guests, the queen will be livid." Del smiled ruefully.

Aela stepped forward suddenly and took Brynne's hand in hers. "It was a pleasure to meet you, Lady Halloran." Aela bowed emphatically to match her haughty, mocking tone. Her hand was hot to the touch, despite the chill from the falling snow.

Brynne tried to look in any other direction but the warm brown eyes staring her down. "Likewise," she stuttered, as Aela dropped her hand and stalked away across the dance floor. Turning back to Del, she remembered Charmaine's advice and plastered on her best smile.

"You're going to want to finish that," he said, gesturing to the glass in her hand. "Trust me." Brynne drained the glass and set it aside. She held out her hand for Del to take and let herself be led onto the floor to pay lip service to the city's aging aristocrats and gossipmongers.

WALKING BACK INTO the throng of people crowding the edges of the dance floor was stifling. Brynne took a deep breath, but was barely able to exhale before a tall woman with grey hair twisted in an elegant bun descended on her. The woman grasped Brynne's hands with her wrinkled ones in an uncomfortably tight grip, though her gaze was locked on Del.

"What a beautiful wife you've found, my prince." She grinned, her teeth a stark white against skin like parchment. Del smiled meekly.

"Thank you," he said. "Brynne, this is Graella, one of my father's councillors."

"It's lovely to finally meet you," Brynne said, recognizing the woman as Charmaine's mother, the council's representative of the Merchant.

Graella squeezed her hand in response. Her eyes were honey brown, but without softness. She shifted focus from Brynne to Del with the sharpness of a hawk. "Reza, sweet prince, I believe the queen has been searching for you." Del glanced around warily at these words, opening his mouth to speak, but Graella continued on, determined. "Please, leave this lovely girl with me so we might speak woman to woman. I promise I won't let her out of my sight."

Del frowned. He placed a supportive hand on Brynne's back. "I won't be long." He walked away across the dance floor, dodging couples in the midst of a waltz. As soon as he disappeared behind a pair of dancers, Graella's grip tightened painfully, causing Brynne to whip her head back towards the old woman.

"My, what a deal your father must have made to hoist you up to this height," she said, as Brynne struggled.

"Ah—" She winced, slipping her hands out of Graella's death grip. "I don't know what you're talking about."

"Don't be a fool," she said, her thin lips shaping a sharp tone. "Wife of an heir, that's not a position to be given lightly, and certainly not without the benefit of both parties. Even you must see this decision seems slightly lop-sided—daughter of a peasant, no foreign princess, no great scholar, no brilliant beauty..." Her voice was low and forceful, her painted eyebrows narrowing.

Puffing out her chest, Brynne tried to raise her head high. "My father gave his life for his king. Is that not enough?" She tried to arch a haughty eyebrow like Charmaine would have, though she felt the effect might have left something to be desired as Graella sighed ruefully.

"Stars, I had hoped that you were somewhat sharper than popular opinion, but it seems you truly are dull as they say." Brynne recoiled slightly as the woman reached out and placed a withered hand on her shoulder. "For your sake, I hope you figure this city out quick, or you won't last another month."

Brynne opened her mouth to speak just as a massive arm reached out and pulled Graella into a reluctant embrace.

"Miss Halloran, I see my fellow councillor is giving out more of her expert advice!" The cheerful voice of the Royal Blacksmith rang out as Graella tried ungraciously to extricate herself.

"Good evening, Alphonse. To what do I owe this pleasure?" Her voice dripped acid, but it was no match for his enthusiasm.

"I saw this young girl talking your ear off, and I thought I'd come rescue you before something else dislodges, you old corpse!" He grinned widely, his mouth appearing with the gesture from behind a massive unruly beard. Brynne had never heard someone insulted so cheerfully, and her hand flew up to cover her mouth as she stifled a laugh.

Alphonse turned to Brynne, holding out a massive hand. It made hers appear miniscule as they shook.

"How is your evening going, my dear?" he asked as Graella coughed out a polite excuse and stalked away.

"Frightening," Brynne said, opting for honesty. She had only spoken to the blacksmith once before, at her father's funeral, but there was an undeniably comforting aura around him.

"Ah. I feel the same about these events," he said. "Have you met my husband, Doyle?" The lorekeeper stepped out from behind Alphonse, as if appearing from thin air. Stick thin, with massive glasses perching atop his nose, he seemed almost like an old mantis. Brynne tried to ignore that thought as she curtsied.

"Lovely to meet you, sir."

"Ah, my dear. I do believe I've seen you roaming the library stacks before. How are your studies going?" He smiled, wavy blond hair bobbing across his forehead. As he spoke, he moved his hands in overwrought, animated gestures. "I see you've been spending a lot of time in the biological sciences."

Brynne blushed. She didn't think anyone had been keeping tabs on her as she walked through the dusty shelves.

"Very well, thank you. I'm finding everything to be quite fascinating."

"Everything?" Alphonse boomed. "Even the political histories?"

Brynne smiled politely. "Oh yes, it's so interesting to see how the monarchy structure has changed since our forefathers came across the sea," she replied as Doyle agreed enthusiastically and Alphonse began to imitate a heavy snore.

As Doyle launched into a tirade about the quality of record keeping, Brynne felt herself grin, not out of politeness but out of appreciation of these two men, who seemed genuinely interested in her thoughts. As they conversed, she forgot about Aela's appearance and Graella's harsh words. She simply listened and enjoyed the fact that for once she didn't feel like a fish on land, struggling to breathe.

At the end of the night, as the prince walked her towards the lift, Brynne still had a smile on her face, remembering Doyle's enthusiasm and Alphonse's jokes. Del took her hand and she blushed. He looked away.

"Thank you," he said.

Brynne furrowed her brow, confused. "For what?"

"I'm not sure I would have made it through this tedium without you," he said, gazing up at her, earnestness startling in the lantern light. Brynne smiled timidly.

"I'm glad I could help," she said, relieved when he returned her smile.

AS THE LIFT chugged upwards, Brynne removed her shoes, her feet aching. Finally the night she had been preparing for had come, and it hadn't been a total disaster. The prince was nothing like she had expected. She had imagined a hardened soldier, handsome but humourless, authoritative and arrogant. Del was clever and shy. He was tentative and uncertain, but he treated her as an equal.

This life that her father had wanted for her would be all right. It would be manageable. For his sake, for his memory, she knew that she would make it work.

As she reached her floor at the top of the city, she stepped out to find that she was not alone. The door of the chamber down the hall was ajar, and beside it, a slim figure sat, leaning against the wall, legs stretched out in front of her.

"I didn't realize we hadn't met," Aela said darkly, glaring up at her in the dim light.

Brynne paused at her doorway. "I think that would be for the best." The certainty inside of her moments ago began to drift out of reach. Her hand on the doorframe, Brynne hesitated as Aela walked towards her.

"I understand, Bee. You wouldn't want to jeopardize your new lot in life," she purred, stepping in close so that her body pressed against Brynne's. "And neither would I." Her lips met Brynne's cheek. Up close, Aela's skin smelled like leather and sweat. "Don't worry. I won't be staying up here to haunt you."

Brynne closed her eyes, heart sinking as Aela stepped back. When she opened them, the corsair was walking away, hips swaying as she disappeared into her chambers.

She returned to her own room and lay curled up on the bed, trying to fight the memories that flooded her mind. She could feel Aela's presence on the other side of the stone, knew what it felt like to spend the night with those arms wrapped around her. But looking back, she also knew that no matter how powerful and pleasurable the nights were, in the morning, Aela would always be gone.

Chapter Nine

SHE WALKED DOWN the endless hallway, each step bringing a new stab of pain that flashed like a bolt of lightning between her temples. The voice ground into her mind like a pestle, reverberating through her skull and rattling her brain.

"Come, my child."

Aela winced. She knew that she shouldn't be there. She knew she could resist the mysterious voice drawing her forwards, but she could not remember how. The stone above her head and below her feet sloped downwards, sinking deeper and deeper into the mountain.

"You will find me. I know it. You are my daughter."

Blinking rapidly at a sudden surge of pain, Aela gasped for breath as she felt her body slump against the stonework, exhausted.

"Get up! Keep going! You must do this!" The voice cracked, snapping like a brittle bone reduced to shards. Beads of sweat rolled down Aela's forehead as she pressed a cheek to the cold stone only to feel it blossom with heat at her touch. A cry escaped from her mouth as the pain pressed on, thick and heavy, blinding. Flexing to bring the feeling back into her fingers, she struggled to stand, slapping one hand against the wall. She heaved herself upwards and carried on into the yawning darkness, her palm trailing a dark red smear against the stone.

"Good."

AELA WOKE IN a burning sweat, tangled in the linens, her palm stinging. She released a handful of fabric and held her hand up to see a series of gouges where her fingernails had dug into her flesh and left blood spattered across the clean white sheets. Dim light filtered in from a high window, a mote-filled shaft stabbing down into the centre of her chambers, casting shadows across the room.

It was better here. That room at the top of the city might have been closer to fresh air, but it lacked the strange peaceful hum that Aela had noticed when she first arrived. It echoed through the stones during the day from some unseen source but abandoned her when the sun fell. She'd been having tumultuous dreams for four weeks, ever since she moved into her father's old chambers. Her first move had been to take down that ridiculous tapestry. She concealed the hole in the masonry with one of the many bookshelves that lined the walls, unsure if she was trying to keep others out or herself in.

She had barely seen Brynne since the queen's ball, but the more distance between them, the better. While she couldn't deny the continued attraction between them, Brynne had made it clear that those days were over. Evidently, she had come to Ghara for one reason only, and even if she could be led astray, Aela knew it wasn't worth damaging her friendship with Del just because she couldn't keep her pants fastened.

Aela leapt up at the thought of Del, remembering that they were supposed to meet at the blacksmith before her training session with the king. Living in the capital was a life unlike any Aela had known. She had places to be and appointments to keep for the first time in her life. She had to give herself extra time to get anywhere because of her propensity for getting lost in the city's countless halls and chambers.

Aela threw various garments into a pile and grabbed them before stepping out the freshly replaced door and striding down the hall in the nude. She was the only one who ever walked these halls, and even if she wasn't, she was never one for modesty. When she reached the doorway of the spring-fed pool, she tossed the clothes down on the semi-damp floor and dove into the cool water. This was her greatest discovery. It was as if the little cenote had been made just for her, the way the ice-cold water warmed around her as she plunged under its surface. Quickly, she scrubbed the drying blood from her hand and then grabbed hold of the convenient iron ring and hauled herself out onto the stone like a harbour seal.

After pulling on the simple black leather armour that made up her uniform, Aela ran her hand over the seal of the king that sat embroidered in violet over her breast. The king had kept his word so far, but Aela still felt like a hypocrite. Living here under the thumb of a monarch, wearing his seal—she mocked others for their fealty, for kneeling to anyone other than themselves alone. Ignoring the nagging thoughts that surfaced daily, Aela finished dressing and walked towards the lift, her mind working to recall Del's directions to the smithy. When she had told him that she would stay "for a while," even she was not sure exactly what that meant. Now, a month later, she often thought of leaving, and yet each morning, she found herself waking up in that same little room.

GHARA'S ARTISAN QUARTER bustled with activity as Aela made her way to the smith. Merchants and their workers ran carts back and forth between their suppliers' workshops and their own stalls in the even busier market quarter. The air was thick with the smell of freshly tanned leather and the tang of expensive dyes.

Following the clang and clatter of metal on metal, she wove her way along the crowded avenue to a large chamber at the very end. A massive storeroom sat perched on the edge of a precipice, extending onto a wide balcony at the mountain's edge. In the centre of the balcony, a large figure stood looming over an anvil as he brought his hammer down again and again onto a shaft of hot red steel. Sparks wicked off with each impact, spiraling out into the air only to land on the snow that gathered on the balcony, their fire immediately snuffed out. For a few moments, she stared, transfixed by the way the embers danced.

"Alphonse!" Del's voice rang out behind Aela as she stood watching the blacksmith at his work. Startled, she looked back to see him approach, moving slowly and with a pronounced limp. She placed an arm around his shoulders, giving him something steady to lean on.

"What's wrong?" she asked. He had seemed fine the previous day when he came down to the bowels of the city to continue to teach her to read her native tongue. He kept in good humour even as she grew increasingly frustrated, trying to navigate the inscrutable shapes in her father's old tomes. Now Del leaned against her, seemingly grateful to have a relief from his own unsteady weight.

"Alphonse! He gets so absorbed in his work," Del said, ignoring the question as he tried again to hail the blacksmith.

"I'll get him," Aela said. She steered Del towards a nearby crate and eased him down onto the rough wooden surface before striding out towards the blacksmith on the balcony. Ducking low to avoid the backswing on his hammer, she moved alongside the anvil into his line of sight.

Alphonse's hand froze as he spied her. His demeanour softened as he brought the hammer down without force and laid it on the anvil beside a semi-formed blade. He grabbed the still hot blade with a heavily gloved hand and thrust it into the nearby snowbank, causing a burst of steam to release into the air.

"Well, hello again, my dear," he half-shouted, smiling wide. He removed his gloves, reached up, plucked a pair of wax plugs from within his ears, and placed them in a pocket of his leather apron. "Here for your new toy, are you?"

Aela winced at the familiarity in his voice. She gestured back to Del, sitting on the crate. "Couple of things to pick up, if you don't mind." She liked the big smith, even though he treated her as if they were old friends. In his mind, they probably were. Del had told Aela that he used to watch them as children and taught them to play-fight with blunted wooden blades when they snuck down to visit his workshop. To Aela, it seemed she had only met him once before to go over her weapon designs. He was skeptical at best, but her excitement about her roughly sketched schematics seemed to amuse him.

"Right you are. Let me just see if I can't figure out where I put those." Running a hand through damp, sweat-soaked hair, the blacksmith bustled off to a side chamber in search of their goods.

Aela walked back towards Del. He had taken his boot off and was in the process of removing his prosthetic—this one made of solid wood. It was worn and a bit battered, grooves running up and down the wood grain.

"Ahh—" he muttered as he freed the attachments and placed the contraption beside him on the crate.

"What's up?" Aela asked, eyebrow raised. Del smiled despite gritted teeth.

"I've been using 'ol' birchy' since Alphonse has been working on the new design, but I'm afraid I've outgrown it. Just a little bit tight around the knee." He moved his hands across the bottom of his limb, rubbing the tissue where the tight leather cuff had bit into it.

There was discomfort in Del's expression, and he flinched as his thumbs dug into sore muscles.

"Would ice help?" she asked, gesturing to the snow that lay piled on the balcony.

Del shook his head. "Heat is better."

Aela got up and crouched down in front of him, placing her hands around his leg. Concentrating, she let the heat blossom from her fingertips as she rubbed in slow circles.

"What are you doing?" he asked, sitting straight up in surprise.

"Helping you, asshole," she replied. She meant it. Del had stayed true to his word since she came to the city. He dedicated himself to helping her understand her past and her people. She regularly joined him in the library to study old Sarkany texts, though often the sessions ended in frustration for both of them as Aela quickly grew bored of dusty tomes and ancient facts. It was a task she was still not sure she wanted to pursue, but if it would help her understand the king's motives, then she would do it.

Moving her hands across the end of Del's leg, she worked to focus her heat, trying not to let it grow too hot.

"How's that?" she said.

"I can feel the heat all the way to my toes," he replied, closing his eyes.

Scars stretched across the surface of his skin, strange patterns etched into his flesh beneath her fingertips. They seemed like the ridges formed by waves against the sand.

"What are these marks, Del? They look like—"

"Fingerprints?" he said. "They are. From when your father cauterized the wound."

Aela raised her eyebrows, staring down at her own hands as she withdrew them. She rose to stand before Del, confused. "Is that even possible?"

"Turns out, yes. Lucky for me."

"Yikes..." Aela said, as Alphonse approached behind her. Del glanced past her to hail the blacksmith as he came closer.

"Good morning, Alphonse! Is my new leg ready?"

"That it is, my little prince," Alphonse boomed as he neared, carrying two similarly sized bundles. He set them down on a nearby stack of crates, opened the first one, and lifted out Del's new prosthetic. Like the one ruined by the river, it was lightweight metal, his own aerodynamic design, with a few improvements made this time around.

Del took the new leg from Alphonse and ran his hands across the body.

"It's perfect, Al," he said, lighting up at the sight of their handiwork. "Your finest work."

Alphonse smiled in response, opening the other package. "Oh I wouldn't say that too soon. You haven't seen hers yet." He hefted the weapon and handed it to Aela with a flourish. She slid her hands across the barrel of the speargun, almost identical to her old standby but with a few upgrades. Instead of rough sailor's rope in the spooling mechanism, there was a different kind of line, a suggestion from Alphonse. It was strong but smooth and elastic, and unlike anything Aela had ever seen. The spear tip that protruded from the barrel was beautifully crafted and sharp as any blade. Aela grinned wide, her finger teasing the release mechanism as she aimed towards the balcony.

Alphonse reached out to rest a hand on the barrel and lowered the weapon.

"Whoa there," he said. "You save that firepower for someone who deserves it. I've made you a handful of replacements spearheads, but don't you go burning through them."

Del stood up from his crate, weight balanced steadily as a result of his own fine engineering.

"Thank you, Al," he said and shook the big man's hand.

Aela smiled enthusiastically as Alphonse took hers in turn. "I'll think of you when next I spill some blood."

"Why thank you, little lady," he replied, shaking her hand with a gusto that reverberated through her entire body.

Unable to bite her tongue, Aela continued. "I'm not a lady."

Beside her, Del broke out into a smile at the same time Alphonse shook his head in mock sorrow.

"You never were, kiddo."

Aela frowned at Del as he waved goodbye to Alphonse and steered her out of the shop, new weapon in hand.

"It's good to have you home!" Alphonse called out behind them as Del and Aela stepped out into the busy underground avenue.

THEY PARTED WAYS in the middle of the market district. Del disappeared into the crowds, making his way up two floors to his favourite haunt, the city's cavernous library. Since she had agreed to return to the capital with him, his passion for the study of old Sarkany tomes seemed to have increased undeniably. Each time they met, he had new information to share, a new theory about the demise of the people who once inhabited this city.

Aela made her way solo through the merchant's stands, eyeing up the wares of shopkeepers occupying their tiny alcoves along the walls. The rush of people and the smell of fresh fruit reminded her of the bright souk in Marinaken, but the stone walls and torches reminded her of the silent marketplace that she and Del had narrowly escaped. She tried to imagine it busy, like the one she passed through now. The waterfall would have spilled down into the river, curious children catching the spray as their parents shopped. Lit by dancing torch flames, level after level would be filled with people walking, browsing, chatting, and eating. They weren't her people, but they were people like her, bodies filled with heat, eyes with flame.

She stopped just once, at the courier's stand, to send a letter to Timlet. She hoped it would reach him. He would still be in Marinaken if he knew what was good for him. She had written a full page with Del's help, mostly bawdy jokes but some well wishes also. She thought often of Timlet's freckles and shy smile, still sorry at his foolish actions in the square. She passed it over to the courier with a handful of silver coins.

As she turned to leave, Aela spied the fruit stand next to the courier. Grinning, she reached out and grabbed a ripe peach. She greeted the fruit seller and tapped the king's crest on her chest.

"Gonna have to confiscate this. Royal business, you understand." She sunk her teeth into the fuzzy flesh, then wiped away the juice that dribbled down her chin as she made her way to the lift. If she was going to wear the royal colours, she might as well make the most of it.

THE LIFT SUNK down to the carriage house. She strode purposefully across the mud and dung to the great craggy opening and then onto the alpine meadow. The sun shone down onto the frosted grass as it stretched from the castle looming overhead out to the mountain's edge where the ground dropped away sharply. The earth seemed to just end there, continuing on as open blue sky as the stone below rumbled down to meet the foothills.

Aela looked out on the horses grazing lazily in the field, acutely aware of several people approaching from behind. She turned to see King Reza, accompanied by Pompadour and Dimples.

"Ready to begin?" he asked and then continued past without pause, striding out onto the grass with his guards in tow.

"Dying to," she said as she turned to follow. "Gotta try out my new friend here." She lifted up the speargun, the sharp metal tip glinting in the sunlight. The king strode a half step ahead, but he turned back and squinted at the weapon in her hands.

"You won't be needing that," he said.

Aela pursed her lips. "I thought you said it was finally time to do some training," she replied with frustration as she hoisted the speargun into the leather holster strapped across her back.

"I did, and you will, but you won't need a weapon," he said, continuing his march across the alpine meadow towards a carved lintel set into the rock on the other side. The sound of hoofbeats echoed against the natural stone walls surrounding them. Aela looked sidelong to see two horses moving at a refined canter, one slightly unsteadily. Recognition dawned as Aela saw soft ginger curls bouncing across the shoulders of the better rider. Quickly she glanced away before Brynne caught sight of her. Who the other woman was, Aela didn't know. She seemed to have trouble keeping control of her horse, probably because she was riding like she had a massive stick up her ass. Aela smirked, sneaking one more peek in their direction only to meet Brynne's eyes from across the meadow. Grimacing, Aela dropped her gaze and focused on their path to the doorway ahead of them.

AS THEY REACHED the other side, the two guards bore down and ground their shoulders into the heavy stone door. They shifted it aside, revealing a slim hallway. The king ushered Aela in ahead, commanding the guards to stand watch outside. He grabbed a lit torch from just inside and followed behind Aela as she stepped into the dim tunnel and down its slight slope. The king's boots slapped against the stone behind her.

"Tell me what you know about the naga," he said, his tone direct.

"Big. Shiny. Angry."

He did not reply.

She tried again. "I used to think they were just big dumb beasts that hunkered down in the mountains and toasted anyone idiotic enough to try to live up here." Her tone was as light as her footsteps.

"I trust your perspective on this has changed?" Reza asked pointedly.

"Yeah, now I know they never shut the hell up," she said, wincing at the memory of the naga's voice reverberating inside her head as they fought.

The tunnel opened into a large chamber. The king moved ahead of Aela and lit a series of torches around a central pillar, spilling light towards the edges of the room. Large stone pens lined the walls, punctuated by the occasional doorway.

"In point of fact, they are very intelligent and incredibly vicious. There's a reason your ancestors chose to live underground north of the green belt. Unfortunately, all their safeguards weren't enough."

"What do you mean?" Aela asked.

The king beckoned Aela forward and gestured to one of the pens just as a blast of steam jetted up towards the ceiling from inside. As she leaned over the edge, her eyes met that of a young monster. They were jet black but shone like the tightly packed scales that covered its form. Its protective mail was a burnished green that reflected the torchlight where it flickered across the creature's body. It was longer than she was tall, but coiled up in the corner of the pen, it seemed much smaller. It hissed, and small geysers of steam erupted from flared nostrils. An iron collar gripped it around the neck, tethering the beast to the wall of its pen as its wings curled close around its body.

"What do you think happened to your people, Aela?"

"Does it matter?"

"They tried to share a homeland with creatures who don't know the meaning of the word, and in exchange, they were hunted to the brink of extinction. Burned to ash and bone."

Aela's mind jolted as she remembered the alcove in the underground market. Thick black ash had covered every surface, from the carved stone walls to the decaying rubble. Of all Del's theories, this particular scenario had never come up.

The king walked to the other occupied stall and opened the door to reveal a chubby piglet. It lay wiggling on the floor in a mess of hay and dirt. Nearby, the young naga let out a sound somewhere between a growl and a bark and then snapped with long teeth.

"If you would be so kind." The king gestured to the pig. "I believe our friend knows it's mealtime."

Frowning, Aela walked to the pig's pen, bent down, and hefted it up in her bare arms, covering her leather tunic with mud and other fouler smudges. As she approached the naga's enclosure, the little pig began to snort and flail, almost struggling free of her arms before she dropped it unceremoniously into the beast's pen. The naga peered up at her with dark curious eyes before taking a mere heartbeat to unfurl its body and pounce on the pork. One last abrupt squeal and it was done. Blood smeared across the floor, spatter glistening on the naga's scales as it buried its snout into its meal.

"This one's quiet," Aela said curiously, having just realized that her mind was free and clear despite being within spitting distance of the thing.

The king nodded pensively. "It won't gain access to that ability until maturity. It is also unable to create flame just yet. The steam is created as it generates heat against its salivary gland."

"How do you know that?"

The king gestured towards the other empty pens. "Our medicinary team have been able to learn a great deal over the past few years about their physiology. Amazing what you find when you look beneath the surface," he remarked conversationally.

Aela absorbed his meaning and stared down at the feasting naga. "Is that what will happen to this one? You'll cut it up to find out how it works?" Her tone was combative.

The king turned to her, his voice cut with steel resolve. "Aela, exploration is the root of knowledge. How do you think this nation has been able to advance in the field of medicine so quickly when our rivals are still pressing leeches to their skin for every little ailment?"

Aela furrowed her brow. It was true that Thandepar's medicinary achievements were well known across the sea.

"But to answer your question, no, we will not be dissecting this specimen. This one is yours." The king laid his hands on the edge of the stone pen, his eyes catching hers.

She wrinkled her nose. "Mine? What am I gonna do with this little maniac?" Aela looked over at the naga, its head buried in the stomach of the pig, blood dripping from its long teeth.

"Like it or not, you have a connection to these creatures, developed over time by your kind in order to survive. You need to learn to use it as an advantage. It helped your father a great deal." The king stood, arms crossed as he stared down at Aela with a stiff expression.

"Yeah, well, last time I fought one of these, I barely escaped with my life."

"But when you let your gift take over, you could anticipate its movements, correct?"

"I guess so. It kind of felt like we were...sharing a mind." Saying those words aloud felt foolish, even though she had relished the feeling as it was happening. It had washed over her like a rushing river; she had felt whole and unstoppable.

The king's face remained impassive, as if this was all familiar ground. Aela supposed that it was. After all, Sarus must have become quite used to the experience, protecting the populace from these monsters on a regular basis.

"Indeed," the king said, breaking her train of thought with his crisp tone. "If you can learn to control the connection, you can control the beast."

"Control them...for what purpose?" she asked, staring up at the king. As she asked the question, she found she knew the answer: anything he wanted.

"To keep this land safe, of course," he replied, placing a gloved on her shoulder with a firm grip. His eyes drilled down into hers, and her chest filling with unease.

Aela frowned, her neck like a loose hinge. "Of course." She tried to regain her composure and fight down the feeling in her gut.

The king released his grip on her shoulder, a smile carving its way across his face. "Well, you've got a lot of work to do, and so have I, so I'm afraid I must be on my way." He brushed off a few specks of blood that had spattered onto his sharply pressed sleeve and turned to leave.

"King Reza?" Aela said, hesitation sitting on her tongue.

"Your Highness," he corrected.

"Sure. How come the people of Thandepar don't live below ground? Aren't you afraid of what happened to the Sarkany?" She didn't expect a real answer. It seemed the king was the type to tell people what they needed to know and nothing more.

"The people of Thandepar come from a land that was green and fertile. Living above and working the land is part of who we are."

"Uh..." She raised an eyebrow. It was a Bureaucrat's answer, blandly patriotic and resolving nothing.

The king nodded sharply to signal the end of their conversation before turning on a heel and disappearing down the tunnel. A sickening crack turned Aela's head back to the pen in time to see the naga snap a rib in half with its powerful jaws and swallow the shards whole. Its liquid gaze swivelled up in her direction as it licked blood from the stone floor with a cautious tongue.

"So you're pretty dangerous, huh?" She leaned over the barrier between them. It didn't seem so tough. It actually looked a little pitiful, its wings splayed out on either side, curling up against the walls of the too-small pen. Smirking, she hoisted herself up, swung her legs across the stone wall, and planted them inside the enclosure between the beast and the remains of its meal.

"Lucky for you, I'm a big fan of danger." Boots sliding on smeared blood, Aela squatted down in front of the naga. Their eyes locked. It skittered backwards, the sound of its claws matching rhythm with the chain that hung down from its neck as both bounced across the floor. In one quick movement, it thrust its wings upward and pulled them down around its body, cocooning itself in leather and scales.

Aela cocked her head to the side. The naga followed suit. She chuckled at it, losing her balance a little. She stuck out a hand to stay upright and planted a palm directly into the thin layer of blood coating the floor around the pig carcass.

"Eww!" She held it up to see the deep red liquid smeared across the grooves on her skin. Past her hand, the naga stirred, its nostrils flaring as its line of sight followed her movements.

"This is what you want?"

It stared at her hand, moving forward tentatively as she reached out towards it.

"Be careful, I need those fingers."

A long, pink tongue unfurled from behind razor-sharp teeth and hit her palm with a slap as it worked its way between her fingers and across the heel of her hand. Unable to stop the laughter from rising up inside of her, Aela erupted into giggles as the strange creature's tongue dipped and darted.

"What do you think? You didn't kill anyone, did you? You're just new. You don't know about any of that stuff. So why should it matter to you?" She sighed heavily as the naga stepped backwards, its gaze moving past her to rest on the half-eaten pig.

"Sorry, I'm rude. I'm interrupting." She was surprised the naga hadn't made a move to attack her. Resting on the balls of her feet, she was ready to move away swiftly, but it didn't seem to be treating her as a future meal. She slipped out the knife that she kept hidden in her boot and eyed the creature warily. The last time she did this, it was purely on instinct, as if her body knew it was the right thing to do. Now she wasn't sure what was right.

Drawing the knife across her bicep, she felt it bite into her skin, igniting her inner fire. As her eyes kindled their flame, it was like looking at a fresh perspective—one that was not just her own. All at once, she could see the naga in front of her, but also, she could see her own form from its perspective. She moved left. It moved left. She moved right. It moved right. She could see, or rather feel, that it didn't see her as a target. It was curious, marking her movements, trying to copy her instincts. She laid a hand across its snout, knowing instinctively that it would recoil but moving faster than it could react. Its scales were warm to the touch. When she tucked her face in close, her own flickering irises reflected in the beast's black eyes. Its consciousness moved alongside her own, the two of them in tandem.

She closed her eyes, focused every fragment of awareness she could muster, and projected them towards the creature.

"Blow."

A low growl escaped from its throat. Aela could feel the beast resisting, its mind like a brick wall.

"Blow."

She stared the creature down, mere inches from its snout. Focusing again, she hurled her mind against that brick wall, trying to knock something loose.

"Blow!"

The beast screeched out in pain with a rush of hot air and gruesome breath, one forearm lashing out to swipe across her shin. With ringing ears and gritted teeth, Aela stood her ground as the naga's claws bit into her. A hot surge of blood pumping through her body, she focused on the pounding in her temples. Usually when she slipped into this state, the only sound she heard was that of her own heart slamming against her rib cage. This time, in the silence of the cave and the resounding din of her mind, she picked out the second heartbeat that hammered across her senses. Pulling it into the forefront, she reached out and placed either hand on the iron ring that bound the naga's neck as her mind leapt forward.

"Blow!"

A jet of steam burst from the naga's nostrils like a small geyser, clinging to her cheeks and forehead in humid drops. Sudden pain cracked across her brain like a thunderclap, and she fell backwards onto the blood-smeared stone floor, her fire fading. The naga growled low, stepping towards her as she scrambled back onto her feet. It lunged, teeth snapping, just as she sprang upwards and vaulted out of the pen. Their eyes met as she leaned against the stone enclosure to catch her breath. Dark and empty, it stared up at her for a bare second before attacking the remains of the pig, long teeth flashing as it grasped the intestines in its powerful jaw, pulling them foot by foot from the carcass.

Blood landed in a hot spatter across her cheeks and arms. Without hesitation, she turned and walked from the chamber, not stopping to douse the torches. She kept walking until she reached the afternoon light that stretched over the meadow. She sank down to her knees in the grass. The alpine breeze blew across her, but it wasn't the reason that the hair on her arms were standing tall, punctuated by gooseflesh.

She realized now what the king was asking of her. When the naga had let that steam spray from its nostrils, it wasn't obeying her command and it hadn't given up control. She had taken it.

Getting to her feet, Aela fought to shake off the memory that was rising in her mind. She struggled it all the way across the grass, boots slamming into the soft ground. She tried to push it farther and farther down until it rose like a body through dark water. With one hand on the opening back into the mountain, her nose pulling in notes of hay and blood and manure, she gave in and let it break surface.

Up on the ridge, after she left Del bleeding from the nose, Tern had called her a monster. There were many that felt that way about people like her, no matter how few and far between they were these days. Now, for the first time, Aela Crane was not sure she disagreed.

"Aela?"

She glanced up sharply to see Brynne standing a few feet away beside the stalls, tying her horse. The chestnut mare snorted, big damp nostrils flaring as it dipped its head down to the water trough.

"Are you all right?" She moved towards Aela, her loose hair swaying in the light. Or was it Aela that was swaying? She wasn't quite sure. The ache inside her mind was spreading out to all corners, pressing against her. She felt her legs go slack beneath her as she slumped down against the stone.

A soft scent snuck into her nose as Brynne knelt down beside her. Warm fingers brushed the damp curls from her forehead, smearing the light layer of sweat that marked her brow. Brynne gazed past her across the meadow, in the direction she had come.

"I'm fine," Aela murmured, as she tried and failed to fake a smile.

"You don't look fine. You look like shit," Brynne said, honest as always. She leaned over Aela, her eyes clear and blue as the day they met.

"Then I'll be fine." Without thinking, she reached out a hand and laid it against Brynne's cheek.

Brynne exhaled, moving to slump down beside Aela, her back against the wall as their shoulders brushed.

"Bee," she said, pausing to savour the taste of the name on her lips. "Do you remember that day in the souk?" Aela rolled her head to the side, face pressed against the cold stone as she stared at Brynne.

"Of course. You stole a peach from our stand. I had to pay out of pocket for it."

Aela smiled, genuinely this time, as Brynne furrowed her brow at the memory.

"That's not the part I was talking about," Aela said, her smile fading as her eyes flicked across Brynne's freckled cheeks. Her head was clearing, the pain easing from her temples, but inside her chest, it held hard like a summer squall. Something behind her ribs was aching, a painful pulse pounding for every moment that she wasn't touching the beautiful girl beside her. She reached out and took Brynne's hand, intertwining her scarred brown fingers with paler, softer ones.

"Sometimes I think I'm still paying for it," Brynne said with a sigh.

Aela searched her expression, trying to read Brynne's honest eyes. She didn't like what they told her.

Brynne's body repeated the message as she extracted her hand from Aela's and got to her feet. "Come on."

Aela grabbed the hand that Brynne extended and let herself be pulled to her feet. After shifting her speargun holster back onto her back from where it had slid beneath her armpit, Aela adjusted her uniform, walked past Brynne, and let her feet take her all the way to the lift. Looking over her shoulder was not something that Aela Crane did, but suddenly she found herself struggling not to turn.

Chapter Ten

DEL'S SALAD FORK clinked against his gold-veined plate, the sound bouncing across the lofty dining chamber, an echo of countless meals spent in stern silence. Holding his breath, he looked up across the table where Brynne smiled politely as she attacked her dish. At either end of the long table sat his mother and father, their usual stiff posture presiding over the meal.

Between crisp bites, Brynne launched into polite conversation, asking the queen about her life as a courtier in the Southern Isles before she had become engaged to the king. He admired the way that Brynne combated each clipped answer with increased enthusiasm, her bright voice stretching out across the hall. Del released his breath as they spoke. The girl sitting across from him was so warm, so kind. He felt lucky. From the moment they first met, he had enjoyed her company, and his fondness for her had only grown during the weeks they'd spent together since his homecoming. Long ago, when they still spoke, his mother had told him that was all that mattered in a future spouse. Having no hand in whom one spends their life with is not easy, but it is a necessity for those who rule, she said. Becoming the partner of a monarch is not a choice born of emotion, but a job, a position of power. Tucking him into his bed at night, her long hair drifting across his nose and filling it like warm perfumed breath, she told him that as long as he could enjoy the time he spent with his future partner, he would have no trouble.

As he grew older, Del realized that while his mother did feel that way about the king, it did not cause her any shortage of trouble. More importantly, he learned that while a person can enjoy somebody's company, it does not guarantee that they are kind.

There was a lull in the conversation as servants brought out the main course. The smell of roasted meat filled the air as several artfully stacked platters were placed onto the long table. They featured more food than the four of them could eat in one sitting, culled from the king's personal herd of bison. Fair few folks of Thandepar would see a meal like this in their lifetime. For Del, it was typical, but even the hearty scent of the ginger, garlic, and yogurt marinade couldn't dislodge the discomfort in his chest.

As portions were served onto clean new plates, Del turned to his father to broach a topic he had been thinking about much since returning to the capital.

"I'd like to hold a public funeral for the soldiers we lost up on the ridge," he said, his tone direct.

The king raised his head and met Del's eyes with practiced indifference. "Absolutely not."

"They died honourably, at your orders. They were good men, and they deserve any respect that we can afford them." As Del made his case, he could sense his father's displeasure rising. Slicing through his rare meat with practiced flair, the king flicked his gaze across the table to his wife.

"If I 'afforded' a royal funeral for every individual that saved your life, we'd run out of coffins in a fortnight," he replied. His voice was light and free of anger, but Del knew better. Across the table, Brynne's eyebrows were raised. She stared at Del, the freckles across her cheeks lost in a rich blush.

"Then we should at least present their families with some kind of compensation for their loss." Del pressed the issue, his dish untouched.

His mother put a delicate hand to her forehead. "Reza, please. Now is not the time." She sighed as the king's grey gaze hardened.

"Your bleeding heart does you no favours, Delphinium. There is no reason that a handful of dead farm hands should be accorded additional fanfare for doing their job. Their families will receive the same as any others who lose a child during their conscription."

"Tern's parents relied on his return. His work in their smelting shop provided an increase in income that they cannot survive without. How is a casting of the royal seal going to replace what they have lost?" Del continued, pulling up a specific example. The truth was, most families needed their children to help produce for the family in order to offset the monthly tithe.

"Then they can sell the seal. I'm sure the gold will net them some reward," the king said, putting down his knife and fork with a clank that rang out against the vaulted ceiling.

"The seal that is meant to represent the sacrifice of the child that they've lost?" Del knew that it was time to ease off. He could see the veins begin to stand in relief on his father's forehead like the gold shot across their dining plates, but he couldn't stop himself now. The indignation was building up inside of him. He thought of Aela and the way she lost control in anger, giving herself up to the fire of her people. He was tired of worrying about angering his father and upsetting his mother. He wanted to stand up for the things in which he believed.

"This conversation is over," the king said, before returning to his meal. His knife darted in and out of his roast, thin slices sliding off with bloody red centres.

"I guess I just find it farcical that you can hoard gold while denying the simplest respects to those who have died to serve your whims." The words leaping off his tongue before he could shut his teeth to block them. On one side, his mother pressed a napkin to pursed lips, her brows knit together. On the other side, his father didn't respond. He stared at Del, his marble eyes alive with contained fury. His father was so many things to so many people. A sovereign, a leader, the son of saviours who brought their people to this land. To Del, he was a thunderstorm in human guise, dark and looming. On the rare occasions he released himself, the result was unpredictable and violent. Most of the time, the storm passed silently, while Del waited it out, anticipating the palpable drop in pressure.

They passed the rest of the meal without a word. Del barely ate, occasionally glancing up at Brynne to find her expression troubled.

AFTER THEY LEFT the dining chamber, they walked down the hall in silence, the light sliding from torch to torch until they emerged onto a terraced balcony set into the mountainside. Brynne paused, the moonlight soft against her pale skin, caught in the hollow of her throat.

"He should listen to you," she said, flicking her gaze up to meet Del's. Her lids were heavily lined with dark lacquer, the current trend floating amongst the aristocracy.

"How is it going with Charmaine?" he asked, inquiring about Brynne's tutor. He noticed that she briefly closed her eyes to comport herself before responding. Clearly her instructor was having an effect.

"I feel like I'm making progress. I almost made it through that entire dinner without using the wrong utensil," she said, smiling from ear to ear.

"I wouldn't have minded if you ate with your fingers." Del returned her smile fondly.

"I think the queen might have minded." Brynne contorted her features to match his mother's disappointed scowl.

"You're probably right." Del laughed softly.

Brynne reached towards him and swept the hair off of his brow with a quick flick of her hand as the other one came to rest on his shoulder. Unsteady, Del shifted his weight as she brought her face closer to his.

"I meant what I said a moment ago. But it doesn't matter, I suppose. When you're king, you can make sure that those soldiers get their due." Her voice was low, a whisper. Her nose was inches from his, the powdered blemish concealer visible on its surface. The thick lines along her lids gave her the appearance of a cat, ready to pounce.

Del stepped back, took her hand from his shoulder, and held it in his. His breath was unsteady.

"You're really shy." Brynne giggled. "Did you know that?" She pulled his hands towards her and placed one on either side of her waist, then reached up with her own to straighten the lapel on his uniform. Del's smile faded. She was beautiful and warm, but there was a wariness that he couldn't shake. Something didn't feel quite right.

"We don't have to do this," he said too abruptly.

Brynne's eyebrows rose high above her painted lashes. "What do you mean?"

"I don't want you to think that just because my parents have maneuvered us together...that it means we have to be anything that we don't want to," he stammered.

"And if I want to?" she asked. The words slid over the edge of the balcony, falling away into the night sky. She leaned forward and pressed her lips to his, soft and sweet but meaningless. As her lips brushed upon his, he felt an absence he couldn't explain.

He pulled away, removed his hands from Brynne's waist, and let them hover in the air for a moment, unsure of what to do.

"I thought you said you liked me," Brynne asked, the confusion plain on her face.

Del glanced to the side, over the edge of the balcony where the mountain sloped down sharply before splitting into countless rolling foothills. "I do. I did. That girl I met before, on the balcony before the ball, the one who spoke her mind—" he began, trying to figure out his feelings.

"She doesn't belong here," Brynne said, looking down, her voice thick and harsh. There was the quiver, the rising tide. He understood, he had hurt her feelings.

"I think she does. In fact, I think that she and I could be great friends. Partners."

"But only that?" she asked, raising her face to meet his gaze as the liquified black lacquer had only just begun to track patterns down her cheeks.

Del didn't reply. He stood solemn, something strange and sudden stirring inside of him.

Brynne pursed her lips, hooded eyes damp and blazing as she turned to go.

"Fine," she said over her shoulder as she stole away down the hall, leaving Del alone on the balcony. As the echo of her heels on the stonework died away, he crumpled.

IT SEEMED AN unreasonable task to pull himself out of bed the next morning. Del stumbled to the small balcony off his quarters, twisted the tap on his water tank, and let it fill his stone basin. His own design, the tank was a reservoir for collected rainwater. He preferred it to the heated water that flowed inside the city's walls. After splashing cold handfuls onto his face, he blinked the drops from his long eyelashes and ran his damp hands through his hair. It had grown shaggy and unkempt over the course of his journey with Aela, and he had not cut it since his return.

Del dressed and made his way towards the library. He stopped in the market to pick up something to break his fast. He exchanged a few coins for a honey-soaked pastry and a copper cup of thick dark coffee and tried to ignore his father's stern face staring up at him, stamped upon the pressed gold.

He jogged double-time up the stairs to the library, spilling a little coffee on his sleeve. Already he could hear from the commotion ahead that Aela had arrived for their lesson.

"It's singed." Del heard the stiffly contained outrage in Doyle's voice. He passed through the carved double doors to see the Keeper of Lore holding up a book in front of Aela's nose, pointing out the aforementioned offence.

"It made me angry," Aela said matter-of-factly, arms crossed over the mahogany countertop that separated Doyle's office from the rest of the cavernous room.

"*The Littlest Bison* made you angry?" he said, and then shrewdly, as if noticing for the first time, "This is a children's book."

Rolling her eyes, Aela threw her hands up in the air before slamming them down on the countertop.

"I know! The stupid little bison loses his pack, and he just lies down in the rain and weeps! I mean, get it together, bison. Move on!"

Doyle stepped back and put the offending book down as if expecting Aela to swoop over the counter and attack it.

"Still charming everyone you meet, I see," Del said, stepping forward to try to cut the tension.

Aela looked over at him, her fury dampened as a smile cut across her face. "I'm not paying for the damage."

Doyle shook his head, staring out in confusion over the top of his half-moon glasses.

Del smiled apologetically at the exasperated Keeper of Lore. "Charge it to the crown," he said, passing Aela and leading her back into the stacks.

THE ROYAL LIBRARY was, without a doubt, Del's favourite place in the entire city. Several stories high, it was set directly against the side of the mountain, an entire wall of windows letting light spill over the maze of stacks. Some shelves reached all the way up to the ceiling, accessible by rickety ladders, while others still were only reachable by hidden staircases leading to jigsaw mezzanines.

Stuffed onto the shelves was every yellowing text salvaged from the halls of old Ansar. The escaping monarchy, led by his father's father's father, had carried over what they could, but Del could only imagine what they had to leave behind. He had never seen his homeland, and given that it was now covered in a caustic igneous crust, he probably never would.

After passing by shelf after shelf, he turned a corner and jetted up a thin set of steps, not much wider than his own shoulder span, before emerging onto a suspended platform that he considered his private reading room. Books were piled across every surface of the nearby desk. Two overstuffed chairs sat beside the window, a copper spyglass resting between them. Aela dropped down into one of the two chairs with a puff of dust, the spill of motes illuminated by a shaft of light.

Del brushed aside a pile of books to set his coffee down and glanced up, suddenly noticing Aela's physical state. "Uh, what happened to you?" he asked. Now that the sun was pressed up against her, he could see the singed flesh rippling across her arms. On her left bicep, stark cuts raked through her flesh like claw marks. From their appearance, they had begun to heal; maybe a week old.

"Barfight," she said, spinning the spyglass in its stand. The look in her eyes said she knew that he was aware that was bullshit.

"With a naga?" he asked, half-joking.

Shaking her head, she wrinkled her nose. "Being your father's pet project has its ups and downs."

Del narrowed his eyes. His fingers tightened around the spine of the book in his hand.

Aela sprung up from her chair, pressing her eye to the spyglass and pointing it out the window. "Hey, I can see Marinaken," she said, swivelling the copper contraption to peer out over the hills below.

"You joke, but you don't know what he's capable of," Del said darkly. Aela rolled her eyes and grabbed a nearby book.

"He's a snake, but I'm not sure he's the villain you make him out to be," she said, flipping through the pages casually.

Frustration ignited in Del's chest and spread impotently behind his ribs. "I'm just saying, the things he did to your father—" He took a step forward.

"I'm not my father," Aela said, snapping the book shut.

"To me," Del followed up.

She softened, rising from her chair. "If you told me, then I would know."

Del shook his head. "Let's just get started." He picked up a stack and carried them, teetering, over to the other chair as Aela sunk back into hers.

"Deflecting," she said, not ready to back down.

Del sat down with a tight smile, flipping through the titles on his lap. "Let's see: agriculture, law, Sarkany religious rites...what do you feel like learning about?"

"You mean what do I feel like struggling through?" she groaned. "I still can't read for shit without asking you every other word."

"That's called learning," he said, dropping the pile of books onto her lap. "Pick one." He tried to calm himself as she sifted through the different titles, squinting at the ancient language. It bothered him that they seemed to argue so often about his father. It wasn't that she took the king's side. She just refused to believe that he was any more sinister than the sellsword captains she was used to dealing with. Del knew better.

"All of these are from before the fall," Aela said, dropping the heap on the ground beside her as Del cringed.

"You need to be more careful. Those are some of the few remaining Sarkany texts we have." He bent down to inspect the covers for tears. The books were so old that some had torn pages, stitched back together with sinew or thread. Only he and Doyle had ever touched the collection since they found it hidden in a dark corner. They'd spent many afternoons together deciphering the ancient language.

"Are there any books about what happened to the Sarkany?" she asked.

"There are books that speculate, but no one really knows for certain. I mean, between an epidemic, starvation—"

"Your dad was pretty certain," Aela said, her eyes catching the sunlight as it filtered across the mezzanine.

Del wrinkled his nose. "What do you mean?"

"A few weeks ago, he told me they were all slaughtered by the naga." She said it like a question, her brow furrowed as she stared at Del. "Aren't there any books about that?"

He searched the volumes around his feet, picking out a slim tome about the beasts. "This is the only Sarkany book that mentions the nagas in detail. I mentioned it to you when we were in the mountains, remember? It refers to them as the Daughters of Balearica." He carefully turned the delicate pages to the relevant passage.

"Who's Balearica?" Aela asked, already glazing over at the sight of the inscrutable text.

Del ran a finger across the words, trying to find further mention of the name. "I don't know. Some kind of matriarch, maybe?" He stopped sliding abruptly, holding the book closer to read the miniscule footnotes. "It just says 'Balearica—the heart of the mountain.'"

"Do you hear that?" Aela asked. Del looked up to see her staring across the room. He sighed dramatically. She was a terrible pupil, using any excuse to avoid a lesson.

"Now who's deflecting?" he said, closing the book with a snap.

She narrowed her eyes, still staring off into the distance. "I'm serious. It sounds like...drums. You really don't hear that?"

Del shook his head as she lifted a hand to her temple and gritted her teeth. He couldn't hear anything but the scratching of Doyle's quill at the far end of the room.

"Are you okay?" he asked, growing concerned.

Aela shook her head suddenly, staring back at him, slightly shaken. "I'm fine. It's gone now. Does that book say anything else?"

"Just general facts about nagas and their behaviour." Del scanned the remaining pages, but nothing useful jumped out at him.

"Right. Flying about, breathing fire, stealing gold."

"Stealing gold? Naga will steal livestock for food, but I've never heard of them taking gold." Del raised an eyebrow. "What would they use it for?"

"Damned if I know, but that naga I killed had enough gold to set a certain scoundrel up for life. She said she earned it." Aela shrugged, stretching out her beaten limbs like a cat in the sunlight.

"That's strange," Del said, staring at Aela. How long until she planned on telling him that?

"I snatched a piece of it, actually. I've still got it," she said, as if it had only just occurred to her. "You want to see?"

Del assented, putting the book down gently before reaching down to help Aela up, only for her to spring past him.

"Save the gentleman crap for your betrothed." She smiled, the edges of her mouth falling slightly as she saw his glum reaction. "Whoa, everything okay in the princely marriage bed?"

Del grimaced, turning and heading down the stairs ahead of her. "C'mon, I've got a shortcut." He led her down a slim shelf-lined hall to a stone doorway. He pushed the door in and revealed a staircase spiraling up and down into the farthest reaches of the city. "Hope you aren't sick of stairs," he said as he descended them two at a time, as if he could leave any conversation about Brynne far above them.

SEVERAL STORIES LOWER, they emerged from the stairwell and headed for Aela's chamber. Del was impressed that she had managed to make it seem less musty, but he also felt a tinge of sadness realizing that she had removed any sign that this room had once belonged to her father. The tapestry was wadded up in a dark corner, gathering dust.

Aela opened a small set of drawers and lifted the bottom to reveal a magpie's treasure trove. Naga might not have been prone to stealing gold, but it seemed like the swarthy corsair had a habit of collecting anything she came across.

She reached into the back of the hidden compartment and produced a thick, roughly pressed gold coin.

"Wait. You grabbed that from the naga's cave?" he asked, suddenly confused.

"Yeah, why?"

"How come you didn't lose it in the river?" he asked. Their packs had been lost when they jumped into the swollen subterranean rush, their clothes nearly torn off from the force of the meltwater.

Aela flashed a fox's grin. "I'm a corsair." She flipped the coin in the air, catching it deftly. "We know how to smuggle." She winked as she tossed the coin towards him, laughing as he barely caught it.

"Ah..." he said, turning it over in his fingers as his disgusted grimace turned swiftly into shock. "Aela, this isn't a Sarkany coin."

"It isn't?" she said, stepping over for a closer look.

"It's Ansari." He held it up, trying to read the date in the low light. The numerals were hand-carved, not stamped like modern currency. "From before the exodus—this coin is from Old Ansar."

"So, I bet there are lots of old coins still lying around somewhere." She shrugged as Del shook his head, his mind racing.

"No, there aren't. There was no time for the crown to bring its fortune over so an entirely new currency was minted when they arrived here." He glanced up, eyes wide. "You said the cave was full of coins just like this?"

She frowned, wary now from the concern in his voice. "Like I said, a fortune."

"Or a payoff," he said, suspicion rising.

"What are you talking about, Del?"

He slumped down against the bed, gears turning and ticking inside his head. "My father told you that the Sarkany were killed by the naga.

How would he know that? Nobody knows for sure what happened to your people."

"Maybe that's just his pet theory? I mean, it made sense. Remember the thick layer of ash covering that market place we found?"

"I'm not saying it didn't happen. What I'm saying—" Del said, his eyes drifting up to meet Aela's. "Is that it happened for a price."

Aela rocked back on her heels, chewing her lip as she absorbed his words. "You think your ancestors paid off the naga to destroy my people."

Del nodded, still processing the concept himself.

"Wouldn't that be common knowledge? Wouldn't people know?" She gestured to the city, resting above them like a stone hornet's nest.

"Who would tell them?" Del asked. "This would have happened generations ago."

"Why, then?" Aela shook her head. "Why?"

Del understood her reluctance. She was searching for any reason not to believe him. Even if she could pretend not to identify with her people, this conception of their demise was too gruesome to ignore.

"Why does anybody do something terrible? Because they're jealous or they want revenge or they think it's righteous. If this is something my ancestors did, I wouldn't be surprised. I think it might even be in our blood."

The more he thought about it, the more sense it made. Old Ansar was verdant but volatile. The kings of old must have known it was only a matter of time before their mountains revolted, spewing hot and heavy blankets of magma across farms and cities alike. Their trading partners, the Sarkany, had a land that was frigid but rich beyond measure, with gold hiding in every corner of the earth.

"Of course," Aela said, shaking her head. "I should have known you would have a way to make this crackpot theory about your father." She sighed, stepping forward to put a hand on his shoulder. "Del, you're sailing into a storm here. Turn around."

"Come with me," he said. If she didn't believe what his father was capable of, he would have to show her. He grabbed her hand and pulled her along behind him as he stalked out of the room and down the hall.

"You know I've killed people for less than this, right?" she asked as he brought her into the room with the glacial pool.

"When I was younger, my father became obsessed with his jealousy. He was convinced that my mother was cheating on him with Sarus, that she had been for years. He even believed that I was illegitimate, but he had no way to prove it." Del stumbled over his words but was determined to get them all out. He dropped Aela's hand and walked towards the pool in the centre of the room, resting his boot on the rusted iron ring.

"Del..." Aela said softly from behind him. He stared into the depths of the ice-cold pool, an unwelcome shiver running up his spine.

"Until he found a way," he said, his throat growing more sharp and raw with each word. "He thought that the betrayal was hiding dormant inside of me and that if I stayed under long enough..." Del's eyes began to burn as he kicked the iron ring with the toe of his boot, feeling the matching manacle cut into the flesh of his wrist, a bitter memory. "That it would rise to the surface, proving him right." He turned to Aela, his jaw tense, teeth gritted. "But it didn't."

He looked up to see her staring at him with concern, dark curls limp against her forehead. No arms crossed, no raised eyebrow. No tough pretense. She stepped towards him, but he held out a hand.

"Don't," he said.

"That's how you lost it?" she asked, staying at arm's length. "Because you didn't have the Sarkany blood to heat yourself?"

Del felt himself smile, ugly and forced. "I'm my father's son, after all," he spat, dropping his arm.

Aela moved forward, her posture awkward and uncertain. "You aren't. You're nothing to do with him. You could leave now and never give him another thought." She hesitated for a moment. "We could go together."

Del shook his head and swallowed, forcing himself to hold it in. He gestured to his prosthesis. "It still hurts," he said, hating the weakness in his voice. "But it has to. I couldn't use it otherwise." He wasn't making sense and he knew it, but he couldn't find any other way to express what he needed to say. "The painful reminder can take the weight, but an absence can't. I need the ghost...to move forward." He stared at Aela. She had changed so much since they were children, but looking at her now, he realized that they weren't so different. "Do you know what I mean?"

She stepped back, light reflecting across the myriad of scars that shone on her skin. "No," she said emphatically, shaking her head. "I don't."

"Your past, your people..." he stammered, desperate to make her see. He held out the coin, and she took it from his hand.

"It always comes back to this, doesn't it?" she said, the anger giving her voice a steel edge. "It's not my past, and I don't need it to find strength. In case you hadn't noticed, I've plenty of that." She turned to leave.

Del shook his head. How many hours had he spent, weighed down by dusty tomes, trying to understand the past, all to find some clue to where she might be. Now she was here with him, but he still couldn't seem to let it go.

"But now that we know what happened—"

"If that even is what happened," she said, jagged tone interrupting his train of thought. "And not just a story you've made up to explain your father's cruelty."

"It makes sense," he insisted. "All the pieces fit." If he could only find a way to prove his theory, he was sure that she would care. Together, he knew that they could find a way to right the wrongs of his forefathers. He stepped towards her, reaching for the gold coin.

Aela blinked, sidestepping quickly as he moved towards her. Her eyes ignited in a flickering bloom. She reached out with uncanny speed and grasped him by the throat, and Del could feel his trachea tighten. Her fingers against his neck grew warm, then hot, until they burned like searing brands against his flesh.

"The pieces are broken," she hissed, "and jammed into place." As she spoke, she lifted him up bodily by the throat, until his dangling legs skimmed the surface of the pool.

"What are you doing?" he choked, staring her in the face as she held him out over the water, the veins in her arm standing out in relief. The coin in her free hand shimmered as she flicked it into the air. Del heard it hit the water with a splash, the only piece of evidence in his search for the truth sinking quickly into the unknowable depths.

"Aela, please—" he sputtered as her fingers tightened around his windpipe.

Chapter Eleven

AELA'S HAND, AS if of its own volition, tightened around Del's throat. His eyes wide and mouth sagged open, gasping for breath as he stared at her.

"Aela..." His words cut across the surface of her awareness, almost entirely blocked out by the resolute pain pounding between her temples. It had begun in the library, growing in intensity and rhythm until it was all she could hear, all she could feel. As if watching through another's eyes, her own arm stretched out in front of her, smooth dark skin broken by ripples of scar tissues from her shoulder to her fingertips, where they choked the life from her only true friend.

"Why—" he sputtered, his pupils rolling up into his head as her own widened in shock. She didn't know why. She didn't know what or where; she barely knew who it was struggling beneath her slender fingers. She knew rage and pain and fire coursing through her body, hotter than any conviction she'd felt before. His bangs pressed against his forehead, damp and matted, as he struggled to say her name one last time before his head lolled to the side.

And then she knew. Her irises flared and then blinked back to their usual brown as her brow dropped like a stone, mouth hanging open in slack horror. Releasing her grip like recoil, she dropped Del and lunged forward to catch him moments before he hit the water. She gently lowered his limp body to the stone floor and lay over him, fingers searching his throat for a heartbeat. Nothing. Just soft skin, smooth against her fingers. And then—there it was, faint. Her head still ripped through with a resounding tattoo. His pulse was weak, but he was alive, no thanks to her. His eyes flickered open, grey marbles in the dark. He took a ragged breath, and she jumped a foot and scrabbled back across the floor until the wall pressed at her back.

"Aela—" he tried, lifting one hand to his throat, fingertips lingering across the tender skin where a bruise would surely begin to bloom in no time at all.

She didn't reply. The wall hard against her back, she leaned on it for support as she stood up on shaking legs. Hot and hard, the lump grew in the back of her throat. She couldn't speak, couldn't think, couldn't stay here, knowing what she was capable of.

Shaking her head, the closest to an apology she could get, she turned and left the chamber, the sound of Del's ragged breathing falling away behind her.

SHE POUNDED UP the narrow spiral stair, taking her up and away. On instinct, she continued running, taking a passage off a low landing until the familiar smell of hay and blood wafted towards her. Following the scent, she emerged into the old stable, looking around the dark chamber. She had never come there through the city's passages before, always across the meadow, the way the king had led her that first time.

Two orbs flickered at her in the darkness.

"Kera—" Aela muttered, rummaging in her pocket for the flint and steel she kept. She lit a torch and the warmth spread across the young naga's cramped quarters. He had grown so quickly, already too big for his pen. He lay in the centre of the chamber, a new metal collar and chain keeping him close to the stone pillar.

Approaching cautiously, Aela bent down to greet the young monster. Over the course of the past few weeks, she had taken a liking to the creature, and it seemed he felt the same. Despite the brutality she had employed during that first encounter, they had reached a steady truce. She had not tried a second time to control the beast, opting instead to play with him. Of course, her version of play was fighting or wrestling, and he was nothing if not rough. She would always come away with some fresh bruise or scrape, all the better to let the king think that she had received them while trying to master her new charge. When she was pained and exhausted, she would sit beside the beast and talk, watching the soft warmth grow behind its eyes as she shared tales and thoughts.

Now she slid down against the wall of a nearby pen to rest on the floor, minding the blood that crusted the floor from past meals.

"Kera, I don't know what's happening to me," she said, staring at the hands that moments earlier had, seemingly of their own conscience, tried to stem the life from someone she cared deeply for.

Kera snorted, shaking his head from side to side as thin columns of steam blossomed from his copper nostrils. Aela let her head drop into her untrustworthy hands, warmth radiating from Kera as he curled as close as the metal chain would allow, his burnished scales pressing against her thigh. She had never lost control the way that she just had with Del. It was as if she didn't even know what she was doing even as her grip tightened around his throat. Was that how the young naga felt as she exerted her control over him?

The dull ache in her head refused to subside. Before that day, she felt like she was making progress in understanding the fire that flowed inside of her. Spending time with Kera had helped her figure out how to tap into it at will, allowing her to feel his heartbeat contrasting with her own. It was a skill that would have come in handy if she had been able to figure it out as a corsair. Instead of constantly reining herself in for fear of her true nature emerging, she could have used it as a tool, only when necessary. She summoned the flickering feeling in her chest, letting her eyes catch and kindle. Her heart beat strong in her ears, the blood pulsing. She swallowed hard and pushed her own pulmonary rhythms to the back of her mind, listening hard to Kera's slower pulse, matching the rise and fall of his copper chest. She pressed her head back against the stone pen wall, letting the two rhythms play against each other in her mind. Though Kera was still too young to invade her mind, she had begun to feel him probing at the edges, bare hints of emotion getting through her barriers. Now concern drifted softly at the cusp. He peered up at her, and she placed her other hand on his great horned brow.

"I'm sorry. I wish I could tell you everything was going to be okay."

Kera growled low as a sharp pang hit Aela. The pounding in her mind started afresh. As new pains hit in rhythmic beats, Aela opened her eyes wide. Lain against the already busy noise of her mind, she was finally aware of what it was. A third heartbeat was pulsing inside of her head. And while her own was pushed towards the back and Kera's calmly pounded along with it, this one was different. It was loud and sharp and furious, and it beckoned to her painfully from beneath them.

Aela stood unsteadily and brushed her hands over the beast's warm scales once more before heading down a dark passage. Kera whined at her retreating back, but she ignored him, focusing hard on following the mysterious beating into the depths underneath the city.

AELA FOLLOWED THE thumping of the heartbeat until it filled her mind, an unending din. Twisting through passageways, taking doorways on instinct, stumbling down slim stairways, her feet pounded on until the smoothly carved tableaus of the city gave way to uncarved, untouched rock walls. The ceiling held no artistic arches, just sharp stalactites, hanging ominously above her head. Her feet were sore, her throat was parched, and her hands were covered in scrapes from using the uneven walls as a guide in the dark. She couldn't see the state of them, but she could feel the raised welts and smell the coppery scent of her own blood, somehow stronger and heavier than the stuff drying on Kera's stable floor.

All at once, words ripped through her mind.

"Come, daughter."

The voice was feminine, rich and deep. It seemed to echo through the hall, but Aela was certain that anyone else would not have heard a word. She shuddered against the wall as her body threatened to buckle under the weight of the ache in her head.

"So close. You are almost here. Come, daughter."

It reminded her of the naga at the top of the mountain, the way it spoke into her very mind, but she could tell that this was different. No mocking edge to it, it seemed to call the very core of her onwards. It was like the feeling that embraced her in her father's quarters, multiplied by a number to which Aela surely couldn't count.

Stumbling forward, she pulled herself along as if an invisible rope guided her. The rough passageway seemed unending, the thick air growing hotter every second until a sweat broke out across Aela's brow. Finally in the distance, the passage turned. The stark unbreakable darkness of the undermountain was shattered by flickering light reflected on the curve of the stone. Desperate steps took her forward until she turned the corner to an unbelievable sight.

The passage opened into a cavern bigger than any she had ever seen. Larger than the open court, larger even than the naga's nest on the ridge. Her feet were just steps from the edge of a great crevasse. Aela could see that it extended up to a dark unseeable ceiling, as well as down into an endless abyss. Brimming out of the rift in the ground, swirling and crackling up into the air was a towering inferno. Red flames slapped and licked against the stone, rearing up into incarnations of gold and scarlet. Within was a white-hot centre, holding a strange solid sphere that pulsed like a distant star, though it seemed close enough to touch.

The stone walls that rose on either side of the chamber towards the dark were punctuated with narrow openings, angling off into the rock. The choking smoke siphoned into them in dancing eddies, carrying hot air up into the city. A kind of maddening hypocaust, Aela thought, her gaze drifting up into the dark. No wonder the city was so comfortably warm for the Ansari who adopted it as their home.

"*Adopted?*" the voice hissed from inside Aela's mind. "*Invaded. Claimed. Conquered.*" The flames snapped angrily with each word, as if to punctuate. They seemed to be speaking to her from the mass in the centre of the inferno. It looked like a cluster of rock and towered over her like a megalith. "*Come closer, daughter, there is so much to speak of.*"

But Aela hesitated, standing with her back against the wall, a mere three feet of rock between her and the edge of the chasm.

"So it's true, then. The Ansari had them killed?"

"*Yes! Your clever little prince was right. Pity you didn't choke the breath from him when you had the chance. After all, his ancestors had yours slaughtered like your dear Kera's piglets.*" The voice brightened and cracked.

"You know about Kera?" Aela asked, curious now. Whatever was dwelling in that strange enclosure seemed to know a lot about her. It seemed to share the same connection to her as the naga that she killed, but it felt much more personal.

"*Of course. The one you call Kera is my child as much as you are.*"

"Who are you?" Aela asked, stepping forward and feeling the immense weight of the heat roll over her body. Fire had never made her feel this way before. Usually the warming glow matched her own inner temperature, but this was far more intense. It was choking and oppressive, scorching her face and her throat. Before her eyes, the dark stone that sat in the centre of the flames seemed to ripple and reform as something within tested its boundaries.

"*Sweet daughter, you know so little of your own history. You have your father to thank for that. The one boon he granted you was to send you away rather than let you serve your enemies as he did.*"

"Did you know him?" Aela asked. The smell of brimstone itched at her nostrils as tiny ashes fluttered down to rest among her curls.

"*Know him? Poor, weak Sarus.*" The voice lost its comforting edge and became angry and cruel all at once. Aela felt but an echo of the rage that had raced through her body as she held Del's life in her hands. *"We spoke on more than one occasion. Too smart to ignore the truth, but too cowardly to help me set things right. But you...you have a chance to correct our legacy."*

"You seem to know a thing or two about me," Aela shouted. "Maybe you've picked up that I don't give a shit about legacies." She knew that the voice could hear her every thought, that to speak out loud was pointless, but it helped her nerve to formulate the words in her own steadying voice.

"Ah yes. I had forgotten the ignorance of youth. But you are my child, and you will help me to repair what has been broken and to break those who deserve it in return. I know that you will."

"Can you just tell me what the fuck you're talking about? Like without being all prophetic and obscure and shit?" Aela wiped the sweat from her brow. It was starting to sound like a conversation with Del, a pang of guilt pinning her heart to her spine. "Just answer my question!"

"You know who I am," the voice insisted.

Aela thought back to anything and everything she had ever learned about Sarkany lore, until it hit her like a ton of white-hot bricks. "Balearica... The—" Of course. "The heart of the mountain." Of course. All ancient Sarkany texts seemed to have a penchant for asinine metaphor. Aela blinked the stinging smoke away, trying a different tack. "Okay, *what* are you?"

The fire roared high and hot, reaching up into the very highest reaches of the unfathomable ceiling as wave after wave of heat rolled off of it. *"I am flux. I am your maker,"* it hissed in the very back of Aela's mind, and an anxious tremor in her empty gut told her it was the truth. This broiling ball of rock and fire and anger, it called to something deep inside her, to the heat that flowed through her body like spite.

"What exactly are you asking me to do?"

"I want you to help me avenge your sisters. To rip the very throats from the Ansari dynasty. To show them what it feels like to lose your children. The very same thing I asked of your father before he took his life."

Aela swallowed hard, realizing that she had never asked Del how her father had died. Her anger had been too great to care.

"Can't you just avenge them yourself? You seem pretty powerful. Just look at you, all billowy and hot." Aela swayed on her feet; the smoke and heat were getting to her. Her curls pressed down around her neck, drenched in sweat.

"*I need something from you, my child. Just a drop of the blood that runs hot through your body.*" The flames shot forward, reaching for her as Balearica spoke. Aela's mind swam as the heat blurred her vision. Was she trapped within the stone at the centre of the fire, or was she the fire itself? Why hadn't Aela paid attention during any of Del's discussions of Sarkany lore? She thought back to the only thing she could recall—that Sarkany myths were all about transformations. Nothing could ever stay the same, change was the only constant. It had never occurred to her that change might require a catalyst.

Aela edged back towards the safety of the passage, away from the fire and its stone chrysalis, trying to escape the reach of the flames.

"You know, I don't think I'm going to do that," she managed to choke out. "I'm not really the honourable revenge type. More of an opportunistic slash-and-grab girl."

"*Just come a bit closer, daughter. I see you've scraped your hand. Just press your palm against this form that I occupy. That's all I need— just a taste. You'll feel no pain, and I will be born anew.*" The flames reached for her, pulsing along with the heartbeat that thrummed against her skull like a tympanic corona. The rock amidst the frames seemed on the verge of fracturing, its sharp edges glinting like naga scales in the firelight.

Aela glanced down at her hand. It was indeed torn up from the journey towards the cavern. Still, gifting her internal fluids to a bloodthirsty deity seemed like a choice that should be given some pretty serious consideration, and she felt far from straight-headed.

"Okay. I'll do it." Aela's voice rang out across the depths. The flames crackled victoriously as she took a half step forward. "Just tell me one thing."

"*Anything.*" It sighed, long tapers of fire reaching out to stroke the ground before her feet.

"How did you get trapped down here?" Aela asked, one eyebrow raised.

A low laugh erupted against her mind. "*Unfortunately, my daughters didn't much care for me meddling in their affairs. The Ansari offered them endless piles of gold to do away with the younger siblings they had always felt jealous of. For them, it was an obvious choice.*"

Aela tried to parse through what she was hearing. Balearica was referring to the nagas and the Sarkany as siblings. It seemed to make sense, given the effect they seemed to have on each other. Was it possible they both came from the same source—and was it truly the one she was speaking to right now?

"And for you?"

"I was overpowered and driven underground, where I could do nothing but listen to wretched screams as my eldest decimated their younger brothers and sisters. No one to speak to but the ancestors of their assassins."

"You mean the king. He knows about you?"

Again, the dark laughter lapped at the edges of her mind. *"But of course, daughter. We've spoken many a time. He was very eager to hear about the powers you might possess and how they might aid his army. In fact, it wasn't until he came to me that he realized just how foolish he was to let you and your father out of his sight."*

Aela's jaw tightened. The king was just as much a pawn in this ancient game as she was. Balearica convinced him that she was indispensable, so he spared no expense to find her, all so that this great flaming ball of hate could draw her into its maniacal revenge plot.

"Come a little closer, daughter. Isn't it time we set this indignity to rights?"

Aela stared hard at the form in the heart of the inferno, letting the rage and pain in Balearica's voice wash over her. In all Del's lectures about history and ancestry, she didn't think this was what he meant when he spoke about her responsibilities to "her people." Gritting her teeth as she remembered how this very rage had poured through her body as she throttled Del, she stepped back from the flames and turned away.

"Sorry. Just doesn't seem worth my while." Aela began the grueling walk back up into the dark passageway. Behind her, the fire seemed to lash out in anger, the chrysalis within it shaking and shivering as if about to explode, but there wasn't a blast.

However, Balearica's voice still raged inside her mind for quite a distance, calling her a coward like her father, begging, pleading, wishing her demise. It was only when she began to climb back up into the city that it faded away, leaving her with only her own thoughts, her own heart pounding in her ears. Finally, she came across a familiar sight. A pile of loose stones cluttered around a jagged opening in the wall, blocked from within by her own bookshelf. She pushed it aside with some difficulty and stumbled into her own dusty quarters with sore limbs and a raw throat.

SADLY, IT DIDN'T take Aela long to pack up as the light of the moon slanted in from her high window. The things she needed to take with her were few and far between, some spare pieces of clothing, a small cache of coins, and of course, her speargun. She felt the sharp sting of guilt as she ran a hand over the barrel, remembering the joy on her tongue as she described the weapon to Del and Alphonse while they planned its construction.

Aela walked swiftly down the hall and dropped her pack and her weapon at the entrance to the small shimmering room and continued over to the edge of the pool. There was no sign of her recent struggle. Del must have left of his own volition once his airways recovered from her grasp. She couldn't see the bottom of the pool, though she knew that the old Ansari coin rested somewhere down there in the dark, the only proof that Del's ancestors had once paid to have her own mercilessly slaughtered. How many long nights had he spent in that cavernous library, his nose hovering over dusty tomes as he tried to divine the truth of what had happened in this sad, strange land. Aela shook her head. It was better that the truth stayed hidden, just like the vengeful flames burning brightly beneath the city. She wouldn't be responsible for any more destruction. In fact, the farther she could make it from this place, the better. If Balearica could affect her enough to nearly wring the life from Del, it was only a matter of time before she found herself pressing a bloody palm into the centre of those flames, held under its strange control. It was for the better of the entire city if she left—or at least, that's what she continued to repeat to herself in moments of wavering resolve.

THE SCRAPE OF a heel against the stone pulled Aela out of her reverie. When she turned sharply, she was surprised to see Brynne standing at the entrance to the room, hefting Aela's speargun in her freckled hands.

"You're leaving," she said. She was dressed in the part of the princess that night. Tight silk the colour of jadestone wrapped around her ribs, billowing out into numerous layered skirts around her hips. Her breasts were hugged by the dress, their bare horizons rising above the dark fabric. Auburn hair was piled atop her head, twisted and oiled into submission. She stared at Aela from dark painted lids and pointed the loaded spear across the room, one pale finger caressing the trigger mechanism.

"Put that down, Bee. It's dangerous." Aela took several strides forward until the spear's point was mere inches from her breastbone.

"I've been wondering about this thing since I saw you carrying it in the stables that day. Is this a common weapon for a corsair?" Her eyebrow was artfully arched to match her haughty tone. Aela suspected that the lessons with her tutor were going a little too well.

"No," Aela said. "Just for me." Her heart jolted as she saw Brynne's gaze harden, her jaw tighten and tense. "I had Alphonse craft it for me," Aela continued, uncertain of Brynne's motives. "To replace the one I used to have. I took it off a southern whaler."

"So," Brynne said, pressing the weapon forward until the spear tip poked cold and sharp against Aela's skin directly between her humble breasts. "If someone washes up on the coast with one of these in their back, it's a pretty clear sign that you pulled the trigger."

"There's a damn good chance." Aela felt the point of the spear press against her, hovering above her heart, not quite enough force behind it to the break the skin. One slip of Brynne's finger and she'd be skewered.

"Funny—" Brynne shuddered, drawing in a thin breath as she lowered the gun. "—as that's how they found my father." She tossed the speargun aside, and it slid across the floor with a clatter.

"I've never met your father." Aela took a step back. He was thankfully never around during her many visits to Brynne's bed in Marinaken. He was a merchant captain if she remembered correctly.

"Really? Because it sounds like you were the last person who ever did." There it was again, the hard edge in Brynne's voice, her words biting at Aela like barbed wire. Stepping back farther, Aela racked her brain, trying to understand Brynne's words. A spear in the back wasn't her style. She had mostly used the weapon for swinging between ships during a raid, preferring her knife for close combat. Breaking from Brynne's accusing gaze, Aela scanned the surface of the glacial pool as the memory hit, cascading over her like cold water.

She had stood at the railing of the merchant ship, Timlet at her side as the violet-coated captain swam fruitlessly away through the ice-laden water. She felt the recoil shudder through her palms as the spear launched, finding its target with a thud. She heard the tear of the rope as she cut it free, happy to be rid of the man. She shot him to make sure he didn't survive the swim, because he had seen her true nature and he knew what she was. But it had all been a ploy, hadn't it? That wasn't a true merchant ship. It held false cargo: Dreadmoor's payment from the king for her safe delivery to Marinaken's docks.

"It was a suicide mission," Aela said, still refusing to look at Brynne as the memory chewed at her innards.

"What?" The response was harsh, more pained than Aela had ever hoped to hear from her old lover.

"Yes, I killed him. No, I didn't know that he was your father. I thought he was just an easy mark, some merchant bearing cargo. I'm a corsair. That's what I do." Finally she brought her gaze to meet Brynne's, immediately regretting it as her heart seems to shrivel and shrink inside of her chest. "That's what I did." That beautiful girl stood before her, wrapped in uncomfortable luxury as her eyes welled with the pain of betrayal.

"But I was wrong." Aela stepped forward, kicking the speargun back towards her pack as she gauged the depths of Brynne's anger.

"What do you mean?" Brynne choked out, her arms crossed against her chest. Her haughty attitude had been sapped from her. Instead, she stood before Aela, a broken doll, the fresh trappings of her royal station like a chipped mask.

"He wasn't there as a merchant captain. He was there for you. Haven't you wondered how you got here? The daughter of a crofter and a merchant, somehow rising above her rank to join the royal family?" Aela tried to keep the spite from her tone, her chest still aching from the pain written clearly across Brynne's face. Pain that she had caused, as always.

"Of course I have. Everyone has," Brynne choked out.

Aela narrowed her brows, not savouring this revelation. "It was a bargain struck, Brynne. When Dreadmoor gave up my location to the king, they would have needed someone to deliver the payment, but it had to seem like an ordinary corsair attack. That means no man left alive. Your father must have offered to captain the ship, in exchange for your betrothal." As Aela spoke, she could see the wheels turning behind Brynne's widening eyes.

"I don't understand," she said, her voice nearly a whisper. "Why not just order someone to captain the ship? The king has an entire army at his disposal."

"Because king and country only mean so much when you're being asked to give your life. If you want something done right, ask a man who has something to gain."

Brynne shook her head bitterly. "He went to all that trouble, just to get you in his grasp." She reached up with her hands to wipe beneath her eyes, smearing the dark liner that rimmed them. "I would ask what the king sees in you—" She left off.

Aela stood silently, taking in every aspect of the girl before her. Every inch of pale skin was familiar. She could almost feel the soft touch beneath her fingers. Her chest begged her feet to close the space between them, to press her body against Brynne's, to hold her inside her arms and cling on for dear life. Somehow, with the day's revelations, it didn't feel the right thing to do. She settled for reaching up to place a hand on Brynne's shoulders, a static shock running through her body as her fingers found that old familiar resting place. Brynne looked over at the hand that lay on her shoulder, her lip beginning to curl with distaste.

"I should hate you," she said, spitting the words at Aela like they left a poor taste on her tongue. Stepping forward, Brynne reached out and pushed her away. Aela let her body fall back and stumbled to a stop a few steps from the pool. It felt good to let herself be pushed, to not fight back. She was so tired of fighting back. She sighed as Brynne strode forward, arms up to give her one more solid push. This time Aela reached out to encircle her assailant's wrist, pulling her along as she fell back into the chilling waters of the pool with the slap of their combined weight on the water.

AELA BROKE THE surface as Brynne wrested her wrist free of Aela's grasp and struggled to find her way above. Aela took a deep breath, plunged her head beneath, and slung her arms around Brynne's satin-swathed waist to pull her upwards. Brynne thrust her head up and broke the surface tension. Aela followed a second later. The ghost of a smile crossed her lips to see the state of Brynne. Her neatly coiled hair had escaped its prison, damp cascades falling across her bare shoulders. Brynne's teeth began to chatter as the initial shock of falling wore off and the cold reality of the water hit her. Aela pulled her close, gripped Brynne tightly, and swam to the edge of the pool. With one arm around Brynne's waist and one gripping the iron ring just beyond the lip of the cenote, she willed her Sarkany warmth to rise to the surface and move between them. As the water around them began to take on heat, Brynne shook her head, loose hair tangled against the flesh of her neck and gazed deep into Aela's eyes.

"I should hate you," she said again. This time her voice was weak and tired. Aela moved in close, pressed her cheek against Brynne's, and let the heat penetrate her chilled skin. Close to her ear, Brynne whispered, "Why don't I hate you?"

A shiver ran through Aela's body despite the spreading warmth. She pulled her head away and stared at Brynne for a moment, their eyes locked in dark understanding before Brynne lunged forward to lock her lips against Aela's, rough and rasping. The length of their bodies pressed against one another beneath the water as Brynne moved her mouth against Aela's, close and desperate. Aela's mind cleared blissfully as they kissed, every awful moment of the day forgotten, sinking beneath them to the bottom of the pool. She let go of the iron ring and trusted the buoyancy of their bodies as she plunged her hand below the water, running it down the curves of Brynne's body in its soaked satin dress. The jolt of teeth against her lower lip brought her focus back above the surface and she pulled her lips away from Brynne's. Not wasting any time, she moved along Brynne's chin, pressing light kisses every inch until she reached her neck. Baring her teeth, she delved into the soft peach skin, letting the play of her tongue and lips create warm suction as Brynne flattened her hands against Aela's back, pulling her closer. A soft moan fell from Brynne's lips into her ear, and her chest swelled at this favoured sound. Not content to let that be the last one, she moved her hand down from Brynne's waist and fought through the layered skirts that drifted like seaweed until she managed to find her way beneath them. Slipping her hand into sodden undergarments, Aela pulsed and probed, grinning as she was rewarded with a pleasured gasp. She moved her mouth back up to find Brynne's and savoured each soft brush between their lips, the heat of her body radiating out into the pool.

LATER, WHEN THEY climbed, sopping, from the pool onto the still warm stones, Aela burrowed her way beneath those voluminous and dripping skirts. As she spread more warmth and pleasure through Brynne, the sounds she received as restitution brought her all the way back to the smell of warm hay on a summer afternoon. She disentangled herself and couldn't wipe the smile from her face as she crawled up her lover's body, letting Brynne's deft hands unlace her leather tunic. Finally free from all the fabric that separated them, Aela exhaled into Brynne's hair as their skin moved beautifully in sync. This had always been her favourite place. Letting Brynne move her hands across her arched back, she knew that this was the closest to home she had ever felt.

Chapter Twelve

CURLING THE BLANKETS around her more tightly, Brynne burrowed her face into the pillow, letting Aela's smell surround her with rapture and nostalgia. She reached out to wrap an arm around her bedmate and her heart instinctively dropped like a stone when she found nothing but an empty space beside her. She opened her eyes and took in the shape of Aela's room, just beginning to pull in the morning sunlight.

She was alone. Again and always. There was no sign of Aela, her pack, or the speargun. The very thought of the weapon sent a ripple of pain through Brynne's chest, followed by a flood of guilt. Hadn't she begun to suspect weeks ago that it was no random corsair who had sent that spear into her father's back? And now, upon confirming her worst fears, the first thing she had done was give herself to Aela, unable to ignore the unstoppable charge between them. Brynne bit her lip and found it tender and sore from the previous night's reunion. It was impossible to know how to feel. Every conceivable emotion flooded into her mind at once: sorrow, guilt, betrayal, pleasure, joy...love? Brynne choked back that horrific notion. How could she possibly love the woman who had killed her father? Even if it was a setup, even if Aela didn't know the man's identity when she shot him, how could Brynne let the hands that pulled that trigger touch her the way they had last night? It was too much, far too much to deal with. And Aela was gone, just like every morning-after, and as always, Brynne wasn't sure that she'd ever return.

Just as she was trying to pick through the wreckage of her emotions, there was a knock at the chamber door.

"Aela!" A thick, masculine voice shouted from just outside. Pulling the blankets closer around her body, Brynne didn't make a sound. Desperately, she hoped that if she kept quiet, they'd move on and search elsewhere. The compromising nature of her situation hit her very suddenly. Being caught naked in the bed of someone who was decidedly not the prince would be very bad indeed. It would certainly give the court something new to talk about instead of how she had snuck her way into the royal family in the first place. Brynne held her breath and listened for retreating footsteps. Instead, another louder knock jarred her senses.

"Aela Crane! In the name of the king, open the door or we're breaking it down." Barely a moment passed before Brynne heard a heavy weight hit the door with the telltale crack of splintering wood. Thinking quickly, she rolled off the bed and hit the floor, wedged into the slim space between the wooden frame and the wall. The bed was too low to hide beneath, but through the dusty slit, she could see the door come down with a thundering crash as three pairs of military boots followed it into the small chamber. Biting her lip, she held her breath to hear their words.

"No sign of her," said the voice. Brynne recognized its husky timbre and the lilt of the one that followed.

"There seems to be an opening behind this bookcase. She must have taken off in the night," Gerard said. If it were just him and Sam, Brynne might have revealed herself. They had always been kind to her, and it wouldn't have been so awful to be caught there by them, but there was no mistaking the voice that responded next. She would recognize that cold, calculating tone anywhere.

"I don't think she's gone far. She cares far too much for the boy to leave for good." As the king spoke, a chill crept down Brynne's spine.

"That's not what it seemed like to me," Sam answered warily. Brynne focused on keeping her breath calm and still, despite the heavy dust that lay on the stone floor just beside her nose. Closing her eyes, she waited.

"Let's see where this passage leads. Remember, if you find her, she's not to be harmed. I need her alive." Three pairs of boots moved towards the bookcase as Brynne opened her eyes with relief, only to find herself eyelash to whisker with a particularly grizzled rat. She let out a squeak of surprise before she could stop herself. The sound seemed to hang in the air for an eternity as the feet on the other side of the bed paused.

"Did you hear that?" Gerard asked, his footfalls growing closer as he rounded the edge of the bed. As he came into view, Brynne could feel the flush of shame swell her cheeks. She stared up at him, hope rising in her heart that he might not give her away, but it shriveled and died at the hard arch of his brow and the deepening disgust in his expression.

BRYNNE CONSIDERED HERSELF lucky that the king had even allowed her to dress before they hauled her away. Because her silk gown was a ruined, sodden lump at the foot of the bed, she pulled on a pair of Aela's leather trousers and a loose tunic. The pants were a tight fight, as Aela cut a much slighter figure than Brynne, whose curves seemed to resent the unforgiving leather. She had pulled them on as a rosy blush spread over her entire body. Only the king turned away, his gaze sweeping across Aela's humble living quarters.

She had seen the king cross, and she had seen him frustrated and dismissive towards Del, but she had never seen him as livid as he was upon discovering her in this compromising position. When he turned back around, his face was almost purple, his grey eyes tight with rage. He gave a curt order to Sam and Gerard, and they immediately moved to flank her. They dug their fingers tightly into her upper arms as they forced her down onto her knees. The king strode forward, raised one delicately gloved hand across his body, and brought it down swiftly upon Brynne's cheek with a strong backhand. As the sting of her cheekbone grew sharp like the lump in her throat, the king's mouth curved into a gruesome smile.

"I should have known," he said, shaking his head as if to chastise himself. "Just like her father, never satisfied with what I so generously gave. No, they just have to take and take and take. And you, ripe and willing to be exploited." He exhaled a drawn-out sigh. "I can't help but blame my son as well. I should have known he wouldn't be able to keep a girl like you satisfied. What's that old saying about Marinaken whores?"

Brynne felt shock as the king spoke. The disgust he felt for her was written on his face.

"I'm asking you a question, dear." The king stared Brynne down. She hung her head, limp hair falling against her temple as she stared at his impeccably shined boots.

"Any port in a storm," Brynne muttered, remembering hearing the phrase bandied about her mother's market stall by sailors and corsairs alike as they searched for a warm place to spend a night. At the sound of his tongue clicking, she raised her head just in time to catch a hot wad of spit on her cheek, right where his hand had connected.

He gestured to the guards and turned. The dam broke, and hot tears began to flow soft and silent down her stinging cheek as Brynne was lifted bodily. Sam and Gerard wrenched her forward, then marched her between them, following the king past the bookcase and into the hidden passage.

THEY WALKED FAST, following the king as he stalked through the halls and paused occasionally to inspect any sign that Aela had been past. Finally, after an endless march, he stopped before a rough expanse of wall. Brynne wasn't sure where they were, but they seemed to be descending, even though the air grew warmer with each step.

A few steps ahead, the king peered closely at the rock, his torch lending a flickering glow. He handed the light off to Sam and carefully peeled the glove from his hand. He stroked one slender finger down the wall and then pulled it away to inspect some dark residue as he rubbed it between his index finger and thumb. The king lifted it to his nose and smelled the substance briefly before holding his index finger up to the light. In the dim glow, Brynne could see it had a deep red hue. Her heart sank into her stomach. Had Aela gone this way? Was that her blood?

With a raise of his brow, the king turned to Gerard and Sam, something like fear hiding just behind his regal exterior.

"Take the girl up to the holding pens and see that she stays there until I can deal with her. I have something I must attend to." With that, he turned on his heel and strode quickly away down the dark passage.

EVEN WITH THE large amount of wandering she had managed to do between her lessons, Brynne didn't recognize any of the passageways her silent guards pushed her along on their way back up towards the city. Each one was strange and novel, and none of the carvings seemed familiar to her. The king mentioned holding pens, but she had never heard of anything like that, let alone what they might be holding.

Finally they reached their destination. Gerard pulled out a keyring, released her left arm, and stepped forward to unlock a large ornate door. He swung it open, reached back, and grasped her again before shoving her forward into the dark room. She skidded to her knees.

"Wait!" she called. These men had been friendly to her once. Maybe they could be again. She turned back and moved towards the door, reaching out to Sam.

"Please don't...."

He frowned, shaking his head as she held a hand out towards him. "Stick to the edges. That's the only advice you'll get from me." He stepped out of her reach and closed the door behind him, cutting her off from the torchlight. There was a scraping sound as the key turned, locking her in.

Alone. Again and always.

She turned to sit with her back to the door. As she squinted into the dark room, trying to get her bearings, the drying tears made her cheeks feel tighter than Aela's pants around her thighs. She ran her hands up the smooth leather, remembering how they'd peeled down Aela's damp thighs the night before. Raising her hand up to touch her throat, she remembered the heat of Aela's breath on her skin. Now, Aela was gone, and here she was, waiting for whatever punishment lay in wait for adulterous princesses. Drawing in a shuddering breath, Brynne's shame turned quickly to fear as a burst of light flickered several feet away in the darkness. Holding her breath, she listened. Something moved across the floor towards her, bearing the unmistakable sound of metal scraping on stone. A rank smell reached her nostrils, drawing up bile in the back of her already raw throat.

Another burst of light proved to be the telltale flicker of fire, this time bright enough to illuminate the room for a brief second and leave Brynne frozen in terror. Just a few feet away lay a rising pile of burnished copper scales and razor sharp claws, the dying light issued in jets from twin nostrils set beneath a pair of reptilian eyes.

Brynne scrambled back against the door and drew her body upwards to stand on perilously shaking legs. On either side of her, she reached out to feel low stone walls. She moved to the left and climbed over one and then felt around to find herself in an empty enclosure. The low wall seemed to continue along down the room. She crouched down behind it and peered over towards the beast in the centre of the room.

Another jet of flame burst from its nostrils, reflecting light on the metal collar that bound it to the wall by a short length of chain. It sniffed at the air, moving towards her. Brynne ducked down, turned away, and pulled her knees up to her chest. Would Del wonder where she was? Had someone already told him she was unfaithful? And would he even blame her, considering how he had turned her away? He certainly didn't seem interested in her, not the way that Aela was, anyway. She cursed Aela's name but found the words fell flat coming from lips that had so recently said similar with a much different tone.

From behind her, she heard a low keening noise, almost a whine. Brynne brought her forehead down to her knees, grinding her teeth in the darkness. She couldn't help but wonder if this was the person she had been before she came to the capital. Would that girl have stayed locked in the dark, pathetically holding her breath for whatever fate awaited? Would she accept punishment for something that had felt so right? Brynne wiped the grime and tears from her face and stood, a little more resolute. With one hand trailing the stonework and her eyes locked on the naga's resting place, she made her way around the edge of the room, searching for another exit. She had just climbed over the other side of the low pen wall when the first of the tremors hit.

SUDDENLY, THE STONE itself seemed to shudder beneath her hands and feet. A great loud rumbling sounded from somewhere deep beneath her, shaking the masonry as Brynne struggled to stay upright. Just as one subsided, another hit, and another, each successive wave building in strength and power until she could no longer keep her balance. The ground jittered beneath her feet, sending her sprawling away from the wall. The naga gave off a panicked blast of flame, revealing its coiled form only a few feet away from her. Its eyes flashed with fear.

Brynne scrabbled away and found a new handhold to grip as the shaking calmed again. Keeping low, she waited a moment and then another to see if it would begin again. When the world stayed still, she rose on shaking knees, her stomach roiling with something like seasickness.

No sooner had she regained her balance than the entire chamber seemed to blast apart with a thunderous crack. Chunks of stone crumbled and fell from the walls and ceiling, cascading down over the floor. Suddenly, the floor pitched beneath her, and Brynne found herself lying face-up, staring at the ceiling with the wind knocked from her lungs. A strange light poured across the chamber where it jutted in from above. The rift had released a choking storm of dust that hung in the air above as Brynne dizzily realized it was daylight slanting down from the caved-in roof. She wasn't sure how long she lay there, her mind slow and sluggish. At some point, she became aware of how sore her limbs were, and the dull ache in her back from the hard stones beneath it. Pushing chunks of debris from her body, she rose to see that she'd gotten off lucky. Mere feet from where she fell, the central column of the room had come crashing down, creating a crater in the wall where it landed. Now bathed in the light of day from the broken ceiling, she could see the extent of the damage. Chunks of rock lay in piles across the chamber. In the corner, something stirred.

Brynne held her breath as the naga unfurled itself. Its chain hung loose, scraping against the floor as it moved towards her. The beast was free, she realized with a start. She gave a quick glance around and her chest began to ache, partly from the deluge of rock and partly because she could see that there was nowhere to run. Standing stock still, she sucked in a shaking breath as the naga reached her. It was longer than she was tall, and came up roughly to her navel. Up close she could see the long teeth that lived between its jaws, razor sharp and flesh-ready. She sucked back a whimper and stood her ground. Calmly, it pressed its nose up against her thigh, eliciting a soft snuffling sound as it took in her scent. It turned its head and nudged its cheek against the softness of her stomach, causing it to lurch in fear.

"Please, just make it quick," she said, surprised to hear her own voice as she looked down at the beast. As it peered up at her, she felt a strange familiarity. She was no stranger to eyes like that. How many times had her heart warmed as she gazed into them?

As soon as the thought hit her, she felt the warmth of the naga's head leave her side. Its tail brushed against her shins as it turned away. With an agile leap, it jumped up onto the fallen column and continued up to slither through the crack in the roof. Cautiously, Brynne followed the creature. Her hands shook as she climbed on the great stone pillar, keeping her body low as she made her way up its length to emerge on a rocky outcropping just above the alpine meadow.

Or at least, where the meadow used to be. Instead of a wide expanse of soft grass and dew, there was nothing but a smoking hole. An endless chasm was all that remained of the former riding grounds, yawning up at Brynne. She crouched down and grasped dizzily for a handhold. As she peered over the edge of the rocking outcropping, it seemed to her as if the world had fallen away before her feet, leaving an absence in its wake. Behind her, she heard a strange noise and turned to see the young naga standing at the edge of the mountain. Stretching its leathery wings, it released an echoing cry and lurched forward, swept away on the breeze. She stood, staring at the chain swinging from its neck, each metal link shining in the sunlight.

WHEN THE BEAST was nothing more than a dark speck against the sky, Brynne broke her attention away from the sight. She searched for an escape route and spotted another rift in the rock just ahead. As she crawled across to it, she was all too aware of the steep drop-off on all sides. After taking a moment to peer down into the dark chamber beneath, she gathered her bearings and swung her legs over the edge, using every ounce of bravery to push the rest of her body over and down into the dark.

She landed with a jarring thud, her legs nearly giving out beneath her as her teeth smacked together on impact. Peering around through filtered half-light, she allowed herself a small smile. She had come down in the hallway just on the other side of the locked door that led to the naga's pen. She turned on her heel and stalked in the opposite direction, trying to retrace their steps back to Aela's chamber.

Unfortunately, the labyrinthine passages she inched her way along in the dark were just as unfamiliar the second time around, especially with no light to guide her. Even worse, numerous stairwells and hallways seemed to have been blocked by rock and stone, probably knocked loose by the same tremors that had destroyed her holding cell., She continued on with shaky legs, taking any passage that she could squeeze her way through. Every now and then, she came to a passage that simply ended, the floor ahead giving way to the same endless pit that she had seen from above. She tried not to look down, instead focusing above at the circle of light that hung overhead like the surface of a pool.

Retracing her steps, it seemed to Brynne that she was picking her way around the chasm, back to the castle proper. Eventually, she reached familiar passageways, lit by lamps at regular intervals that lent their yellow light to familiar tableaus carved into the walls. Her thighs ached from the effort and her throat was sore and parched, but she pushed herself onwards until she found a familiar stairwell and began to climb, despite her exhausted body.

BRYNNE KNEW IT might not be safe to make a detour up to her chambers at the top of the city, but there were a few things that she wasn't willing to leave behind. She expected destruction and disarray, but what she didn't expect to find was Charmaine, standing in front of her door, more than a hint of frustration hiding in her perfectly practiced smile.

"What are you doing here?" Brynne asked, glancing quickly around for signs of damage as she entered her chamber.

"What are you wearing?" Charmaine asked in response as she followed behind, looking Brynne up and down with a disapproving expression. Brynne turned, suddenly aware of the tight leather hugging her skin. These were not her clothes. Shaking her head, she brushed aside the question and went to the old wooden chest that sat in the corner of her room. She opened the lid and reached inside and then glared back at Charmaine, standing in the doorway with her arms crossed.

"Again I ask, what are you doing here?"

Charmaine's expression hardened for a moment before she could blink her decorum back into place. "We were supposed to meet this morning for your first dance lesson. You still have to make it through the wedding, remember? If you think I'm going to let you shuffle-step your way through the royal waltz—"

Brynne let Charmaine's tirade wash over her. She was the picture of elegance. Her dress was smooth and wrinkle-free. Her hair stood piled atop her head, not a single strand out of place. Except for the bitterness on her tongue, Charmaine was everything that Brynne had tried her very best to become.

"Fuck. I'm sorry. I completely forgot," Brynne said, thinking that dance lessons would have been a kind alternative to what she actually spent her morning doing. "Wait—" She paused. "You were waiting here for me, and then when the entire city started falling apart, you just...stayed put?"

When Charmaine didn't reply, Brynne turned back to the old wooden chest. She reached inside to grab a string of black pearls, feeling her chest swell as she held them coiled in her palm.

"I didn't know what to do," Charmaine said from behind her.

Brynne turned to face her tutor and raised her eyebrows in surprise.

Charmaine drew in a slow breath and continued, her haughty facade beginning to slide away. "I was scared."

Never show weakness. That was the first lesson that Charmaine had taught her. Not in so many words of course, but it was in the way she held herself, the way she was always perfectly composed, no matter the situation. Now, for the first time, Brynne could see the girl underneath the courtly training showing through. Stray curls of hair had fallen down on either side of her face to frame her dark brown eyes, which shone in the sunlight that came in through the window. She no longer stood with her hands on her hips. Her arms were wrapped around her now, sending wrinkles rippling across her perfectly pressed dress.

"It's going to be okay. Come on. Let's go see if we can find someone who knows what we're supposed to do." She stepped towards Charmaine and held out her hand, but hesitation sparked in the other girl's expression. Extending one soft, perfectly manicured hand towards Brynne's own, dirt-smeared and scraped as they were, she managed a small smile.

"I think we've got to clean you up before we go anywhere. You're supposed to be a princess, and you look like shit." Charmaine smiled slightly as she stepped towards Brynne, dragged a thumb across her cheek, and held it up to show a thick layer of dirt, grime, and smudged eyeliner. Brynne couldn't help but grin back self-consciously as Charmaine set to work, wiping her face clean and running a comb through her lank tangles.

A FEW MINUTES later, Brynne and Charmaine made their way down to the open court. They took the stairs, not trusting the integrity of the lift. A bit more comfortable, Brynne made her way quickly down the steps in a simple tunic and a pair of roughspun linen pants left over from her days in Marinaken. Charmaine had tried to coax her into another gown, but Brynne wanted to be able to move freely in case the tremors started up again. Everything had been calm and quiet since she climbed out of the holding chamber, but her nerves were still shuddering under her skin.

They could hear the voices rising as they descended the last few floors, but stepping out into the open court was like nothing Brynne had ever seen. The entire space was filled with panicking citizens, moving from one group to another as they shared concerns and speculation on what had caused the ground to give way. At the far edge of the court, one of the pillars holding up the great carved ceiling was cracked through and listing dangerously.

She turned away to gaze up to the royal balcony, which overlooked the teeming masses, her breath hitching as she saw a familiar figure standing hunched over the railing. Brynne grabbed Charmaine's wrist and pulled her along as she made her way through the press to the side chamber and up the stairs. Brynne breathed a sigh of relief as she reached the topmost step. There were no royal guards standing back in the shadows, just Del, alone at the edge of the overlook.

She motioned for Charmaine to stay back by the two massive thrones that stood vigil against the back wall and walked forward to stand beside the prince, resting her forearms on the railing as she had the night they first met.

"Are you all right?" she asked. She got her answer before he even said a word.

Del turned to her, his eyes a dark maelstrom. Just below the curve of his chin, an aura of bruises stood out across the front of his neck, colours running from just slightly darker than his clingstone skin and all the way to a deepening purple. She drew in a sharp breath before reaching out to place a hand over his.

He raised his eyebrows as he stared back at her, as if taking her in for the first time. He reached out and ran his fingers over the skin of her own neck.

"Who?" he asked. Brynne realized with a rush of embarrassment that the bruised marks left by Aela's skilled mouth must be standing out in stark relief on her own pale flesh.

Bowing her head, she drew her hand away from his as she replied. "Aela." She refused to acknowledge the blush of shame that spread across her cheeks. The surprise on Del's face was almost more than she could take.

Quickly, she changed the subject. "What happened to you?"

There was a wince at her question. He appeared as if he had been full-on throttled. "Aela." His answer came through gritted teeth. His voice was so weak she could barely hear it, just above a whisper and rough as sand.

Brynne couldn't stop the gasp before it escaped from her lips. "It looks like she tried to kill you!" Brynne pointed to the bruises that spread across his throat. She knew better than anyone that Aela had issues with control, but she could never imagine her hurting someone she cared about so much. Not physically, at least.

"Not her," Del rasped. "Well, yes her, but she wasn't—right. Not herself. Where is she?" He glanced around as if expecting her to materialize from the shadows.

Brynne shook her head sadly. "She's gone. Left during the night. Took her stuff with her." Brynne gazing down at the railing as she replied. She knew she had some explaining to do, especially with the way she and the prince had left things before. She had practically launched herself at him and he had turned her away. Tears of guilt and embarrassment brimmed in her eyes as she looked back up at him. "I lied," she said, turning away, "when I said we hadn't met before. We've been familiar for a long time. Since before I came here."

"How familiar?" he asked, curiosity cutting through his painfully strained voice.

Brynne bit her lip, unsure of what to say. "Carnally," was all she said. The story was too long to tell at a time like this. She couldn't quite bring herself to look back at him. "Are you mad?" Brynne felt a bit like a child, lost and sorry, but not quite sure why. He was quiet for a moment, and then Brynne felt the warm weight of his hand on hers. "I told you, I don't belong here," she whispered, glancing back to see a small enigmatic smile resting on his lips.

"I disagree," he replied with a slight wheeze. "Love whomever you want, hold whomever you want. We're still partners."

"How can you—" As she spoke, that familiar rumble grew beneath her feet as the ground began to shake, breaking the words off as they rose in her throat. From somewhere overhead, there was a strange sharp sound, like a keening scream, but unlike anything she had heard before. It didn't sound as if it had come from a person. Over the balcony, the buzz of conversation on the court floor rose into a chaotic clamour as fault lines spiderwebbed their way along the smooth marble, cracking beneath the feet of those who stood on it.

"It's happening again," she said, glancing over at Del. "Do you know what's causing this?"

He shook his head, looking around as a fine dusting of stone rained down over their head. He stepped swiftly away from the balcony and led her back towards the stairs, motioning for Charmaine to follow as the shaking stilled.

"Have you seen any guards?" he croaked.

"No," Brynne lied. He didn't need to know how she had spent her morning. Not right then. As they reached the top of the stairwell, two very unwelcome faces materialized out of the dark, climbing up to meet them.

Brynne could feel hostility from Sam and Gerard as they reached the top of the stairs and fanned out to either side to make way. Behind them, Graella, Alphonse, and Doyle came up into view, relief breaking out on the latter two at the sight of Del.

"There's m'boy!" Alphonse cried, pulling Del into a bone-crushing hug as Doyle patted him tentatively on the back. All three of the councillors looked a little worse for wear, clothing ripped and covered in chipped and dusted stone. Alphonse had a shallow scrape running across his left cheek, and Doyle's knuckles were bruised and battered. Of the three of them, Graella was the most put together. Her delicate dress had sustained some damage, but her immaculately painted face was perfect, except for the permanent scowl that graced it.

"Have you seen my father?" Del asked, his voice strained and sore as Alphonse released him. Brynne saw Gerard and Sam share a pointed look behind the backs of the Arch Council members, probably thinking about his last known whereabouts deep below the city. Alphonse shook his head.

"No. We've been trying to locate both him and the queen in order to evacuate them from the city." A fresh rumble echoed through the small semi-closed chamber.

"What about the citizens?" Brynne asked, hearing the panicked shouts from the court below. Graella snapped her head up, teeth bared in a grimace.

"Our only concern is protecting the royal family. The people of this city will have to make their own way to safety." Graella's gaze moving across Brynne's body, narrowed at the princess's unseemly country rags.

"Come on. We've got to go," Doyle said, reaching out a hand to help Del down the stairs. Arms crossed, Del stood his ground, shaking his head vigorously.

"No," he shouted in breathy tones just as his voice deserted him entirely. His mouth moved, but the only sound he could seem to release was cold mountain air scraping against his vocal cords. Gesturing frantically back at the crowd gathered in the open court, he caught Brynne's eyes, his own flashing desperately with concern. She understood, agreeing wholeheartedly.

She rounded on Graella and moved her body between Del and the councillors. Placing her hands on her hips, she adopted the haughtiest Charmaine-inspired tone she could muster.

"Forgive me if I'm wrong, councillors, but the king is missing. Now I seem to remember that if an urgent situation should arise, the mantle of command falls to the heir, in this case our own Prince Reza." Graella was taken aback, and Doyle seemed in shock, but Brynne desperately hoped she wasn't imagining the proud smirk that seemed to be gracing Alphonse's lips.

"And as the prince seems to be unable to give orders at the moment and he has no heir to speak of, I believe, if I recall my extensive studies in political custom, that means that chain of command falls to myself, his wife. Wife-to-be, in our case." Behind Graella, Charmaine stood, shaking her head vigourously as if to warn Brynne off her tirade. Brynne steeled herself, knowing she had come too far to stop now.

"So, now that we've established that, here's my command. We will evacuate every single person in this city. The prince and I will not be going anywhere until we do." Beside her, Del stepped forward, nodding vigourously as he crossed his arms. She glanced to the side and caught his eyes, something like pride swelling in her chest.

Before her, Graella sputtered.

"Surely we're not taking orders from this dockside slattern?" As she glanced from Alphonse to Del to the guards, Charmaine burst forward to stand beside Del and Brynne.

"Dockside slattern? Mother, that's your princess you're talking about. Have some decorum." Brynne found herself suddenly coming to appreciate Charmaine's penchant for a withering glare, especially when it wasn't directed at her.

"Miss Halloran is right. With the king missing in action and Prince Reza in this state, she's our de facto monarch. I'm not about to waste time bickering over archaic law. We've got to move fast if we want to get everyone to safety." Alphonse stepped forward to put an end to the argument, Doyle at his side.

"We'll have to get everyone down to the under roads—" he began.

"And pray that the entire city doesn't come down on us before we make it out," Alphonse finished. "So let's move."

He turned and headed down the stairs, Doyle and the guards hot on his heels and followed begrudgingly by Graella. As Charmaine headed down behind them, Del's hand grasped hers. He pulled her into a hug.

"Thank you," he whispered. "Partner."

Brynne smiled, a lump rising in her throat as she returned his embrace.

WITH THE HELP of the blacksmith's booming voice, it didn't take long to begin the exodus. People moved towards the numerous stairwells in groups, with palpable relief that some kind of order had been restored. Sam and Gerard fanned out into the city with a group of guards, searching for any stragglers. They remained passively hostile towards Brynne, but they didn't seem inclined to share the events of that morning either. The memory rising hot on her cheeks, she couldn't help but reach up to brush the string of black pearls resting against her collarbone.

"I think that's everyone," Del said, looking around at the cracked floor in the centre of the open court where they stood. The councillors waited for them by the stairwell as the last few citizens disappeared down into the dark.

Brynne opened her mouth to speak just as something heavy slammed down on the roof above them. That strange scream rang out again, closer this time, as the listing column at the end of the row broke free and came crashing down on its neighbour, threatening to domino the entire line. Above them, the roof still held, but it seemed only a matter of time. Out of the corner of her eye, something dark hung down off the edge of the roof, swinging back and forth through the air. The swell of success in her stomach quickly turned to hot, briny fear. She turned to Charmaine.

"Go," she said, pointing towards the stairwell where the councillors waited. Charmaine hesitated, glancing around nervously.

"What about you?" she asked, unwilling to move an inch.

Brynne gripped her shoulder reassuringly. "We'll be right behind you."

Charmaine stood still for another moment before turning and walking quickly away towards the backs of the retreating stragglers. With Del at her side, Brynne focused on the familiar shape hanging over the edge of the roof. A long, sleek tail ending in a viciously barbed tip cut through the air, its cool, green scales sparkling in the sunlight.

"I think it's safe to say what's causing this," Brynne said to Del, as she pointed towards the naga tail. He swallowed painfully and squeezed her hand. The stone above them groaned with the pressure as the massive beast launched itself off the roof and cut through the air just beyond the balcony.

Brynne gasped as the beast wheeled across the sky into her view. It was massive. Far bigger than the naga she had been trapped with earlier. Bigger, in fact, than any creature Brynne had ever seen. It was truly a monster. Jet black scales gleamed over every inch of its body, except for the smooth leathery wings that stretched out on either side as it flew away from them, growing smaller by the second.

It wheeled around towards the court and rushed in their direction as Brynne and Del stood frozen in fear. It grew in perspective, flickering red eyes glowing like bonfires above brutally sharp teeth, each one easily as long as the sword that hung at Del's side. Steel rasped beside her as he drew it, though she couldn't tear her attention away from the beast speeding towards them. There was something hanging from those gleaming fangs. From a middle distance, it seemed like nothing more than a limp doll, but as each inch closed between them, its form grew larger and more familiar.

Brynne and Del braced for impact just as the naga hit the edge of the open court, smashing into the structure with all its weight. Every pillar groaned around them as the beast reeled back, its long foreclaws grasping around the balustrade as it deposited its prize on the edge of the balcony and took off again. It sailed straight up into the summer sky before turning back yet again to wage private war on the myriad stone turrets and towers above them.

Del raced forward before Brynne could think to hold him back. She followed close behind as he threw the sword to the ground and skidded to his knees in front of the body sprawled across the floor. She reached him just as he thrust one arm out to take a pulse, two fingers pressed against a limp throat. He glanced sidelong at her, shook his head, and pulled his hand back, recoiling. Rivulets of blood ran down across the golden skin and an immaculate military uniform, still seeping hot from the deep puncture wounds dealt by the naga's teeth. Del reached over the lifeless form and closed its eyelids, hiding those grey eyes for the very last time.

King Reza Ansari III lay before her, dead.

King Reza Ansari IV kneeled beside her, hunched over his father's body, his expression torn between resignation and relief.

Chapter Thirteen

THE SHARP SALT air hit Aela like a homecoming as she jumped from the wagon and planted her feet firmly in the Marinaken mud. If there was one thing Aela Crane was good at, it was running away.

Or rolling away in this case. As luck would have it, there was still one wagon driver awake by the time she made it down to the carriage house in the dead of night. It only took the mention of her official title to get him to agree to a nighttime trip to the coast and a small bribe to keep it off the books. By the time they eased into the port city, dawn was breaking pink and gold over the water.

Aela flipped another coin towards the shabbily dressed carriage driver and stomped off into town, stepping from mud onto ancient cobbles as she made her way towards the docks. There was only one thing on her mind, and that was finding a ship to take her far away from this stupid rock. The warmth of Brynne's touch was still an echo on her skin, but every time the memory crept back into her mind, she pushed it away. There were only so many times she could tread over the same painful self-flagellations. Yes, she had killed her lover's father. Yes, she had tried to choke the breath from her closest friend. Yes, both Brynne and Del were far better off without her.

And worst of all, the thought of the raging inferno dwelling beneath the both of them—it didn't bear thinking about. She was leaving so that they would never have to find out.

Aela's old instincts kicked in and she found her feet taking her through a well-worn shortcut as she turned into Marinaken's souk. Styled after the traditional covered markets of Old Ansar, the open-air marketplace seemed a jumble of stands and kiosks, all covered from the elements with colourful sheets of fabric or panes of hand-blown glass. Tradesmen of every kind could be found in the massive complex, from metalworkers with their finely curved copper to those selling produce fresh from the green belt. Even merchants from over the sea came to set up shop, bringing special delicacies from the Southern Isles or even farther away.

Aela's boots picked out an old familiar route through the deserted rows as early-rising merchants arrived and set up their stalls. Suddenly her heart lurched in her chest as she found herself before a shabbily appointed stall. It stood empty, wooden baskets barren as they waited to be filled with that day's orchard pickings. The scent of ripe peaches lingered in the air as a memory rose unbidden in her mind.

SHE WAS A *young corsair, still finding her swagger. Back then, her arms were not the only part of her with fewer scars. She crept through the crowds, keeping her head low. The scent of earth and fruit swelled as she drew closer to the stand. She reached her destination, popped up into view, and shouted loudly, causing the girl behind the counter to jump a clear foot into the air. Her short orange hair was a frizzy halo surrounding dirt-smudged cheeks and clear blue eyes. As the shock subsided, she took in the sight of Aela, her expression changing from fright to shy excitement.*

"You've been gone months! I sure hope you didn't come back empty-handed."

A sly smile slid across Brynne's face. Aela reached into her pocket and wrapped her fingers around her latest prize, taken from the hold of a southern pleasure-craft. She held it up in front of Brynne's eyes and relished the swell of her chest as Brynne assessed the gift. It was a string of jet-black pearls, each one as smooth and perfect as she was.

AELA CHOKED BACK the painful heat rising in her throat and turned on her heel, pointing herself towards the docks. Refusing to allow herself a backwards glance, she made her way quickly towards the calm familiar freedom of the sea.

The square next to the docks was the same as the last time she saw it, when her nose had been pressed to the cobbles by a troupe of Ansari soldiers. She noticed that someone had seen fit to clean the red sweep of Timlet's blood from the stones. The grim memory resurfaced as her feet passed over the place where he had tried to play the hero. He had never responded to her letter, but with any luck, he had learned from his mistakes. She hoped he was settled down somewhere with a slightly less dangerous profession. One that suited him better.

Stepping lightly onto the salt-crusted planks of the finger docks, Aela breathed in the brine, having missed the sensation of wind-burnt lungs. She crept down the length of the jetty and looked at the vessels docked on either side, trying to determine who might be most willing to take on a mate of her disreputable skill.

She slid by a couple of inland traders loading up with necessities bound for the river valleys in the north, and as she passed the next empty slip, she noticed the wake rippling out across the water. Ahead, a tall ship drifted lazily towards the mouth of the harbour, aiming for the gap between two long tongues of land that kept the mooring waters calm. The sight of that brigantine sailing away, its familiar flag flapping in the breeze, conjured more emotion than Aela knew what to do with. Nostalgia pressed against joy against rage as she instinctively broke into a run, her boots smacking against the dock, each stride bringing her closer to the end of its reach. She whipped her speargun from its holster on her back and hefted it in her arms, then pulled the trigger as she leapt from the edge of the dock, trusting the truth of her aim. Her body soared over the sunlit waves as she heard the familiar thunk of her spear hitting wood. She shifted her weight to the now-taut line reaching between her weapon and the ship's mast, and swung towards the vessel, her toes nearly skimming the ripples. Beneath her, the faint silhouettes of jellyfish swam just below the surface of the water, the sight falling away as she swung swiftly up along the arc of the line. She rose over the deck of the ship to land with a shuddering smack on its oddly pristine deck.

At least she landed on her feet, she thought, wincing at the jarring pain that radiated from her knee joints. She straightend up and took the lay of the land. Several faces stared back at her in surprise. Not all of them were familiar, but they all belonged to corsairs of ruthless measure, each one reaching towards their weapon. She pressed the powerful retraction mechanism on her gun's shaft and stood her ground as the spear dislodged from the mast, sped back towards her, and returned to its home in the barrel with a satisfying click. Sinking into a ready stance, she silently reminded herself to thank Alphonse for the added oomph before it suddenly struck her that if things went as planned, she'd never see him again.

"Dreadmoor!" she shouted aloud, as if her furious tone alone could call him forth to face her. "Get out here before you've no one left to sail your ship."

The corsairs stared her down, stone-faced and ready to shift into action. She knew immediately that this was by far one of the stupidest things she'd ever done. She was so far outnumbered that it would be a miracle if she made it out alive, but there wasn't a single part of her that cared. The only thing that mattered, that reverberated through her veins and echoed in her arteries, was the sweet song of revenge. Her former captain had betrayed her, and she would make sure he learned the mortal price for that mistake.

"Last chance!" she shouted, sighting down the barrel of the speargun the three men and two women assembled on the deck, each one appearing as violent and brutal as she felt inside. They had been her family once. Her brothers and sisters. Even those she didn't recognize were part of the greater family of outcasts to which she would always belong. She shifted her aim to a brutish bruiser from the Southern Isles, pulled the trigger, and sent her capital-polished spear plunging into his rib cage as the remaining four descended on her with wicked daggers raised.

Aela gave a deft tug to the rope, ducking low as the woman on her left swiped through the air above her with a rusting blade. The line retracted towards her and she caught it midway, using the extra length to whip the rope before her like a propeller, creating a barrier between herself and the corsairs. As it spun, the blood-soaked spearhead spattered dark red drops across the lot of them.

Her arms began to tire as she continued to fend off jabs and parries, the fancy line from her new gun whipping through the air as each backwards step brought her closer to the ship's edge.

"Stand down." A familiar voice boomed out from the hold of the ship. The clomp of heavy footsteps preceded the man as he emerged onto the deck. The mates lowered their weapons hesitantly and stepped aside. Dreadmoor stood behind them, cocky and confident as ever. He looked good—half a lord, even. Fancy threads had replaced his mouldy captain's coat. He was clean-shaven, scars and age lines standing stark where the long grey beard had once haunted his face. He didn't smile, but there was an irksome twinkle in his eye as his fingers caressed the hilt of an expensive sabre.

Aela let her barrier drop, retracted her spear the rest of the way, and stepped forward between the parted sailors. *Another mistake*, hissed the urgent voice inside her head. Never let them see your back.

"What can I do for you, my dear?" he asked, opening his arms in a welcoming gesture.

Aela's jaw tightened as she stepped within a foot of him, gun aimed at his heart. "You can die," she said bluntly. Behind and beside her, she could hear the shuffle of the corsairs as they readied to take her down, their movements stalled at a signal from their captain.

"Now now," he said, a ghost of a smile gliding across his lips. "Why all the hostility, Pip?"

Aela shuddered at his former pet name for her. She had once vied for that vicious smile, a token of his approval and fatherly affection. "You know why. You sold me out." The memory of his betrayal rushed hot and fresh like blood between her ears.

Dreadmoor stood his ground, giving her a bemused once-over, his stare grazing her body from tip to toe. "Well, m'dear, it does seem as if you've done all right for yourself regardless." He smiled again, his attention resting on the king's crest that graced on her uniform, positioned just over her heart.

Aela shook her head in disbelief. Was he really going to pretend he had done her a favour? "As do you. I don't have to wonder where you got the money for the fine clothes and care. Not to mention the extensive refittings." She gestured around to the ship. It was certainly in much better care than it had been at last sight. Fresh timber now lay beneath their feet where there had once been worn and rotting planks.

"And I thank you for your generosity," Dreadmoor said, adjusting his lapels as he eyed her warily.

"Don't thank me just yet," she growled, taking another step towards him as he held up a hand to keep her at arm's length.

"Aela, my darling. There's no need for this madness. You know you're desperately outnumbered. And I don't want to see you dead," he said sincerely, his focus shifting to the corsairs that stood behind her, sharing secret signals. But Aela couldn't seem to find the strength to care that this might be her end as well as his. She could only hear the rush of her own blood, could only see his spilling forth in sweet retribution.

She shrugged. "If I cut your throat before they reach me, at least I'll die happy." Breaking left, she slid a long dagger from her sleeve as she ran towards the forecastle. The pound of boots and the scrape of knives could be heard as the corsairs followed close behind. Trusting the muscle memory in her legs, she leapt up and swung onto the railing above. She stood for a half a second to lock onto her target before she leapt at Dreadmoor. Her dagger slid through the air towards his throat. One hand gripped his shoulder as she landed on him and knocked him down with a knee to the groin. He grappled for purchase on her body as they tumbled down to the finely refitted deck, but just before she could plunge her steel into his throat, a dark shape came flying down from the rigging and sent her sprawling onto her back.

With the wind knocked from her lungs, she stared straight up at her assailant, who rose to stand silhouetted against the sun. The lithe figure glanced over at Dreadmoor as if waiting for orders, but the wait was not a long one. With a sharp nod to the captain, the figure pulled free a knife and flipped it in the air and then smacked her in the head with the butt end just as she tried to rise. A sharp throb of pain was all she felt before the bright blue sky overhead turned to swift blank black.

WHEN THE WORLD returned, it came with a dry mouth and an aching temple. As Aela opened her eyes, the place where she had been struck pulsed with pain, making her thoughts sluggish. Her hands were bound behind her back with rough knotted rope. Her arms were lashed tight against her body, which was backed up against the mainmast, facing out over the starboard side of the ship. To the left was the forecastle, and to the right were the mountains of New Ansar, sliding away behind the waves. She had meant to get as far away as possible, but this wasn't exactly what she had in mind. Behind her back, she moved her wrists against the rope, checking for even the slightest bit of give or wear. No luck. Story of her life.

A shadow fell over her, lending a bit of shade from the hot sun overhead. Glancing up into Dreadmoor's old decrepit face, she bit back a clever retort. What she needed right now was a strategy, not a loose tongue.

"I trust the accommodations are to your taste?" he asked. Aela let her anger wash over her, trying not to give in. The control she had learned during her training with Kera kept her focused and restrained.

"Where are you sailing for?" she asked, not giving him the satisfaction of an answer. She kept her voice light, as if they were two old friends catching up over a pint at the local.

"Oh, got myself a nice little hideout down south. Thought I'd take a little rest, catch up on my reading." He stared down at her, something like pity in his eyes.

"I'd love to see it," she ventured, testing him.

"Pip, you'd love it. It's just the little hideaway you always dreamed of." He glanced out over the side of the ship and sighed. "It's just too bad you'll be dead before we get there." He grimaced theatrically, as if it truly were a shame.

"I thought you said you didn't want to see me dead." She focused on the movements of her breath to keep any fear from edging into her words. He did look surprisingly morose for someone so ruthless.

"And I meant it. Your father, may he rest, would never forgive me if I killed you. So that honour will go to my first mate."

"Shingles?" she asked, straining her head to try and see the familiar shape of Dreadmoor's hunchbacked old first mate. A weather-beaten old salt, he had taken a bit of a shine to her as a young girl. With a little gusto, maybe she could turn the tide without too much sacrifice of her dignity. She stared back up at Dreadmoor, but he shook his head as a familiar shape jumped down from the rigging. This time, with the sun behind her, she could see the face of the boy who had knocked her senseless. Her heart lurched up into her throat at the sight of his shaggy red hair.

"Timlet—" she said, her voice breaking off. He was different. He was a little taller, more muscular, but the main difference was his face. His eyes were dark and sullen. An angry rope of scar tissue reached across his throat. Shifting his gaze from Aela to Timlet, Dreadmoor pulled the sabre from his belt and handed it hilt-first to the boy.

"Make it clean. Dump the body. Let me know when it's done." He turned away as Timlet merely grunted in assent. As the passage to below decks slammed shut behind Dreadmoor, Aela sighed with relief.

"Thank the Corsair, it's you. Quick, untie me, and we can take one of the dories back to Marinaken," she said, relieved to see him. A relief he clearly did not share, based on the way his brow narrowed as he squatted down on the deck, the sabre standing between them like a sharp and shining shield.

"Come on. Hurry." She gestured with her chin down towards the ropes that bound her to the main mast. A terrible feeling was growing in her chest as she looked back at Timlet, expanding rapidly every second that he stared her down, sabre in hand.

"You left me," he hissed. His voice was harsh and throaty, somewhere between a whisper and growl. So that was the price he paid for being the only one willing to stand up for her. He moved forward with lightning speed to close the distance still between them and pressed the cold sabre against her throat.

"Timlet. I had to leave. I made a deal—" She paused, shuddering at the feeling of the blade against her windpipe, biting into her with each word, each breath.

"Didn't come see me. Didn't say goodbye. You just left." He pulled the sabre away slightly, but his glare was as sharp as any sword. It cut right through her to have him regard her as an enemy.

"To protect you!" she said, barrelling on as she felt her frustration rising. He was supposed to be on her side. She had done him a favour, leaving him behind. "And if you knew what was good for you, you would have stayed in Marinaken, found yourself a safe place and a pretty girl and left me and this life well in your past."

He shook his head, red hair scattering unevenly across his sunburnt brow.

"That's not your choice to make. I'm a corsair. Always have been, always will be. More than I can say for you." He spat at the deck, looking with disgust at the king's crest she wore. Aela sucked in a breath and bit the inside of her cheek as her frustration surged, her focus unravelling.

"So that's it then. You're just going to keep crewing for the man that sold me out to the king." She tried to gouge at him with words instead of the hands that were still tied tight behind her back.

"At least he came back for me!" Timlet shouted, his voice rough and rasping as he rose back up on to his feet.

Aela glared up at him. He didn't understand, he was still just a boy, playing at being a man. The words flew out of her mouth before she even considered their meaning.

"The only reason you're still here and I'm not is that I was worth something." He took a step back as if he had been slapped, the colour draining from his already pale face.

"And I'm worthless." He finished the thought, flipping the sabre in the air and catching it. "I guess that's why you didn't come back for me."

He slid towards her with a ruthless grace, the sword coming straight for her as she bit her tongue and tasted the tang of blood against her teeth. A rush of power ran through her as she called on the fire her ancestors had left behind, kindling in her blood. She burned through the ropes that bound her wrists, shook them free, and reached up with one hand to clutch Timlet by the throat just as his blade reached her. Blisters blossomed beneath her fingertips. He recoiled with a cry of pain and dropped the sword as she stared him down through flickering irises.

She burned through the rope that bound her to the mainmast as well, but the moment she rose, Dreadmoor's corsairs rushed her, trying to gain back the advantage. Dropping low, she snatched up the sabre and swung it out to the side where the nearest corsair stood over her. She gritted her teeth as it slid through his calves' flesh, and as she wrenched it free, the mates holding her dropped to the deck with a guttural cry.

A vicious woman to her left grabbed hold of her arm and slammed into her with a hip. She wrenched Aela's wrist with her other hand and broke her grip on the sabre, which fell to the deck with a clatter. The woman and the other two remaining sailors held Aela tight as Timlet came back towards her, one hand resting on the raw red pustules that stood out on already pink scar tissue. His glare was made for murder as he picked up the fallen sword, and she knew her time was up. Though her eyes were still dancing with flame, the fight seemed to drain out of her, abandoning her when she needed it most. Just as she had done to Timlet, to Brynne, and to Del. With blood still on her tongue, she hung her head, waiting for Timlet to make his fatal blow. The edge of the blade whistled through the air, but the world seemed to explode before it could find her flesh.

THE DECK REVERBERATED with the impact, and the sound of splintering wood rent the air as something slammed down onto the forecastle as if it had fallen straight out of the sky. The dark undulating mass uncurled itself and threw its head back in a primal shriek as it leapt down onto the deck proper and pounced on Timlet, pinning the boy to the timbers and raising a row of razor sharp teeth over his ruined neck.

"Kera, no!" Aela shouted, desperate to stop the naga from ripping Timlet's throat out. She owed him more than that. Kera looked up at the sound of her voice, dark gaze searching desperately until it centred on her form. A waterfall of scales, he bounded across the deck towards her. Moving on intuition alone, she lowered her head as he spun to a stop, his powerful tail knocking down those that still gripped her arms and shoulders. As they groaned and tried to recover, a blast of flame issues from Kera's nostrils, the intense heat rippling over the deck, flame catching on shirts and sails alike. It pressed against Aela like nothing more than a tropical breeze, blown in from the Southern Isles.

The desperate screams of three human torches echoed into the clear blue as they ran for the edge of the ship, jumping overboard into the freezing relief of the ocean. Aela squinted at the sails above her head, flames crawling up their rough white height as the forecastle door crashed open. Dreadmoor stomped out from below decks, focusing his rage on Timlet, who still lay sprawled across the deck where Kera had laid him out.

"What did I say, boy? Quick and clean. Useless little arse-scrubbing—" He stopped short, taking in the sight of the flaming canvas and, below it, Aela standing free with Kera curled close around her body like armour. Dreadmoor glanced from Aela, down to Timlet. "I knew it," Dreadmoor roared, slipping a long ornate dagger out of his fine new cloak. "I knew you were in league with her. Just couldn't keep the faith, could you, kiddo? I shoulda never let you back on this ship, you soft little mother—"

He reached down with one meaty hand, grabbed a fistful of Timlet's shirt, and hauled him up onto his shaking feet.

"It's okay, son. Don't you worry. I know how to fix my mistakes." Dreadmoor twisted Timlet around so the boy's back pressed against his front and then raised the dagger.

Aela didn't have to say anything. The thought simply arose in her mind, and the next second, Kera raced forward and knocked Timlet aside before sinking his teeth in Dreadmoor's throat. The blissful rush of the kill washed over Aela, humming along the connection between them. She could feel Kera's rapture as his teeth ripped and tore, hot blood pumping out onto the freshly stained timbers. Overwhelmed, she shut him out, extinguishing her power and cutting off the connection before she succumbed to the naga's glee for gore.

Instead she strode forward to where Timlet was keeled over, retching on hands and knees. She placed a hand on his shoulder, and he turned to look up at her. Tentatively, he stood and wiped a hand across his mouth, even though his face was covered with the spatter of Dreadmoor's blood. He stared at her, body swaying unsteadily.

"We even?" she said. He nodded, running one bloody hand across the still-fresh welts on his throat. The anger in his eyes said she wasn't forgiven. She wasn't sure she deserved to be. Before she could stop herself, she threw her arms around him, trying to imagine that he was still the little boy she remembered. He didn't return the embrace, but then, she didn't expect him to.

Stepping away from his still form, she grabbed her speargun from where it rested on a nearby barrel. Breathing in the salt air, she let the power kindle inside her again and turned to Kera.

"It's time to go," she commanded, and he turned away from Dreadmoor's with a blood-smeared muzzle and long red teeth. He loped across the deck towards her and bent his forelegs as she vaulted up onto his back, a little higher than a horse and far less comfortable.

"What about me?" she heard Timlet ask. Turning back to him, she shrugged, unsure of what to say. Above them, the canvas sails were going up quick, but if he was truly a corsair, he'd find a way to get where he was going.

"Well, Captain Timlet," she said, "I hear you've got some prime beachfront property somewhere down south that I pretty much paid for."

He gazed up at her, shaking his head. "So we're even?" he asked, tone still derisive despite the slight lift of relief in his brows.

"Yeah." She grinned. "Let's call it that."

Timlet snorted in disbelief, shaking his shaggy head. "See you around."

Kera dipped his back, extending his wide leathery wings on either side of Aela. He beat them against the air, leapt up onto the forecastle, and took off into the air. Aela was jerked forward, thrown by the thrust of his body, and slid her arms across smooth warm scales to lock them around his neck. Beneath them, the ship fell away, just a tiny flickering toy in the broad sea. Kera pointed himself east, hurtling forward at breakneck speed, as the shores of Marinaken and New Ansar grew near.

She raised an eyebrow, wondering where he was taking her when her mind erupted with images that she had never seen before.

She was in Kera's chamber, the floor shuddering and shaking as the ceiling fell in on them. A stranger sheltered under a fallen column, trembling in fear as he approached. She smelled familiar. She was wearing Aela's clothes. Brynne. Brynne, terrified and bleeding. Brynne, following him up onto the bluffs above. Brynne, standing on a pinnacle of rock, staring down at a gaping abyss below, where the horse meadow used to be. Brynne, searching for a way to escape as Aela soared around her, before wheeling off into the sky.

Aela felt winded, and not just because of the unbelievable speed of Kera's body as they cut through the air, over Marinaken, over the green belt towards Ghara. She had felt the slick danger of Kera's movements as she peered through his eyes, at the moments he had chosen to share with her. Despite the fall below, she had never felt more secure. Her body low and tight against her mount, Aela watched the world pass by below them, grip tightening around his neck as they began to climb, the spires of Ghara rising before them. She tried not to fall as Kera landed gracefully on the bluff where he had left Brynne. Aela climbed off his back and stood, scanning the devastation.

Suddenly a chill crept over her, the hair on her arms rising as a shadow passed behind her, briefly eclipsing the sinking sun. Aela's stomach clenched in fear as it rushed over her head, revealing its massive form. Alight with a wingspan easily the width of a farmer's field, the naga landed on one of the towers that crowned the mountain, and debris fell away as razor claws dug into the already ruined stonework. It was easily the largest beast that Aela had ever seen. Rearing its head, the monstrosity breathed a tongue of red-hot flame up into the sky before pushing off from the tower to fly across the open pit towards her. She stared upwards as it passed overhead, her jaw hanging open as she took in the mass of shining scales that covered its stomach, each one covered in a cracked green patina. It changed direction effortlessly, wheeling around to land on a balcony far below, the concussive force resounding all the way up to Aela's vantage point as it smashed wantonly into the architecture.

"*Welcome back, daughter. So glad you decided to join me in my retribution.*" The voice blasted into her mind like cannon fire, her mind blank as it momentarily blocked out her other senses.

Aela's eyes narrowed.

"Balearica," she growled. Kera emitted a low whine, butting his head up against her shoulder. It occurred to her in that moment that she could just remount Kera and take off into the sky. Together, they could go anywhere. It would be as if she had never been there, never known what had happened to the city that she refused to call home. As much as she wanted to tell herself that this wasn't her fight, that it had nothing to do with her regardless of what blood flowed through her, she couldn't lie any longer.

The night before, she had left because she knew that there was a chance both Del and Brynne would end up dead if she stayed. If she abandoned them now, they were as good as dead already. An involuntary shudder ran through her as she blocked out the thought that she might already be too late.

Chapter Fourteen

DEL'S SKIN WAS firm and frozen. The cold mountain air gusted over him at the edge of the open court. He kneeled on the tiles—a marble statue, struggling to breathe. Air came in great gulps as his heart hammered against his ribs, threatening to break free. His life was over, after all. Any chance of self-determination died with his father. Prone before him, blood soaking into neatly pressed lapels, the body had already begun to haunt him.

Del felt tears gathering, hot and insistent, but it wasn't the king he was mourning. It was the boy who had never wanted that title and never planned to receive it. Beside him, Brynne reached out for his hand. Her touch was warm. Her lips were moving, but the sound didn't reach him. Everything was blocked out by a loud rushing noise, like the sea crashing violently against the shore. The only thing that cut through the din was the scream of the naga overhead, eerie in its persistence as the beast worked to destroy a legacy that was suddenly hanging heavy on his shoulders.

It threatened to crush him like the masonry that thundered down from above. Every bad decision, every cruel act, every misstep his ancestors had ever made would now rest on his head like a rusted coronet, corroded and crude. And if he was right about his suspicions, that weight included the death of tens of thousands who had carved this kingdom from the earth.

Bile rose up in Del's throat as an overwhelming urge shook him. A little voice rose up in the back of his mind. *Stand up*, it said. *Run*, it said. *Jump*, it said, as he raised his eyes, dimly aware of the balustrade that separated him from a sheer drop down the side of the city.

Shaking his head, he tried to get his bearings. He was desperate for freedom, but he was not ready to pay that price for it. Glancing sidelong at Brynne, he recognized the concern in her eyes and squeezed her hand. It was warm and reassuring as it gripped his. He turned at the sound of boots approaching abruptly from behind. Gerard and Sam walked dutifully towards him with brows narrowed and mouths in tight, thin lines.

"We've located the queen," Sam said, gaze lingering on Brynne rather than the body behind them. Del got to his feet, mind hurriedly trying to convince his legs to stop shaking beneath him.

"And? Where is she?" he croaked, his throat still bruised from Aela's grip.

"In the high court. She refused to come with us. She demanded to see the king."

Del turned to gaze down at Brynne, and his heart dropped like a stone at the expression on her face. Cautious, expectant, and concerned all at once. He reached out a hand and helped her to her feet and then stepped towards the guardsmen with a grim expression.

"The king is dead." He made to brush past his guards.

Sam pressed a hand to his chest to keep him from leaving.

"You can't go up there alone," he said, his focus moving to the body behind Del. "We have to get you away from here before the naga returns."

Del glanced over to Brynne for help but found he didn't have to worry. She was already half-cocked with righteous indignation on his behalf. With arms crossed, she rounded on the imperious guards.

"Tough shit. He's going." She paused, glancing around. "Doesn't the castle have any defences we can use to keep the beast at bay until the queen is safely returned?" Gerard and Sam shared an incredulous look. Clearly they weren't used to taking orders from anyone but his father. That would have to change, and not on his behalf.

"There are some pieces of artillery mounted into the stone along the upper balconies. Mortars. But they're ceremonial, purely decorative. I don't even know if they can be loaded—" Brynne shook her head as Gerard stuttered.

"Then you'd better figure it out fast," she replied, removing his hand from Del's chest. "You've got a king to protect." Her voice was high and firm. "See that you do a better job this time." Her biting tone was both a comfort and a curse in the background as he shouldered his way past the two guards and strode towards the stairs.

THE CLIMB UP to the high court seemed to take every last bit of energy that Del had to spare. His footsteps echoed against narrow walls as he ascended the spiral staircase to his father's audience chamber.

She was standing at the foot of the throne, gaze transfixed on the high windows as a dark shape swept past them, pulling sections of the room into shadow.

"Mother." Del wheezed the word painfully. He was surprised when she turned towards him. Her face was pallid and drawn. Tears had tracked heavy makeup down the valleys of her face, giving her the eerie appearance of a tattooed fortuneteller. When she didn't reply, he closed the gap between them and pulled her into his arms. Breathing in the scent of her hair, he fell back through the years, landing in his own bed, no more than a child as she leaned over him, tucking the blankets closer around his small form.

"Where is Reza?" she whispered, her voice low and graveled.

Pulling away, he couldn't meet her eyes.

"I'm afraid he was— He's been—" Del stumbled over words he didn't want to have to say. He took a deep breath and forged on. "He's been killed." It still hurt to speak, but he needed to say the words.

The queen breathed in sharply, but to Del's surprise, she seemed to grow taller, her usual cold composure returning like an ivory mask. She slid two fingers beneath his chin and tipped his head up to look him in the eyes. Hers were soft and brown, warm despite her outward demeanour. Letting go of his chin, she sank down onto one knee. With one hand resting over her heart, she knelt before him, head bowed.

"My king," she said, and Del's chest tightened.

"Get up, Mother." It wasn't a command. His tone was desperate, like a child. "Please get up," he repeated, when she did not rise.

A dark form passed overhead, blocking out the light slanting down through the windows. As it left, he could see the sun was sinking low, throwing tones of pink and gold across the sky.

"Come on, Reza," said the queen as she rose and started towards the door. But Del stood his ground, fingernails digging into the flesh of his palms.

"I overheard you, you know." His voice shook slightly. "I know Father never intended for me to succeed him." He was surprised to see her eyes were glassy with unshed tears.

"It would have broken his oath," she said. "A child borne between us was legally bound to inherit the throne. That was part of our marriage pact, regardless of his feelings about you or me. Any other outcome would have dishonoured both myself and my family."

Del bit his lip as the pieces slid into place.

"No wonder he tried so hard to disprove his parentage," Del muttered, tasting acid as a shock of frigid pain ran up his phantom shin. Looking up at his mother, he struggled to ask his question, not sure he wanted to hear the answer.

"Is that why you've never left him? Your family's honour?"

"Reza...things are not so simple as that. Yes, my parents... They would have lost everything, and I, I would have lost you." The slight accent of her homeland rounding out the corners of her words. "Every day, I have missed my home and my family. Every day, I have thought of its warmth and beauty as compared to this cold wasted land. But I am a woman of my word." The tears had yet to fall from her eyes, heavily lined with dark ink.

"Don't play the martyr," he said, the words darkening on his tongue. "You love him. The things he's done to me, to you...and still you loved him." He wasn't surprised when she nodded, her arms crossing in front of her body like a shield.

"Someday, Reza, you will know what it is to love somebody who causes you pain." Her hair was held in a high, tight knot, still sleek and smooth despite the state of her. He knew what traits he had inherited from her. His optimism, his doggedness, his desire to believe the best in people. She was the reason that he knew he would forgive Aela despite their last encounter. That is, if he ever saw her again. What he inherited from his father, he didn't even want to consider. The man was dead, and as far as Del was concerned, the memories could die with him.

Shaking his head, Del walked forward past his mother. "You should have left him," he said, as his shoulder brushed hers. He could hear her following him out the great wooden doors, down the hallway. Was it his place to judge her decisions? Probably not, but he was too angry to hold himself back.

THE SKY WAS shot with darkening bands of red by the time they reached the balcony near the stairs. The damage was as evident there as anywhere else in the city. The hand-carved stone railing had crumbled away, leaving a yawning mouth that opened onto a dark drop beyond. As Del took his mother's hand and led her across to the stairs, the beast rose up and swept towards them. It slammed against the edge of the balcony, its broad hide glittering. Del and the queen toppled over each other as the floor shook beneath their feet. The beast pushed off and wheeled around, preparing for another attempt.

Del glanced quickly from side to side, trying to gauge the distance. The stairwell on the left was too far. On the right, the passageway back to the high court wasn't much closer.

"C'mon," he half-shouted, throat still raw. He pushed the queen ahead of him and crawled on hands and knees behind a marbled bench, praying to the Guardian that the ceiling above them would hold. He peered up over the edge as the massive naga raced towards them, but instead of turning to ram them with a flat expanse of scaled muscle, it reached forward with its forelegs, scraping into the stone on either side of the balcony as it clung on to the stone. A sour smell and a deafening sound slammed into Del as it opened its mouth, sword-length teeth mere feet from his face.

The air took on a strange brittle quality as the temperature soared. Gasping desperately for a last breath of air, Del dove back down behind the bench, sheltering his mother with his own body as the flames erupted on either side of them. Flickering and dancing, they razed everything in sight, threatening to converge and cover him in a deadly embrace. Del gasped for breath in the unbearable heat of the inferno.

Just when he thought he could take no more, a fierce cry rang out and the fire died off. When he hauled himself up painfully to look out over the bench, Del was met with a strange sight. The naga was grappling to stay airborne, its wings hitting air desperately as one foreleg flailed wildly, smashing into the architecture with unbearable force. On the other side, its taloned claw was pinned against the side of the mountain, as if held by an invisible force.

Against his better judgement, Del crept forward. In the gathering dark, he could just make out a diminutive spear sticking out between the beast's scales. Stretching away from it, a length of line led to another naga, a tenth the size. The figure atop it was silhouetted against a blood-red sky.

The larger beast pushed away from the mountainside, tearing into the sky as the spear popped out of its flesh like nothing more than a sewing pin. The smaller naga swooped down towards the balcony. Del stepped curiously to the edge of the drop as its rider came into view, a mane of curls flopping in the breeze as she reeled in the line on her speargun.

"Run, you arsehole!" Aela yelled across the void between them. At a loss for words, Del stared at her, his heart swelling at the sight of his friend. Sweeping wide in the evening breeze, she soared off in search of her quarry.

Del turned away, helped his mother to her feet, and led her towards the stairs and relative safety.

AS THEY BROKE out of the stairwell into the open court, the chilled night air hit Del in the face like a slap. Nearby lay his father's body, recovered from the edge of the court and draped in a shroud of fabric. He found he could ignore the sight, but not the strangled gasp from his mother as she rushed towards it.

Over by the edge, he could see Brynne, Alphonse, and Doyle standing, staring up at the vicious battle that reigned in the red sky above. He joined them and put a hand on Brynne's shoulder. She turned to look at him, brow raised.

"You should have evacuated," he said, glancing at Alphonse and Doyle. "All of you. You shouldn't have waited for me." He would have never forgiven himself if they had stayed out of some kind of duty to his impending crown. Brynne pointed up towards the two winged figures dancing around one another in the air.

"We were about to, and then—" She broke off, staring up at two beasts, one dwarfed in size, dodging jets of flame as if they were no more than steam.

"It's Aela," he said. "She's up there."

"She came back," Brynne said, one hand unconsciously moving up to grip the string of black pearls that hung around her neck. Her voice was full of hope and trepidation. Del turned away, unable to watch as Aela courted certain death.

A group of uniformed guards stood clustered around Sam and Gerard. They had recalled their fellow guardsmen to carry the king's body down to the under roads. Together with Del, Brynne, and the councillors, their small group represented the last inhabitants of a city under siege.

"We've pulled back from the artillery. We can't get a shot at it. There's nothing we can do," Gerard explained.

"It's time to go. For your own safety," Sam said, gesturing towards Del and the others.

The guards lifted the still form amongst them as the queen stood alongside, one warm gloved hand reaching out to grasp one still and cold. Del had started towards them when he heard Brynne's voice ringing out firm behind him.

"I'm not going anywhere," she said. The determination in her tone reminded him so much of Aela that he could hardly breathe. She was right, and he knew it. There had to be a way that they could help turn the tide of this impossible battle.

"Neither am I." He stopped short. "Take the queen and my father's body." Nodding to Alphonse and Doyle, he continued, "Get yourselves to safety."

"If you're staying, so are we," Alphonse responded, his voice gruff and full of concern. Doyle laid a hand on his husband's thick forearm as if to shore up their joint resolve. Gerard's cleared his throat severely.

"Prince Reza, I appreciate your concern, but there's no need you to go down with this city. Either come with us willingly, or we'll carry you out of harm's way," he said, Sam standing forbiddingly beside him.

Swallowing hard, Del gave in to the only card he could think to play. "I believe you meant to say *King*, didn't you, guardsman? We may have yet to plan the coronation, but the lines of succession are clear. Now are you going to follow my command, or do we have a problem?" He shuddered at the taste of power on his tongue, but there was no way he was leaving.

Shaking his head, Gerard exchanged a quick word with the guard troupe, and his men turned and marched down the stairs in formation, the king's body suspended between them. His mother stood frozen, seemingly torn between husband and son, before turning to follow the body down into the deep.

Del took a cautious step back as Sam and Gerard approached, sure they were about to rip him bodily from the edge of the balcony and fling him down the stairs. Instead, they came within a pace or two and lowered down onto one knee, bowing before him just as his mother had.

"All hail King Reza Ansari IV. Long may he reign," they said in unison. Del turned to look at Alphonse and Doyle in surprise, only to see that they too were on one knee, heads bowed towards him. Only Brynne still stood, rigid beside him as she gazed up into the sky.

She gasped sharply, and he followed her line of sight as Aela darted away from a swipe of the naga's claws. Her small figure dipped beneath a fresh spray of fire, then flew along the underbelly of the beast, using her size to her advantage. As the naga flipped around in midair, she rose up high, teasing it with her very presence. She flew in lazy circles before zooming straight down in a nosedive, begging it to follow, anticipating its every move. A second too soon, she pulled out of her dive just as the naga came down atop her. Its powerful claws reached out, batting at her. The force of the impact sent her spinning out, plummeting towards them, her mount struggling to regain control as she slumped forward, arms dangling limp on either side of its neck.

"Get down," Del shouted, pulling Brynne to the ground, hoping the others would follow suit as Aela hurtled over their heads to land with a skid across the marble flooring. The beast beneath her let out a low whine as he dug his nails into the floor, leaving jagged marks as he slid to a stop. Aela lay prone before them, her eyes half-closed.

Del pushed off from the railing, but Brynne flew past him as they both ran to Aela's side. She fell to her knees and scooped up Aela's head into her lap. She was rewarded with a groan of pain as Aela's eyelids fluttered. Del knelt beside Brynne and reached for his friend, brushing curls from her forehead as she came around. As she seemed to focus on their faces, her expression greying.

"Are you all right?" he asked, his arm pressed up against Brynne's beside him as a shudder ran through her body when Aela reached up to squeeze her hand.

"I'm so— I'm sorry," Aela said roughly, staring up at him, her focus on the bruises stretched across his neck. He shook his head swiftly, the shaggy hair tickling the nape of his neck where it had grown long.

"Don't. It wasn't you," he said, hoping that she believed his words. He certainly did. Whatever had come over her down in that chamber, he knew that it was not her, his friend.

Aela groaned as she lifted her back up off the floor and pulled herself into a sitting position. "Balearica—" she said, gesturing out towards the dark terror that swept through the skies just beyond the balustrade.

Del turned to look at the scaled beast, feeling dim and confused. "That's Balearica? It actually exists?" Somehow, when he had read the name in his ancient Sarkany texts, it had seemed like a fiction—no more than a warning tale to keep children in their beds at night. Letting out a slight groan, Aela put a hand to her head and rolled her neck from side to side as though it ached. Based on her impact onto the marble floor, it almost certainly did.

"She was trapped in the mountain, beneath the city," Aela said. "Said she needed my blood to free her." She reached up with one hand and wiped a dark string of the very same substance from her lip.

"That's why you left," said Brynne from beside him, speaking for the first time since Aela had tumbled over their heads.

Aela nodded. "I didn't want—this, basically." She gestured at the city, in ruins around them. The roof of the open court was still above their heads, but just barely. Columns were notched and listing, just waiting for a final blow to bring a tonne of shining, intricately carved rock down on their heads.

"And yet it happened anyways?" Del asked, surprised to see realization kindling in Brynne. Her gaze darted from Del to Aela.

"The king, he—he went down into the mountain to find you, Aela. Early this morning. He found some of your blood, spattered on the wall in the catacombs below the city."

"He must have thought I was still down there, must have gone to her, searching for me. Instead, he was delivering her exactly what she wanted." Aela rolled her eyes, a clear sign of recovery.

"Wait," Del said, his gaze locked on Brynne. "You saw the king this morning? You never mentioned that." A deep blush spread across Brynne's cheeks. She withdrew her hands from Aela's and wiped them on her roughspun linen pants.

"Yes. He came searching for Aela this morning, and then locked me up...after he found me in her bed." As Brynne finished, she fixed her gaze on Del, seemingly unwilling to look over at Aela.

The only part of the tale that surprised him was how little it bothered him to hear that his fiancée had spent the night in his best friend's bed. He was fairly certain that was the sort of thing one ought to be upset about. A dull ache was set in his chest, but it wasn't jealousy that grieved him. After all, neither Brynne nor Aela were his.

"What does it want?" Del said, turning back to Aela only to see her eyebrow arched, clearly daring him to have a problem with Brynne's revelation. Her brows relaxed as she absorbed his question.

"She wants what she's already getting. Destruction, chaos, and an end to the Ansari line. You were right about what happened to my people. She won't stop until she's killed the king and you."

"Well, she's halfway there, then. The king is dead."

The surprise that rippled across Aela's face cut through him. "Then you're—"

"Don't." He cut her off. "Don't say it. I can't stand the thought."

Aela shook her head, expression dark and frustrated as she pushed up to her feet, towering over him. "Can't stand what? The pressure? The responsibility? Grow up," she snapped.

Del got to his feet; their gazes locked. Behind Aela, he could see the naga she rode in on, uncurling, undulating across the floor as it came to rest behind her, its shining copper scales pressed up against her back. No longer the little girl he had loved, she radiated power, danger, and heat.

"Do you know why I came back?" Aela asked, her tone sharp. "Because of you. Because of what you said. That you—that I...needed the ghost to move forward. You were right. I can't just run away and pretend that nothing will ever come back to haunt me, because it will. It always will. My past, my ancestors' past, my future? It's time to own the cock-up and make things right. And now, you have the opportunity to do that, and you can't stand the thought? Grow up." She spat the last few words at his feet as Brynne rose to join them, then stepped back a pace with crossed arms. He glanced at her, and her slight nod caught him off-guard.

"Aela's right," she said. "And if anyone can make things right, it's you. It's both of you. Your father didn't listen to your ideas, but I did. They were good. They could make this a better country. For all of us."

Del was taken aback, and sweat beaded across his forehead. The urge to run rose up in him again, bristling in his lungs, willing his legs to take him as far and fast as he could. Just as his feet readied to fly, a sharp pain struck all the way down to his phantom foot, pulling him back to reality.

Looking from Aela to Brynne, he took in the sight of them, the curve of Brynne's soft cheeks, the hard angle of Aela's chin, and his heart swelled in his chest. He wasn't sure that taking his father's place was something he could do, but he was absolutely certain that when he looked at Brynne and Aela, he felt like he could do anything.

"You're right. I know that, even though it's hard for me to hear. But if I'm to try to make any kind of difference, I'll need you two by my side," he said, tasting a tang in his throat as the words fell between them.

Brynne stepped forward and pulled him into a hug. "Every step," she said, then pulled away to glance over at Aela, expectantly.

Aela stared at the two of them, her expression grim and determined. "And every stab," she said, stepping forward to place her hand on Del's shoulder. "But first, we've got to deal with the homewrecker." She jerked a thumb towards the open sky where Balearica still ruled.

Beside her, Brynne opened her mouth tentatively, peering around at the wreckage of the open court. "I think I might have an idea about how to do that." She glanced over at Aela. "If you can buy us some time."

Del raised an eyebrow in question. What Brynne had in mind, he had no idea. Aela, on the other hand, seemed game for anything, despite her fall. Reaching to stroke a hand across her mount's back, she smiled, beautiful and vicious.

"I think I can manage that," she said.

Del reached down and undid his sword belt, handing the leather and steel over to Aela. "This might help. Or at least, it has before," he said.

She smiled warmly, taking the belt and wrapping it around her swashbuckling hips. "This time, we'll make sure it's dead." She winked at Del before reaching out for Brynne's hand. "And you. Are you sure you're willing to let me go again?" Aela ran her scarred fingers across the soft pink skin of Brynne's palm. "Do you trust I'll come back?"

Furrowing her brow, Brynne shook her head. "Of course not. I've learned better." She was about to pull her hand back just as Aela tugged her forwards, pulling her into a firm kiss. Her arms held Brynne close, their bodies pressed against one another as their mouths met, swift and hungry. Brynne's hands moved up to Aela's cheeks as they held one another. Softly, slowly, Aela broke away.

"I'm coming back," Aela said, her voice certain as the tide. Brynne exhaled, pulling Aela's face close to hers, their foreheads rested together, mere inches separating their parted lips.

Del felt the urge to turn away, as if this moment was too intimate for him to witness, but he couldn't tear his attention away from the two women. The pit in his stomach opened, threatening to swallow him whole. He was happy for them, of course, but he couldn't help but wonder if a passion like that would ever be his. Being king already seemed like a lonely business.

Chapter Fifteen

AELA WALKED AWAY from Del and Brynne as if it was the most difficult thing she had ever tried to do. Strange, when so many hours ago, walking away from them had seemed like the only solution.

Behind her, movement buzzed as Brynne's plans were set into motion. Dimples and Pompadour marched away to retrieve the mortars with Doyle's help as Alphonse calculated trajectories with a grease pencil and the tiny notebook he carried, his head bowed together with Del, discussing all possible outcomes. It was an undeniably clever plan, but there was still so much that could go wrong. So much that depended on Aela.

With Kera at her side, she headed to the far edge of the court. The red light of sunset had faded to navy ink, spattered with stars. Del's sword hung heavy at her hip, a reassuring weight to counterbalance the freefall of fear in her chest. Sure, she could distract Balearica, but for how long? All it took was one misstep and she'd be nothing more than a firefly, too close to the lantern's flame.

She grabbed hold of Kera's neck, swung herself up onto his back, and winced slightly at the soreness that spread across her body. Her earlier attempt to distract Balearica had sapped most of her energy. She opened her mind to Kera and felt his mind entwine with hers. Fierce, protective feelings washed over her, and she ran a hand down the creature's long neck. Aela leaned down to brace herself as Kera tilted forward into a run and leapt over the balustrade. His wings extended wide on either side of her body as suddenly there was nothing but dark sky above and an invisible drop below.

The moon hung in the sky over their heads, a shining crescent. Aela picked out the stars that formed the Corsair, its dagger pointing towards the sea. The wind rushed through her hair as they rose and turned back towards the city, where she could just make out the dark form of Balearica curled around the topmost turret. Willing Kera forward, she tried to guard her mind for the inevitable. It came like a thunderclap, the voice crackling through Aela's skull with lightning clarity.

"*Come back for another round, daughter?*" the monster asked, her form stirring as she unfurled herself from the top of the city. Stone crumbled down into the darkness as Balearica pushed off from her resting place, impossibly wide wings spanning from star to star.

"*What do you think?*" Aela replied, not bothering to use her physical voice. She knew that Balearica could hear her every thought, so she carefully filed those that needed protecting to the back, letting only her contempt and violent intentions seep to the front.

"*I think that you're on the wrong side. Come, daughter, you may not have been willing to free me, but you must admit that you have a stake in my crusade. Don't you want to avenge your family?*"

Gritting her teeth Aela tried not to think of Del and Brynne far below her as she replied. "*That's exactly what I'm doing.*" Urging Kera forward, Aela pulled Del's sword from its scabbard as the two nagas passed one another in midair. Reaching out, she scraped the blade along Balearica's flank and was rewarded with only sparks as her steel met hard scales.

Kera dropped low and swooped beneath Balearica, and Aela thrust the blade upwards, trying to find some vulnerability, but found her underbelly as well-defended as the rest of her body.

"*How easily I forget that you have the blood of a coward and a traitor,*" Balearica said, flying over the top of Aela and turning on a dime. At the sight of the dim golden glow crawling forward from deep within her throat, Aela and Kera twisted away to the side, narrowly missing the jet of flame that erupted from between her jaws. "*This is a slightly less conventional method than your father took, but if this is what you want, then I will grant you your death.*"

Lashing out with her forelegs, Balearica batted towards Aela with steel sharp claws. Holding on desperately to Kera, Aela dipped and rose, trying to avoid impact while still looking for any potential weakness that she could exploit. Aela ducked beneath Balearica and breathed a momentary sigh of relief before it hit her. The beast's massive tail swung through the air and into Kera. The crack of splintered bone rang out across the sky as it smacked into one of his wings and sent them spinning sideways through the black night.

Aela gripped tight around his neck as the wind rushed past on either side. They fell towards the city, one functional wing still flapping feebly against her leg. Aela closed her eyes tight and held on to Kera, bracing for impact on unforgiving stone. Shock ran through her body as they hit, instead, a wall of glass. It shattered into sharp, glinting shards, blowing back around them as they hit the floor beyond and skidded to a stop against a precariously towering bookshelf.

Unlike their previous fall, this time Aela's eyes shot open immediately. Adrenaline and ancestral fire coursed through her as she rose and walked to the ruined window. More shelves towered ominously on either side of her. They had crash-landed in Del's beloved library. Above and away, Balearica's dark form was silhouetted against the moon, the Corsair's dagger pointing straight towards her heart.

Aela started at the sound of Kera's whine. He lay curled in the centre of the stacks where they had fallen, a mosaic of broken glass surrounding him like a halo as it reflected the starlight. One wing lay crooked, the arcing bone splayed out at an unnatural angle. His thick scales had deflected any wounds from the broken glass, but Aela was not so lucky. Her already scarred arms were sliced and bloodied from bicep to wrist, her torso and legs cut clean through her leathers. Reacting to a twinge of pain above her eye, she reached up and ran a finger across her eyebrow, then brought it back down to find it dripping with her own dark blood.

Fury ran uncaged through her as Kera struggled to rise. She rushed to his side and laid a hand on the warm scales of his neck. "Stay. You're hurt. You can't help me now."

Kera strained his neck to nuzzle into her chest, but she pressed him back down. She turned back to the wall of broken glass and strode purposefully to the edge of the sheer drop, calling out with her voice and her mind.

"You botched it!" she shouted, chest rising and falling with the thrum of blood in her ears. "Don't you want to finish the job?" Searching the edge of the mountain on either side of her perch, she tried to find a way back into the fight. Luckily, just over her head and a little to the left, a balcony jutted out from the chamber next door. Aela grasped the speargun still strapped across her back and freed it from its holster. She pressed her cheek to its cold steel barrel and sighted down the length of it at a stunted tree that sat on the balcony overhead. Aela fired and pulled the line fast once it was buried in the twisting trunk, then gripped the smooth cord and pulled her body weight up the line, rising hand over hand up through the cold night air until she could grasp the edge of the banister above and drag herself over the edge.

As she retrieved her spear and slipped it back in the holster, she scanned the dark sky before her. The night air crystallized into a dull fog before her as a tailwind swept in from the east. A dark shape cut through the cloud below her feet, like a swift-flowing river.

Aela turned to follow and leapt from the edge of the balcony. Her hands caught on the banister of a thin walkway to her right, just above head height, hauled herself up over cold marble, and ran along its width as it wound along the outside of the mountain. She drew Del's sword as she reached the precarious overhang at the end of the line, then threw herself into a running jump over the banister, out into the night sky.

Her legs pedalled thin air as she fell through the fog and landed jarringly on Balearica's broad back. Using the force of her fall, she drove the sword down to its hilt just inches from the beast's spinal column, level with her powerful wings. Gripping the blade tightly, Aela held on for dear life as Balearica soared through chilling clouds that left her soaked to the bone, her cuts stinging.

"If you think a tiny prick like that is going to take me down, you're sorely mistaken." Balearica's voice roared across her mind, shaking her senses. With a sudden jolt, Aela lost her purchase as her feet slipped out from under her, her legs fishtailing as Balearica soared serpentine through the sky, spiraling in the air far above the open court.

"You just can't shut up, can you? Doesn't a thirst for revenge get boring after a couple of eons? Give it a damn rest," Aela growled, doubling down on her efforts to hold on to the sword hilt even as her body was thrown around like a leaf in a hurricane.

"Daughter, you know I can't rest until I've made things right," Balearica said, firm and dangerous.

That makes two of us. Aela let her eyes kindle and her mind open to Balearica. As she unlaced her internal barriers, she was overcome by the raging storm of emotion fighting to get in. Rage, pain, and a powerful lust for payback overcame her. It was stronger than any need for restitution she had ever harboured—towards Dreadmoor or anyone else. Centuries strong, each red-hot brick of hate had been built up over many lifetimes' worth of guilt and isolation. It was intoxicating.

"Just tell me how to get to the newborn king, and this can all end," Balearica hissed, purging her mind of all but a single thought. Aela gritted her teeth as the vision came over her. Looking through Balearica's eyes, she could see Del standing before her, begging desperately for salvation as she released a torrent of flame towards his brittle body.

Aela blinked hard, gasping for air as she tried to free herself of the unbidden joy that vision dredged up in her chest. It wasn't her joy. It wasn't her hatred. She knew that now. She forced herself to think instead of Del as she had left him, standing in the open court with Brynne, strong and kind, awaiting her return.

"Now, that wasn't so difficult, was it?" Balearica screamed, turning so sharply that Aela nearly lost her hold as the beast beneath her dove for the open court, desperate to take her revenge on the only living member of the family that had destroyed her own. *"I believe I do owe you quite a debt,"* she rasped, her eyes glowing with all the fury that she had held in her heart for untold ages.

"Wait—" Aela said, grasping for any kind of bargaining chip as they soared towards the elegant marble court.

"Luckily, I'm quite good at payback." The words echoed in her mind as Aela's sweaty grip on the sword hilt broke, and she slid across Balearica's back as she barrel turned in midflight. Aela's hands grappled at nothing but corroded green scales until she fell from the beast's back, her view that of the stars above as she plummeted towards the land far below.

Her instinct for self-preservation took hold as she grasped her one chance and pulled her speargun free and aimed straight up and squeezed the trigger. The spear arced up and buried its head in the tender spot where Balearica's foreleg joined her protected belly. The line pulled taught as Aela held on to the barrel of her speargun, dragged along beneath Balearica as she flew between the great marble columns and into the open air of the court. It was pure luck that the beast slowed enough to tuck her wings as she entered the enclosed space, which allowed Aela to hit the mountainside below the court at a speed slightly less than bone-crushing.

Aela threw out a hand to brace against the rock before her body impacted, though the pain that shot through her wrist told her it might have been a mistake. As she gripped the rocky mountainside through gritted teeth, her feet managed to find purchase on a slight outcropping. She released her hold on her speargun and let it dangle against the side of the mountain as she pulled herself, hand over painful hand, towards the balcony above where Balearica's tail stuck out, lashing the night air. With any luck, Aela could reach the floor of the open court before it was too late.

Despite the agony of her sprained wrist and her sliced and sore body scraping over the mountain stone, Aela managed to haul herself up and over the banister that surrounded the edge of the court. After ducking beneath Balearica's massive tail, she skirted the right edge of the court and ran along the open-air balcony that wound around the marble floor. Up ahead, she could hear the snap of Balearica's jaws as she tried to get at her prey, who were out of Aela's line of sight behind the naga's hunched form. Double-timing, Aela raced for the front of the hall, hoping she'd make it before the inevitable inferno.

"Now!" Aela shouted, as she reached the inner end of the hall and caught sight of Del and Brynne. They stood at the edge of the throne room that perched over the court, just out of reach from Balearica's long teeth and claws. Alphonse and Doyle stood back a few paces, while the two guards stood at either end of the alcove, each manning one of the city's archaic defence mortars. Ancient copper constructs, they looked like ship's cannons only far more ornamental. At the sound of her voice, the two uniformed men lit their fuses and adjusted their aim towards the marble columns supporting the vast roof above.

Aela skidded out past Balearica's head but stopped short at the sight of an orange glow kindling deep within her throat. She ducked back behind a column and threw herself to the ground at the last moment before the flames poured out of the beast's mouth. The fire rippled across the floor and up towards Del and Brynne, just as the thunderous crack of mortar fire echoed in the air above her. She glanced back towards the far end of the hall where she had just come from as the first columns fell. Already cracked and listing, they toppled easily as the artillery ripped through their elegantly carved height, blowing them apart where they met the ceiling. They fell towards her and the inner sanctum of the city, thanks to Doyle's expert calculations. Each one smashed awry into the next, dominoing down the line towards the last, one of which sheltered her from the blistering heat. The entire mountain shook with each impending impact. Dust and debris exploded out into air already shimmering with the heat from Balearica's desperate flames.

Behind Aela, the columns were quickly coming down the line. Before her, the fire rolled across unblemished marble. Caught between a rock and a very hot place, she took a deep breath and somersaulted forward through the unfathomable heat, letting the fire of her ancestors fill her body instead. Rising up through the licking and flickering flames, she stood, letting the fire wash over her like a summer breeze as the last columns came crashing down, the massive marble roof with them.

It slammed down on top of Balearica, an unstoppable force. An entire history carved into stone lay broken across her broad back. The flames dissipated as thin spirals of smoke curled up into the air, released from the nostrils of the age-old god.

Aela slipped the dagger from her boot and strode forward to meet her maker. A dull flame still burned in Balearica's eye. The enormous orb was like a mirror reflecting the inferno that burned inside Aela. She hefted the blade in her hand and plunged it deep into the flickering sac. Heat poured over her arms and chest as steam rose from the punctured orbit. It smelled like smoke and copper.

Balearica's body writhed with pain as molten blood began to ooze from her wounds, scarring the perfect floor with fissures and fosses wherever it touched. Aela walked around to the other side of Balearica's fearsome maw and followed suit with the other eye, then closing her own still lit eyes, Aela reached out with her mind.

Strong and steady, she could hear her own heartbeat pounding like the drumsman of a warship sailing for battle. Faint and farther away, Kera's came to her, steady as ever. And softly before her, Balearica's own heartbeat faded, ebbing away with each moment. Bending down, Aela placed a hand on the deity's great wide snout and squeezed tight as its last heartbeat thrummed against her temples.

SHE STOOD THERE for a long time, unwilling or unable to move as the cold night air around her met Balearica's boiling blood and turned to steam. *The world should feel different.*

She turned at the sound of fleet footsteps behind her, just in time to catch Brynne in her arms. Folding her close, she relished the feeling of her lover's arms around her. Her hair smelled like gunpowder. Despite some raw red patches on her forehead and cheeks, it seemed she had escaped the worst of Balearica's wrath.

"I told you I'd come back," Aela whispered, shifting her gaze to look at the rest gathered behind Brynne. Alphonse and Doyle seemed to already be planning the revitalization of the city, taking stock of the damage while Gerard and Sam flanked their new king. They eyed

Balearica's still form warily, as if she would rise up at any moment. Del stood between them, his expression inscrutable, even to Aela.

She released Brynne and walked towards him. Stopping a few feet away, she held out a hand to shake despite the screaming muscles that ran up and down her arm. A fleeting smile crossed his face as he stepped forward to meet her, and in her mind, that same smile was shared by a much younger boy. She could see him now, with shaggy brown hair and kind green eyes, ever willing to follow her into any trouble she could manage to find. And she could certainly manage a lot.

Del pulled Aela into a tight hug, which she gladly returned.

"I'm glad you found me, brother," she said, wondering if this was what it felt like, coming home. Regardless, it was a feeling she didn't hate.

Epilogue

IN MARINAKEN, THE crowds gathered in force to witness the coronation of Thandepar's new king. The autumn chill was just setting in as crowds of locals and those displaced from their crumbling homes in the capital clustered around the town square, waiting for Prince Reza Delphinium Ansari IV to receive his golden crown and the power to affect their lives. Even villagers from the high steppes had made the long journey through the under roads to pay their respects.

It was a relatively subdued affair, despite the queen's insistence on the lavish display of fireworks that would soon finish off the night, heralding a new era of revitalization and rebuilding. The king's council vetoed any of her attempts to institute more extravagant decorations, agreeing all around that the repairs to the city of Ghara would keep their coffers relatively empty for several years to come. The council's newest member, Aela Crane, was the first representative for the Corsair in many years, but her expertise was welcome from most of the other councillors.

Rumours abounded about the sudden closeness of the Master of Hunt and their new king. Whispers passed from mouth to ear as merchants, artisans, and pilgrims alike stared up at the wooden platform that had been erected on the cobbles of the square. Strange that such a wild young girl should be raised so high. And the king, so handsome in his deep purple uniform—but didn't he catch her eye one too many times during the proceedings? And his poor queen-to-be, standing so still and beautiful in her delicate gown, did she have any idea what might be going on behind her very back? Speculation on the state of the royal marriage hadn't been this high since the old Master of Hunt took his own life for love of the former queen.

The ceremonial drums began to beat, first soft and steady, before growing to a din that drowned out even the roar of the crowd as Prince Reza sank to one knee in order to receive his crown. The golden circlet rested atop his brow, just above his keen green eyes, framed on either side by brown curls. He rose, born again as King Reza, another name in a long line of the like. With the cheer of the crowd and the blunted echo of the drums against the surrounding wood buildings, he turned, followed by his queen-to-be and the Master of Hunt, and stepped off the stage and into a covered carriage. The mud squeaked beneath its wheels as the team of horses led the carriage away through the town, leaving the townsfolk to their drunken revelry. After all, it had been some time since they'd had something to celebrate.

THE CARRIAGE CARRIED on over the cobbles for a ways, until the terrain under the wheels gave way to a rocky dirt path. Outside, the evening was settling in, the sky overhead a dark and gauzy blue.

"Where are we going?" Del asked. "I don't remember any dirt roads on our way to the square?" He looked across the carriage to where Brynne and Aela sat, hands intertwined.

Brynne smiled wide, excited. "I found us a better vantage point to watch your mother's fireworks," she said, as the carriage came to an abrupt stop. She pushed the door open, and the smell of salt air hit Del like a panacea. He followed her out and dropped down onto the soft smooth sand. The beachhead before him was deserted but for a flaming pyre and a wooden keg. Aela emerged from the carriage behind him and clapped a hand on his shoulder as Brynne grinned at his side.

"Okay, so there's only one keg and no dead whale, but believe me, it's better this way." After slipping off her heeled shoes, she walked barefoot towards the bonfire. Following forwards, Del breathed in the salt as the ocean breeze rushed in towards them from the sea. A few yards away, waves rolled softly across polished shells. Glancing back at Aela, he cocked an eyebrow.

"Shouldn't we have guards or something?" he asked. They were totally exposed. Aela shrugged as she wandered past him.

"I think we'll be protected," she said. Reaching out with her mind, Aela beckoned to the darkness, and the darkness slunk forward. Kera crept out of the shadows and curled up contentedly near the bonfire, the flickering flames reflected on his scales.

Releasing a breath, Del joined his friends and took a seat on a weathered driftwood log. Following their lead, he removed his shoes and planted his feet in the sand. With his eyes closed, he flexed his feet, cold grit beneath the ghosts of his toes.

There was so much work to do, so much to learn, and he was frankly terrified at the new life stretching out before him, but tonight, there was only the sea, the sand, and his family.

A FEW FEET away, Brynne felt goose bumps rise up and down her bare arms, despite their proximity to the fire. Exhaling, she relished the feeling of Aela's arms sliding around her waist, the heat of her back against her lover's chest. It was a strange situation she found herself in. She was engaged to the King of Thandepar, and in love with his right-hand woman, the Master of Hunt. If she broke their engagement, she would lose the opportunity that she had finally begun to embrace, and any chance of helping her people along with it. If she didn't...she wasn't sure what would happen with Aela.

Breathing in the smoky drifts from the fire, she closed her eyes. Soon she would have to make a very difficult decision, but not tonight.

Warm against her back, Aela stared into the flames.

REACHING OUT WITH her mind, Aela pulled at the flames, enjoying their reaction to her thoughts. They danced and moved, twisting into strange shapes that nearly matched her in height. Since her defeat over Balearica, she had been testing the strange power that flowed within her, and she knew now what she had to do. She'd already discussed the mission with Del. She was going to sail out in search of other Sarkany, though few and far-flung, to see if they would return to Thandepar with her, to rebuild. She was ready to find her people and bring them home.

A sharp whistling noise rent the air, a signal that the show was about to begin. Releasing Brynne from her embrace, Aela led her over to Del. The three of them sat, talking and laughing over tankards of ale as the sky overhead filled with brightly coloured explosions. The fireworks burst overhead in endless hues, heralding the start of a new age.

About the Author

A.E. Ross lives in Vancouver, B.C. with one very grumpy raincloud of a cat. When not writing fiction, they can be found producing and story-editing children's cartoons, as well as producing & hosting podcasts like The XX Files Podcast. Their other works have appeared on Cartoon Network, Disney Channel, and Netflix (and have been widely panned by 12-year-olds on 4Chan) but the projects they are most passionate about feature LGBTQIA+ characters across a variety of genres.

Email: aeeeross@gmail.com

Facebook: www.facebook.com/aeeeross

Twitter: @aeeeross

Website: www.ae-ross.com

Also Available from NineStar Press

Connect with NineStar Press

www.ninestarpress.com

www.facebook.com/ninestarpress

www.facebook.com/groups/NineStarNiche

www.twitter.com/ninestarpress

www.tumblr.com/blog/ninestarpress